The Dating List
(A New York Nights Novel)

Jean C. Joachim
Second Edition
Moonlight Books

I0659263

A Moonlight Books Novel
Cover design by Dawne Dominique
Edited by Kathy Krick

Dedication

For my wonderful readers who have helped me find my way out of misery to happiness again, enabling me to revamp this book into a frothy, happy romance.

The Dating List
Jean C. Joachim

Chapter One

NEW YORK CITY, THE last week of December

The doorbell rang.

"Can you get it, Colin?" Grey Andrews hollered from the kitchen.

Wearing only sweatpants, his kid brother padded to the front of the Manhattan townhouse. He whipped open the front door, revealing the most beautiful woman he'd ever seen.

"Do you always answer the door half-naked in winter?" she asked, her gaze scooting up and down his body.

Her beauty robbed him of words. A low whistle sprang from his lips. "I'd know those hazel eyes anywhere. You must be Grey's brother," she said.

His eyes widened. Clothed in a soft, rose-colored, quilted jacket, the lovely, petite woman took his breath away. The white ermine trim on the hood emphasized the rich mahogany of her hair framing her delicate oval face. Her eyes, the color of honey, glowed as they looked up at him. His lips parted but no sound came out.

Finally, he squeaked out a response that he hoped sounded like *yes* while his gaze wandered over her, settling on her luscious, kissable pink lips. Glowing skin with an attractive blush and the hint of tiny laugh lines topped off her perfection. She was, without a doubt, the most stunning woman ever to walk into his life.

"Name?" she asked. Merriment danced in eyes highlighted by artfully smudged black liner and fringed with black lashes.

"Colin," he breathed.

"It's cold out here, Colin. Do you think I could come in?" She raised her eyebrows as a small smile played on her lips.

Her words snapped him out of his reverie. He looked down to see a large red suitcase standing next to the diminutive woman. He picked up the suitcase, placed it inside next to the door, and stepped back.

"Carrie's friend, Leah," she said, offering her small, white leather-gloved hand to him after she stepped across the threshold, closing the door behind her.

He took her hand, squeezed it a touch too hard, causing her to wince, then let go. He watched her gaze move down from his dark brown hair to his hazel eyes and lower until it rested on his bare chest. The deepening of the blush on her cheeks made him aware he had not finished dressing before answering the door. He crossed his arms over his pecs.

"Excuse me," he mumbled as he made a hasty exit, taking the stairs two at a time to the second-floor landing. The last sound to reach his ears before he closed the door to his room was the pleasing tinkle of Leah's laugh.

A few minutes later, Colin returned sporting a red plaid flannel shirt, jeans, Grey's piney aftershave, and freshly combed hair. As he descended the last two steps, he saw Leah had settled into a corner of the sofa. Her slim legs, encased in black suede boots, were crossed. He plopped down next to her. His older brother, Grey, dumped another log on the fire.

Carrie, Grey's fiancée, bounced into the room carrying a small pile of folded laundry.

"Thanks, Grey," she said, heading for the bedroom.

"Housekeeper's day off?" Colin asked.

"You're looking at him," Grey said, closing the screen across the fireplace.

"You do the laundry?" Colin raised his eyebrows.

"Yep. Carrie cooks, and our housekeeper cleans. I have to do something besides shovel snow."

"Wait till I tell Jenna," Colin teased.

"I'll bust your head! I'll never hear the end of it. Our sister, Jenna, is the most awful tease and I'm her favorite victim," Grey said, turning toward Leah.

"Homus domesticus. Carrie, you tamed the wild beast," Colin said.

"Oh?" She tossed her hair. "Was he a wild beast? Tell me all about it."

Colin blushed and shook his head.

"No way. I like living."

"Good answer, Punk," his older brother said.

"How about coffee?" Carrie asked, heading for the kitchen.

As she measured out the grounds, Grey joined her, stopping to grab four mugs. Before long the sweet smell of brewing java filled the first floor of the elegant townhouse.

"Are you staying with us this visit, Leah?" Grey asked.

"I'm bunking in at Nina and Clint's place again. They're upstate for the holiday."

"Coffee?"

"Thanks. It's cold out. By the way, I've got good news."

"Oh? Give," Carrie said as she turned to face her friend.

Leah retrieved a small portfolio from the outside pocket of her suitcase. Colin's gaze followed her, traveling up her legs. When she bent slightly to unzip the pocket, his eyes traced the outline of her behind, nicely rounded but not out of proportion to the rest of her slim frame.

His tongue felt thick. His fingers twitched slightly at the mental image of running them along the smooth skin of her bare bottom.

"Remember, I told you I did some drawings of lingerie?" She flopped the portfolio on the kitchen island countertop. Colin left the sofa to join the others. He wandered over to see what the women were fussing over.

"This is our cue to leave, Colin. Two women and the word *lingerie*."

"Stayin'," Colin replied.

"Your funeral. I'm going to see if there's a game on. Any game," Grey said, disappearing through the den door that opened into the kitchen.

Before opening the small case, Leah flashed Colin a warm smile. A zing flew up his spine.

"Hurry! I'm dying to see these," Carrie said, shifting her weight from foot to foot.

Her friend took out three single sheets of sketches. "The historical romance I was reading inspired these. What do you think?"

Carrie examined the first sheet. Colin kept his gaze on Leah, who stood, chewing her lip. He wanted to do a lot more to that lip. Being six foot two made it easy to look over Carrie's shoulder. He saw a stylized drawing of a woman with long legs, wearing a lacy number that looked like a corset.

"The material is soft, no whalebone. Silk and lace, and it hangs down a whisker below her..." Leah looked over at Colin, then back at Carrie.

"Low enough," Carrie piped up.

Leah nodded, licking her lower lip, her eyebrows knitted.

"Do you like it?" she asked Carrie. "Do you think it's sexy?" She glanced at Colin.

"I think it's amazing. So original, Leah. It's beautiful. I've never seen anything like it. But as for sexy, let's get a man's opinion." Carrie turned to face Colin and then raised her eyebrows.

Heat pooled in his chest as the two women trained their eyes on him. His throat went dry. His gaze dropped down to the picture. The model had hair the color of Leah's. In the drawing, the soft garment, in pink and cream, draped gently around the model's curves. Colin narrowed his eyes to picture it on Leah. He stole a glance at her hips and legs.

He visualized the edge of the lace on the garment barely covering her luscious rear end. Her long-sleeved aqua tunic was cut low enough to reveal a nice helping of inviting cleavage, especially when she leaned slightly in his direction and folded her arms under her breasts. For the neckline of the garment, again he stole a peek, figuring, with quick male calculation, Leah's breasts would fill his hands as well as the bustier. Mentally, he made the switch from the tunic to the top in the drawing. His breathing snagged for a moment.

The heat of the mental image of Leah in the skimpy garment brought warmth to his cheeks and his groin. He shifted his weight, trying to readjust his jeans which had suddenly become tight. He'd have given his right arm to see her in it at that very moment.

"So? What's the verdict? Sexy?" Leah asked, biting a fingernail.

"That's an understatement," Colin said when he managed to control his breath.

Leah clapped her hands together, jumping up and down like an eight-year-old who was told she was going to Disney World. Grey appeared in the den doorway.

"Did I hear someone say 'sexy'?"

"Mister One-Track-Mind has returned!" Carrie teased.

Grey moved over to the counter, resting one hand on Carrie's shoulder.

"What's sexy, besides my fiancée?"

Carrie handed the sketch to Grey.

"Whoa! What's this?" Grey stared at the paper.

"It's one of Leah's lingerie designs," Carrie explained.

"Can I buy this for Carrie?"

"It's only a drawing now but..." She paused, her eyes glistening.

"Give!" Carrie demanded.

"Madame Jeanne wants it. She wants to buy the design and three more of my Wild West lingerie designs. You should see my saloon gal one. It's, well, X-rated."

"Hot, I'll bet," Carrie finished. "You're selling these to Madame Jeanne?"

"Better than that. She's invited me to come to Paris for six months and design for her."

"Ohmigod! Leah! You're going to Paris?" Carrie clapped her hands together.

Leah hopped on tiptoe and grinned, nodding her head.

"Wow. That's the woman who designed the special Christmas present I bought for Carrie," Grey said.

"A Paris designer," muttered Colin, staring at Leah. "I've never met a Paris designer before."

"You have now," she said with a giggle.

"This calls for a celebration! Dinner out," Grey announced.

"Some place French?" Carrie suggested, brushing Grey's sandy-colored hair off his forehead.

"Madame et Monsieur?" Grey asked, cocking an eyebrow.

"That's so fancy," Leah protested.

"It's a celebration." Grey raised his fist in the air. "Can you ladies be ready in half an hour?"

They nodded. Leah wheeled her suitcase into the den. Carrie joined her, closing the door to the men.

Colin put his hand on his brother's shoulder. "I don't have any fancy clothes, Grey."

"You didn't bring a sports jacket and some nice slacks? This is Manhattan, Punk."

"I figured we'd hang out and drink beer."

"Some of us aren't twenty-something anymore." Grey ruffled his brother's hair.

Colin looked at the floor as he felt heat seep into his face. "I don't own a decent sports jacket, let alone a suit. Don't need 'em teaching phys ed in Pine Grove."

"Leah can fix this."

"Leah?"

"Hold on." Grey knocked on the den door. "Leah! Can you come out?"

She stuck her head out.

"One minute."

Grey went to the coffeemaker for a refill. Colin rooted around in the refrigerator for milk.

When the women opened the door, Leah entered the kitchen wearing a low-cut, silver-beaded dress and black patent leather pumps. Colin choked on his coffee when she appeared. Carrie attended to him while Grey took Leah by the elbow.

"This guy has no dress clothes. I can lend him something for tonight, but we have theater tickets, there's the New Year's party, and we'll go out to dinner again. He needs proper clothes. Would you mind taking him shopping? I'll give you my charges at Paul Stewart and Brooks Brothers. You're better at this than I am."

"It would be my pleasure, we can go tomorrow morning," she said before turning to face Colin. "Okay, country boy. I'll get you fixed up fine." She motioned for him to turn around in a circle, casting her discerning gaze up and down his fine form. "We have a lot to work with."

"Now I know how those prize pigs at the state fair feel," Colin said.

"Sweetheart, I'm not buying, but I might borrow." She wrapped her fingers around his bicep. "Hmm. Larger suit size. Forty-two regular?"

"I don't know."

"Don't worry, sweetie, I'll take good care of you. We need to buy everything in time to have it tailored and ready before the theater. And you *will* need some tailoring. Your shoulders are a mile wide."

"Tailoring?"

"With your body? No off-the-rack suit is going to be wide enough for your shoulders and narrow enough for your waist." She placed her hands lightly on his middle, sending a little shock through him.

"That's good?"

Now it was Leah's turn to blush. "I'd say so."

"Come on, Punk, let's find something of mine that fits you."

The men walked up the stairs together, followed by Carrie, leaving Leah alone, staring into her cup of coffee. At the top of the stairs, Colin turned to glance down just as Leah looked up and their eyes met. His gaze held hers for a few seconds before she looked away. He smiled and then followed his brother into the bedroom.

Chapter Two

After a hefty snowfall during the night, Colin and Grey manned shovels and cleared the sidewalk, walkways, and driveway. Carrie insisted they take a break for hazelnut hot chocolate to warm their bones. The men lingered in the fresh air, sitting on the stoop they'd just cleared.

"You think there'll be any hot chicks at the party?" Colin asked his brother.

"Hot girls at Leah's New Year's party? Of course." Grey grinned.

"Not girls, women."

"Oh? And you know the difference?" Grey raised his eyebrows.

Colin nodded and sipped the rich beverage.

"Do tell, little brother." Grey wrapped both hands around the warm mug.

"I'm almost thirty, Grey."

"So? Tell me, I'd like to know."

"Forget it." Colin looked away.

"No, seriously." Grey rested his palm on Colin's shoulder.

"Girls are not as serious as women. They're still talkin' an' worryin' about their weight, their makeup, or stupid stuff like movie stars and shopping."

"And women?" Grey interrupted, raising his eyebrows.

"Women know what they want. They're focused, confident. They talk about something real, like politics, their jobs. They're better in bed too."

Grey hid a smile behind his hand. "And how many "women" have you slept with?"

"Enough." Colin dropped his gaze to his shoes.

Grey laughed. "Name one."

"What? No."

"Can't, eh? Don't remember their names or *her* name?" Grey continued to laugh.

"Okay, okay, yeah, only one. That time in St. Thomas. I was drunk. I don't remember her name, but it was the greatest."

"Best sex ever, huh? And you were drunk?" Grey cocked an eyebrow at his brother, then laughed so hard he spilled some of the cocoa, which immediately froze on the stoop.

"Thanks for your understanding," Colin said with more ice in his tone than on the sidewalk. He pushed to his feet.

Grey placed his hand on his brother's arm. "Sit down, sit down. Don't get all bent out of shape."

"You ought to know what I'm talking about. You were there." Colin stood looking down at Grey.

"I was?"

"Yeah, you took the redhead. Left me with her older sister."

"Guess I took the wrong one, 'cause I don't remember."

Colin laughed, shaking his head before returning to the stoop. "Now who was drunk?"

"Was I?" Grey rubbed his face.

"I didn't think so at the time. You get it—the woman versus girl thing, right?"

"I do. I do." Grey nodded as he took another sip.

"Carrie's a woman, not a girl." Colin stared at Grey, resting his mug on the step.

"All woman." A small smile played on Grey's lips.

"And?" Colin raised his eyebrows at his brother.

"Don't go there. Don't even think about it. Stuff about Carrie is private."

"I can ask, can't I?" Colin broke into a teasing smile.

"Ask all you want, Punk. Ain't happening. Where does Angela fall? Girl or woman?"

"Girl. Definitely girl."

"Sex no good?"

While waiting for a reply from Colin, Grey brought the mug up to his lips for a longer drink.

"Hey! You're not talking, so I'm not talking."

"Have it your way. Thought maybe she left you horny and broken-hearted."

Colin laughed. "Horny, always. Broken-hearted? No way."

"Good," Grey said, clapping his brother on the shoulder.

"I'm still looking for that one woman."

"The one with your name tattooed on her ass?"

"And other places," he said, snickering.

"Let's finish and go inside. I'm freezing my balls off," Grey said, pushing to his feet and draining his mug before placing it on the top step.

"Got a hot date with Carrie? Gonna do her in the kitchen?" Colin grinned at his brother as he set his mug down too.

"What did you say?" Grey asked, picking up a handful of snow from the hedges lining the front of his brick townhouse and then hiding it behind his back.

"You heard me," Colin said, turning to face his brother.

Grey whipped his snow-laden fist around and wiped Colin's face. Colin sputtered, icy water flying. Anger lit up his eyes while Grey's glowed with glee.

"Told you not to go there," Grey said, backing away.

One good face-washing deserves another. Colin took off after his brother. While Grey was too quick for his sibling, Colin managed to rifle enough snowballs at his brother's face to accomplish the same effect. Grey had to retaliate.Soon a snowball fight was in full swing on the front sidewalk. The area they had painstakingly cleaned became dusted again as the men fired back and forth, laughing with glee when they made a direct hit. Carrie came to the front door. She picked up the mugs.

"Hey, you're getting snow all over where you already shoveled!"

Grey stopped at the sound of her voice. Colin rifled one more snowball at Grey's back before he, too, halted. Both men looked at the ground.

"Shit," Grey muttered, picking up a shovel.

Colin followed suit. Within ten minutes, the extra snow was cleared off and the two men, soaked to the skin and shivering, retreated to the warmth of the house.

"Stay there!" Carrie commanded, holding up her hand.

The men stopped.

"Take everything off here. Don't want that wet snow tracked all over the house." She picked up Grey's muffler to slip her hand underneath. "Wet to the skin. Jackets off. All off right here. Wait, I'll get a bag."

While Carrie scooted back to the kitchen, the men toed off their boots and peeled off layer upon layer of wet clothing. When Carrie returned with a large plastic bag, they stuffed their jackets, flannel shirts, socks, and T-shirts into it. With nothing on but wet jeans, both men padded into the kitchen. Grey took off his jeans, went into the bathroom to hang them over the shower curtain bar, and then trudged upstairs. Colin followed.

The men hit the shower, dressed, and returned to the living room. Grey laid a fire in the fireplace. Colin sat on the sofa and stared out the window. Although no more snow had fallen, the landscape looked cold and barren. Unlike Pine Grove, where snow lingered on trees and shrubs, where the gray of barren trees in the forest was lightened by pristine snow covering fallen leaves and clinging to bare branches, the city was stark.

He shivered before moving his gaze to the fire beginning to take.

"Winter is worse here than in the country," Colin said.

"Why do you say that?" Grey asked, carefully loading another log on the fire.

"'Cause you're out in it all the time. I mean, you don't get in a warm car. You're walking in it, dealing with freezing winds, and ugly views. Getting wet and stuff."

"True. But I can get everything in the world delivered to me here."

"Yeah, but what fun is that?" Colin asked. He sniffed the air. "Something smells good."

"Spiced cider," Carrie said. She entered carrying a tray with three mugs of hot cider and a plate of homemade brownies.

She placed it on the coffee table.

"Colin thinks winter here is worse than in Pine Grove," Grey said, rubbing his hands together and then standing up.

"He might be right," Carrie said. "Have something warm."

Grey joined his wife. She passed out the mugs. Colin took a brownie and downed it in three bites and then took a few sips of the hot, aromatic brew.

Carrie snuggled up to Grey, placing a hand-crocheted throw over her knees and Grey's. He slung his arm over her shoulders and drew her close. Colin watched them. Envy lit a fire in his heart. While he didn't want to rob Grey of his great life, he wanted what his brother had.

"I don't know, Colin. This life is pretty darn good."

The younger man nodded. "I see what you mean." Now if he could only find the right woman to cuddle up with, maybe winter wouldn't be so bad anywhere.

THE NEXT MORNING AT nine-thirty, Leah stepped up to Grey's front door. As she pressed the doorbell, she saw a shadow in the snow. Sensing a presence behind her, she whipped around to see Colin standing there. Despite the cold, sweat dripped off his forehead, his hair hung in his eyes and he'd soaked through his T-shirt. His chest heaved. Leah caught her breath at the sight of the handsome young man. His disheveled state made him practically irresistible.

Carrie opened the door. "Come in."

"Running," Colin breathed, stepping inside after Leah, and turning toward the stairs.

"I figured. Put on something easy to take off," Leah tossed over her shoulder as she walked through the living room.

Colin stopped. He and Carrie stood staring, open-mouthed. Leah turned. Grey sauntered down the steps to join them. He looked at Leah and raised his eyebrows.

"What? He's going to be taking off his clothes. Oh my God!" Leah sensed heat in her cheeks. "Minds out of the gutter, you two! Changing—as in trying on clothes! You're something else," she said, shaking her head.

Carrie and Colin burst out laughing.

"Your mind, Colin," Carrie choked out.

"Me? It was you!"

After a quick shower, Colin threw on clean sweats and ambled into the kitchen. Leah took down mugs and filled them with coffee.

"You should get so lucky," Leah sniffed, adding milk before taking a sip. "Sweats won't do. Put on a button-down shirt and slacks." She motioned toward the stairs.

He stopped in the doorway. "Any chance?" The gleam in his eye told Leah he was only half-joking.

Her throat got dry. She shook her head.

"Don't know what you're missing," he tossed off, taking the stairs two at a time.

"What did I miss? I'm always late for these things," Grey said.

Leah handed him a mug and raised an eyebrow. "Chip off the old block, isn't he?"

"I heard that!" Colin hollered from upstairs.

Leah laughed. Energy soared through her. This young man would give her a run for her money. He'd be with her every step. While she'd expected a country boy to be ignorant, ill-mannered, and just plain dull, Colin had surprised her.

She warned herself. His good-natured teasing, quick mind, good manners, and amazing looks were just the kind of poison Leah would lap up. She knew herself well enough to know she might fall for Colin Andrews. That simply could not happen. She had plans. There was Paris, her design career. She'd spent too many years learning her craft and waiting for a big break to throw it all away on a sexually charged, temporary relationship. She chewed on her lip.

She figured Colin would never want a career woman who had her own opinions, spoke her mind, and couldn't cook her way out of a paper bag. Temporary. Yes, it would have to be short-term because men like Colin would sleep with a woman like Leah but never marry her. She let out a breath. That thought comforted her because marriage was simply too all-consuming, and she didn't have time to be distracted. Paris awaited.

Even if she didn't want commitment, she didn't have time for heartbreak, either. Even a fling would take up too much time and energy. She'd vowed to remain celibate, unencumbered emotionally, until her work in Paris had progressed to the point where she could take some time away. Yeah, then, and only then, would she entertain any entanglement with a man. Now was not the time.

After her pep talk, she finished her coffee and looked out the window at the bleak street scene.

Carrie leaned against the kitchen counter. "Something on your mind?"

"Nope. Just hope we find the right clothes today."

"Bull. This is me, Carrie."

"Honestly."

"Come on, Leah. You've never kidded me or yourself before. Colin has already gotten under your skin, hasn't he?"

Leah shifted her weight. "Oh he's a handsome guy. For sure. But I'm not interested."

"Sworn off men?" Carrie cocked an eyebrow.

"For the time being," Leah said.

"We'll see," Carrie said with a chuckle.

"The air is thick in here. What are you two ladies cooking up?" Grey asked, taking his coffee mug to the sink and washing it out.

"Oh nothing," Carrie said.

"Yeah, right," Grey said, planting a kiss on his wife's head. "I'll pull the car around."

GREY'S SPORTS CAR PULLED to the curb. He dropped Leah and Colin in front of Paul Stuart's men's clothing store on the corner of 45th Street and Madison Avenue. As they stepped into the store, the scent of fine wool and good leather drifted to their noses. Leah noticed the lack of noise the minute the door closed behind them. The plush, thick, dark blue carpet absorbed the ever-present sounds of New York City, creating an upper-class hush. As the heat in the store enveloped them, Leah pushed back her ermine-lined hood and opened her coat. Accustomed to much colder temperatures in Pine Grove, Colin hadn't even zipped his coat. A slim man of medium height with steel gray hair, impeccably styled, approached them.

"Can I help you?" he asked smiling, his palms joined together in front of his chest.

"We need to outfit my friend with dressy casual clothes. He's Colin Andrews, Grey Andrews's brother. I believe Mr. Andrews called this morning?" Leah flashed a thousand-watt smile.

"Yes, he did. Right this way. Let's start with a good sports coat and slacks, shall we?"

"Divine," Leah said, putting her hand on Colin's forearm and following the salesman.

"My name is Stan Michaels."

"I'm Leah Golden, Stan...a pleasure." Leah held out her small hand encased in a spotless white leather glove. He shook it and then led them up a flight of stairs. The store was empty at ten-thirty in the morning. Leah located a comfortable chair and draped her coat over the back. A pair of chocolate brown wool pants hugged her hips and flared to boot cut. Her gold top was long-sleeved, stretchy, and low-cut. A slender chain with a gold heart hung just above her breasts. She had a chunky bracelet thick with gold hearts of differing sizes that clinked melodiously whenever she moved. Her shoulder-length dark hair was tied back in a no-nonsense ponytail. The faint scent of gardenia drifted from her.

"Let's start with a sports jacket. Every man needs a navy blue one in lightweight wool. Colin, do you perspire a lot?" Stan asked.

He blushed a bit before answering. "Like most guys, I guess."

Leah turned to address Colin. "Are you allergic to wool?"

"Don't think so. Don't like itchy stuff, though."

"Lightweight wool, then. And slacks, gray, and one in camel. Also lightweight wool. I'll be right back," Stan said.

He hurried away, his highly polished black loafers gliding soundlessly across the thick carpet. Colin shifted his weight.

Leah said, "We'll try the jackets first, then the pants. Once you have a jacket that looks good..."

Before she finished her sentence, Stan had returned.

"I took the liberty of adding camel and a charcoal herringbone to the jacket selection. Noticing the young man's coloring, I thought camel would be especially appropriate," Stan said, hanging several garments on a rack. Stan took the navy jacket from the hanger and held it for Colin, who deposited his coat on an empty chair and shrugged the navy blue blazer over his impressive shoulders.

"Button it, only one button, darling," Leah cooed, rising out of her chair.

She moved over to Colin and stared at his torso, sizing up the fit of the garment. She motioned for him to turn around. A slight pull in the fabric caught her attention, so she ran her hand across his shoulders from left to right. He flinched at her touch.

"A shirt. Stan, he needs a dress shirt. Can't tell about the fit with a T-shirt on."

"Right away, Miss Golden. White?"

She nodded.

"I'd say he's a..." Stan closed one eye as his gaze scanned Colin's torso, "sixteen and a half, thirty-five?"

"Sounds about right," Leah said. Colin nodded.

Before he could turn around twice in front of the mirror, Stan returned, unwrapping a fresh dress shirt.

"T-shirt off!" Leah ordered, waving her hand at him.

Colin handed the sports jacket to Leah and ripped his T-shirt over his head, exposing a well-muscled chest covered lightly with dark brown hair. She coughed to cover her reaction at seeing his fine physique. Her fingers itched to touch him.

"Something wrong?" Colin questioned, his mouth drawn into a frown.

"Shirt, Stan!" Leah commanded before sucking on her lower lip and balling her hand into a fist to keep her fingers under control.

Stan jolted out of his temporary reverie and thrust the shirt into Colin's hands. As soon as Colin finished buttoning, he reached for his belt. Stan put his hand on the young man's bicep and raised his eyebrows.

"Shouldn't you at least turn around or are you and the lady on intimate terms?"

Although he said it quietly, Leah's face grew hot. She faced away to give Colin privacy.

He unzipped his pants, tucked in the shirt, and closed the zipper. "You can turn around now," Colin said, buckling his belt.

Leah spun around slowly. He slipped the navy blue jacket on again. This time she walked around behind him. Her hands slowly and sensuously smoothed out the small wrinkle as the fabric pulled taut across his shoulders. He stood completely still as she ran her hands back and forth.

"This one pulls a little, Stan. Take it off, sweetie."

"With shoulders like that, they may all pull a little," Stan remarked.

Colin took off the jacket and handed it to Stan. Leah stood in front of him and pulled at the sides of the shirt. She touched his ribs which made him twitch and laugh.

"I'm ticklish."

"There? Oh. Sorry." She turned to Stan. "Don't you have anything tapered? This is too baggy on him."

"Of course. We have a new Italian shipment, arrived only three days ago," Stan said as he backed out of the area.

Colin started unbuttoning his shirt.

Leah's breath caught as he displayed his chest. She turned away but not before she heard him chuckle.

"Making you nervous, Leah?"

"Who, me?" She faced him, trying with all her might to steady her pulse since she hadn't seen such a fine body in quite a while.

Colin shot her a sexy grin. She turned toward the wall and pretended to stare at a painting. Stan returned with a tapered shirt and the fitting proceeded.

For pants, Colin retreated to the dressing room. Leah checked the hook at his waist as well as the waistband to see if it was too snug. He cleared his throat as she unhooked it, hooked it up again, and slipped her fingers down between his skin and the material. She looked at the fit in the back, noticing his cute butt. She longed to smooth the material over it but refrained.

Once the suits, sports jackets, and pants were selected, Stan took measurements for alterations. As Colin put on and took off jackets and pants, Leah grew nervous and fluttery. Her body responded to the feel of him under her fingertips. She didn't like it, or maybe she liked it too much.

"Can I take you out for a snack? Coffee, at least?" Colin asked her as they left the shop ninety minutes later.

"Daddy Michael's ice cream parlor is up the street."

"Ice cream on a cold day like today?"

"Need something to cool us down." She chuckled, taking his arm as they left the store.

THE WAITRESS HANDED menus to Leah and Colin. They sat on ice cream parlor chairs, hunched over a small round table. The eclectic décor included old wooden signs, small ornate mirrors, antique dolls, and various knickknacks on the walls. The menu had generous helpings of ice cream in sundaes and other confections, including parfaits and banana splits.

"I don't usually eat this stuff," Leah explained.

"Want to split something? How about a large hot fudge sundae? You can pick the ice cream."

"You're tempting me." She smiled at the double-entendre.

"Come on. Hot fudge and whatever ice cream you want."

"Okay, either chocolate chip or peanut butter swirl." She ran the tip of her tongue over her bottom lip.

"Hmmm. Tough choice. Chocolate chip?"

"Perfect!" She smiled in anticipation of the forbidden treat.

"Coffee too?"

She nodded.

Colin placed their order while Leah looked around. There weren't many people in the place and certainly no thirty-four-year-old women with twenty-nine-year-old men. When an attractive man stared, then raised his eyebrows, she cast her gaze down. Glancing up at Colin, she noticed a mischievous gleam, youthful and full of fun, lit up his eyes. *When was the last time I just had fun with a man?*

"Penny for your thoughts," he said as the waitress set down two mugs of steaming java.

"Thinking how ridiculous a woman my age looks sitting here with a man your age," she blurted out, instantly regretting her candor.

"Really? I think we look cute together. Who cares what other people think? A few years, what difference does it make?"

"You don't care?"

"I'm here with the most gorgeous, talented woman in the place—no—in all of New York City. I'm the luckiest guy alive."

The heat of pleasure rose in her cheeks.

"You even blush beautiful. What man of any age wouldn't give a fortune to trade places with me?"

She looked down at her hands, resting on the table and fiddling with her napkin. His fingers folded over hers. She gazed into his eyes, watching the dancing green flecks mixed with gold. Her resolve to treat Colin like a little brother melted along with the sugar she put in her coffee. His frank admiration broke through her first line of defense. Able to spot a phony a mile off, Leah didn't get those vibes from Colin. Could he be the real thing or was it too scary to believe that?

The arrival of the waitress shattered their private moment. She placed an ice cream sundae piled high with a mountain of whipped cream in the center of the table, then added a utensil for each. Colin scooped some onto the spoon and fed it to her. Giggling like a school-girl, she did the same for him. She turned off her conscience, quieted her mental alarm bells, stuffed her judgment way down deep, and enjoyed the moment.

Chapter Three

"How long are you staying?" she asked. "Just through New Year's. But I plan to come back in February."

"For Valentine's Day?"

"Of course. Love that holiday." His eyes glowed with naughtiness.

"So did I when..." She stopped, swallowing the words *when Hank was alive*. Emotion gathered in her throat, closing it off for a moment. Her eyes wetted.

"What?" Colin took her tiny hand between his big paws. "What's wrong? Did I say something?" he asked.

"No, no. It's not you, it's me. Do you come to New York often?" she asked.

Colin's eyes searched hers, but Leah had regained control, hiding a quick flash of pain behind a soft sigh.

"Didn't used to. How come I never met you before?"

"I'm Carrie's friend. I didn't know Grey before he met her."

He nodded.

"I'll be back more often now." Colin moved his hand closer to hers again.

"Where do you live?" she asked.

"Town called Pine Grove. Upstate. I've spent time traveling and being in the city. I'm not naïve. Don't think I'm going to talk about cows. I'm not a farmer. I have nothing to do with cows."

"Sweetheart, don't go all defensive. I like country boys. Means they know how to do things, fix stuff, and are big and strong. From what I saw this morning, I'd say you fit that bill."

It was Colin's turn to blush.

Was her flattery sincere, genuine appreciation, or was she leading him on? She had no clue.

"In that case, guess I'm happy to be considered *country*." A slow smile raised the corners of his mouth. His hand covered hers. His sweet, sexy expression sent a chill shooting up her spine.

Nervous, Leah focused on the ice cream, eating as fast as she could without getting brain freeze. Keeping eye contact, they ate in silence all the while his heat melted the ice cream and her stand-offish attitude. She chuckled to herself.

"What's so funny?" he asked before putting a spoonful of the cold confection in his mouth.

"Nothing."

"Come on, give." His hand closed around her forearm.

"You're so hot, you're melting the ice cream."

He burst out laughing. "That heat's coming from you, not me, honey."

No one had called her honey, sweetie, or baby in a long time. She blinked back tears. Colin's smile faded.

"Is it all right for me to call you that?" He eased his hand back.

She nodded, afraid to trust her voice.

"Whew! Good. For a minute there..."

"It's fine." She rested her hand on his.

"I didn't mean to step over the line. Your eyes are the color of honey."

"That's...lovely, Colin."

He scooped up a spoonful of the melting ice cream and hot fudge sauce and poised it in front of her lips. She opened, keeping eye contact. They finished in silence.

When the waitress dropped off the check, Colin placed his hand over it to keep her from paying. She shot him a questioning glance.

"It's the least I can do after your patience at the store. Thank you for your time and expertise."

"It was a pleasure."

Once they reached the sidewalk, Leah took his hand and directed him uptown.

"It's not bad out. Shall we walk a bit? Walk off that sundae. Why'd I ever let you talk me into that?"

He laughed. "I could see you wanted me to coax you."

"Oh? All that from my expression yet you hardly know me?"

"A situation I intend to fix." He smiled, sending warmth all the way to her toes.

"Tell me about your work," Leah said, redirecting the conversation.

"I'm a high school gym teacher now, but I want to teach college."

"Phys ed?"

"Environmental Science. I have a master's. I coach the wrestling team too."

"Hard to find a college teaching job nowadays, I'd guess."

"There's an opening coming up at Kensington State next fall."

"Have you applied?"

He shook his head, directing his gaze on the sidewalk.

"Why not?"

"I don't have college teaching experience."

"But you're a coach too. Couldn't that help? Do they have wrestling at Kensington?"

"That's the one hook I have. The dean there told me they want to start a wrestling team."

"So why don't you apply? How many applicants have a master's *and* coach wrestling?"

"Never thought of it that way."

"Well, you should."

"I don't know..." His voice trailed off.

"I'll help you. Let's go to Nina and Clint's, where I'm staying. You need to do this before someone else gets there first."

Leah broke from him, stepping into the street, and raised her hand. She didn't have long to wait before a yellow cab pulled up. Colin opened the door, and they got in.

"Central Park West at 76th Street," she said to the driver, then sat back against the seat.

When they reached the luxury building, Colin got out first, offering his hand to Leah. They picked their way across the sidewalk, wet from melting snow. She threw her brightest smile at Lance, the chunky doorman as he held the door.

Once in the apartment, Colin stopped in the foyer, his jaw hanging open. Leah tossed her coat over a chair and then held out her hand.

"I forget that people aren't used to this place. Coat. Come on."

He peeled off his jacket and laid it across her outstretched arms.

"Is this your place?"

"It belongs to my friends, Nina and Clint. They're upstate, somewhere in or near your little town, I think. They always go there for holidays and the summer. They invited me to stay. I water their plants and enjoy the city."

"Where do you normally live?"

Leah's face reddened.

"I've been living with Carrie's aunt, Delia Tucker, in Connecticut."

"Not on your own?"

"It's a long story. This is such a gorgeous apartment, isn't it?"

"It's a friggin' palace!"

"Let's get started." She tugged on his arm. "When we're done, I'll take you on a tour."

Leah pulled out a chair at the rectangular chrome and glass dining room table where she had her laptop set up. Colin plopped down next to her. For an hour, they focused on Colin's resume and cover letter.

When she was convinced it was the best it could be, Leah addressed it to Dean Mac Caldwell at Kensington State and hit the *send* button. Colin got up and stretched.

"Thank you so much," he said.

"I hope you get the job."

"What about that tour you promised?" He leaned against the thick glass table.

Leah pushed to her feet, stretched her hands over her head, and smiled.

"Right this way." She led him into the large kitchen with stainless steel everywhere, warm wood cabinets, and stunning granite countertops.

The modern living room had a few small tables in chrome and glass. White couches and loveseats provided comfortable seating facing several large windows and a pair of French doors. Vivid, modern oil paintings hung on the walls, adding color. After opening the French doors, Leah stepped out on the large terrace overlooking Central Park.

"This is the most awesome part of the apartment."

"What's in there?" he asked, pointing toward a closed door down the hallway.

"Oh. Okay." Reluctantly, she left the balcony and led the way. Unsure if she wanted to be alone with him in that room, she threw open the door anyway.

"Wow, some bedroom!" he said, strolling in.

He sat down on the king-sized bed.

"Pretty big for a woman your size. Do you sleep here alone?"

Leah's eyebrows shot up. "That's a very personal question."

"To a lady who had her hands in my pants today, I don't think so." His eyes twinkled, and his lips curled up in a devilish grin.

"I didn't have my hands...I was measuring the..."

"Well?" He cocked an eyebrow.

"I'm sleeping alone. If you must know." Embarrassment stained her face.

"Good."

"Oh?" She raised her eyebrows.

Colin took her gently into his arms.

"Maybe I can fix that," he said, lowering his lips to hers.

Before Leah knew what was happening, Colin had his arms around her. His lips toyed with hers for a moment before getting serious. The heat from his mouth zinged through her body, straight to her core. Tingles shot up and down her spine as his tongue swept across her bottom lip. She held her breath, her fingers closed over his wide shoulders as he slowly pressed her body to his. After rising up on tiptoes, she parted her lips. His tongue caressed hers and all thought fled from her mind. His fingers splayed on her back. A moan escaped from her and his hand slid down to rest on her hip, pulling her closer. The firmness of his pecs hardened her nipples.

As quickly as they came together, it ended. Colin stepped back, his breathing ragged, his fingers laced together in front of his zipper, hiding his erection. His eyes darkened with desire.

"Sorry. I got carried away."

Leah waved her hand, trying to catch her breath.

She pretended to gain control. "No problem." She licked her lower lip.

"Please don't do that," he said.

"Do what? Oh, sorry." Her eyelashes fluttered for a second.

"I apologize. I shouldn't have taken advantage. Being in the bedroom with you, I lost my head." He inched closer.

"Don't apologize. It was breathtaking," she whispered, closing her fingers over his forearm.

"You're not mad?"

She shook her head.

"Well, then..."

Leah blocked his attempt to kiss her again.

"You don't know me very well. This is too fast. I'm not a prude or anything but."

He retreated, dropping his hand from her waist. "You're amazing. Please excuse me. I don't usually do this, even on a first date, which this isn't—exactly."

She smiled. *He means it.*

"I've never met a woman like you."

"I'm nothing special."

"Are you serious? You're the most special woman to come into my life—ever," he said.

"Perhaps we should go to the living room." Leah opened the bedroom door.

"Good idea. Good idea," he agreed.

They stood in awkward silence.

"Are you going to come back to Grey's with me for dinner?" Colin asked.

"I was thinking of meeting you all at the restaurant. Can you call me?" She rested her hand on his forearm, briefly.

"Of course."

Colin tapped Leah's cell number into his phone. His eyebrows shot up. "Shit, look at the time! Six o'clock. Grey's going to be furious."

Leah leaned over and glanced at his cell phone.

"You were expected home? Aren't you over twenty-one?"

"Yeah, but they have these dinner plans and he doesn't know where I am. He's a big brother, he worries."

"You run on home. The dinner reservation is for seven o'clock. Call me and tell me where we're going and I'll meet you there." Leah took Colin's coat out of the closet and held it for him to put on.

"Thanks again for everything." He blushed. "I mean, for helping with the clothes and all."

He leaned down, gave her a quick kiss, and headed to the elevator. With a grin that refused to disappear, Leah watched him go. When the elevator dinged and the door shut, an emptiness swept over her. Without Colin's large, cheerful, exuberant presence, the apartment seemed sterile and empty. She sighed as she headed for the shower.

GREY PACED IN FRONT of the fireplace. He stopped to place another log on the embers then resumed striding to and fro, stopping only to glance at his watch.

"Colin should have been back hours ago."

"I'm sure he's fine," Carrie said as she arranged pink carnations with yellow and white mums. "What could happen to him? He's with Leah." Carrie slipped a slender lily into the vase.

Grey snickered. "He could be in bed with her, that's what could happen."

"Oh stop." Carrie gave him a soft punch in the arm.

"Just sayin'—it could happen."

"Isn't he a little young for her? She's thirty-four and he's twenty-nine, right?"

"Colin has the Andrews charm. Women love him."

"Oh? Andrews men wrote the book on charm?" Carrie cocked an eyebrow.

"Won *you* over, didn't I?" He moved closer to deliver a kiss.

"You certainly did."

"Wish he was home." Grey picked up the newspaper from the coffee table and plopped down on the sofa.

Carrie put the last flowers in the vase and placed it on the counter. "I love it when you bring me flowers in the winter. They're so damn cheerful. Reminds me what spring looks like."

"You're as beautiful as spring," he said.

She gestured and he moved over to the counter to accept her kiss then folded his newspaper before picking up half a corned beef sandwich and taking a bite.

"You're right. Artie's does make the best corned beef," he said. Grey sat on a stool at the counter next to Carrie while she cleaned up the cut stems and extra leaves. He leaned over, nibbling on her neck. "After I finish this sandwich, I'm gonna take a bite out of you."

She grinned. "Is that a promise?"

"You bet, baby."

He put his arm around her shoulders and fingered her velour sweatshirt. Carrie leaned into his shoulder. They lingered in a sweet kiss.

"Why are you worried?" she asked.

"I hope Colin didn't do something stupid..."

"Like?" She wiped the counter with a sponge and then raised her gaze to his.

"Like making a pass at Leah."

"He wouldn't, would he?" Carrie raised her eyebrows.

"Didn't you see him stumble all over himself?"

"Yeah, so he was a little impressed by her." She unloaded the dishwasher.

"A little? The boy was practically panting," Grey said, then took another bite.

Carrie laughed. "Come on. Leah is much older than he is and so much more sophisticated. She dates big Wall Street guys. She'd never be interested..."

"You know that, I know that, but Colin doesn't. He's looking for a *woman*, not a girl, and Leah fits the bill perfectly."

"She'll let him down easy." She paused, holding a clean platter to look at Grey.

"Unless he does something stupid." He took the platter from her and returned it to its place on a high shelf.

"Like what?" Carrie asked.

His lips rose in a mischievous grin. "Like this!"

Grey picked her up in his arms and swooped up the stairs. He raced through the hall, into their bedroom, kicking the door shut before dropping her on the bed. Carrie laughed until she almost couldn't breathe. He collapsed next to her.

"And if he should do this," he kissed her, "then this," he cupped her breast, "and this," he yanked up her top with his free hand, "she might very well slap the shit out of him."

"Or she might do this," Carrie said before winding her arms around Grey's neck, pulling him into her arms for a deep, passionate kiss.

He stretched out next to her, easing his leg over hers. After she wriggled out of her top, Grey reached around behind her and snapped open her bra. She shrugged it off while he jerked his T-shirt over his head, tossing it on a nearby chair.

"Much better," he murmured, staring at her breasts as he raised his hands to cover them.

"Is that what Colin said?" she teased him, her eyes twinkling with mischief.

He closed his fingers around her soft flesh as his lips kissed their way down her neck.

Carrie arched into him, pressing her hips into his, her fingers combing through his hair. The slamming of the front door startled Grey, who had his lips on Carrie's nipple.

"I guess Colin's home," Carrie said, reaching for her bra.

"Fuckin' A. The boy never has had good timing," Grey said. "Little brothers...crap. Can't believe he's still showing up at the wrong time." He sat up.

Carrie arched an eyebrow. "Oh? And what inconvenient times did he show up before?"

Grey sensed color in his cheeks. "You know..."

"Not really. Tell me."

"Stop kidding, Carrie." A smile played with his lips.

"Like when you were making out with a girl, trying to get her panties off, you mad seducer." Carrie's fingers tickled his sides, causing Grey to bend and twitch. A roar of laughter escaped his mouth as they wrestled with each other. Grey grabbed her hands and clasped them together in one of his big ones. He rolled her over, subduing her kicking legs by trapping them between his as his mouth blew raspberries on her neck. She screamed, convulsing in laughter as she struggled to free herself from his vise-like grip. He lifted his mouth from her neck and lowered it possessively on her lips. The demanding kiss grew deeper, more passionate. She stopped squirming, relaxing against his hard body, molding hers to his.

The door burst open and Colin rushed in, stopping so abruptly he almost fell over when he saw his brother on top of Carrie, both stripped to the waist. Grey's head popped up. Carrie screamed, crossing her arms over her chest.

"I heard a scream and thought Carrie was in trouble...I'm so...so...sorry," he said, quickly turning away, blushing, and shutting his eyes.

"Colin...you still haven't learned to knock?" Grey raised himself up onto his elbows to pull the bedspread over Carrie.

With his hand over his eyes, Colin backed out of the room, feeling for the door. As Carrie looked at Grey, laughter erupted from her throat.

"You're not pissed?" Grey asked.

She shook her head, laughing too hard to speak. After the bedroom door closed, Grey turned back to face her.

"Now, where were we?" Grey's voice was soft and low.

"Later, lover. Time to get ready for dinner."

Carrie pushed up with her hands, slung her legs over the side, and stood up.

Grey sighed and shrugged. "Where are we going tonight?"

"How about Casa Mia? A little guacamole, mariachi music...it'll be fun," Carrie said.

"And Colin doesn't need fancy clothes. Sounds good. Can I get a raincheck?" he asked.

He put his hands on her naked waist and slid them up and down her sides. Carrie cuddled up to him, pushing her chest against his. She planted a kiss on his lips.

"I certainly hope so. Leave a girl high and dry...wanting." She snickered.

He laughed and squeezed her close to him. "That's why I love you."

She leaned back and raised her eyebrows.

"That and a million other reasons, honey," Grey said, stopping to nuzzle her neck.

Chapter Four

C olin ran down the stairs, all the way to the refrigerator. He grabbed a beer and popped the top. Sitting on a stool at the counter, he took a long swig, hoping his cheeks had returned to their normal color. A few minutes later, the door opened upstairs. He cleared his throat three times and then took a deep breath, but it didn't calm his nerves. Grey and Carrie, wearing bathrobes, joined him in the kitchen.

"We're going to Casa Mia, little brother. Seven o'clock," Grey said as if nothing had happened.

"Carrie...I'm so..."

"Forget it, Colin. I have." She patted his arm and then sat down on a stool.

"Vodka and tonic, babe?" Grey asked.

"Sounds good. Where's Leah?"

"Oh my God! Leah! She said to call with the location of the restaurant," Colin blurted out.

"I'll call her. Be right back." Carrie disappeared into the den and shut the door.

As Grey gathered the fixings for her drink, he shot a sly glance at Colin.

"So, what were you and Leah up to that made you so late? I thought you were only going shopping?"

"Fitting took a while. Seems a great body like mine isn't standard." He cleared his throat again.

Grey chuckled. "Go on."

"Then I had to thank her, so we went out for ice cream, and then we went back to her place and had lunch. And she helped me with a job application...before you know it, it was six o'clock."

"That's all, little bro?" Grey trained a questioning stare at his brother while dumping ice cubes into two highball glasses.

Colin blushed. "What else would there be?"

"Come on. You can't fool me. I saw the way you looked at her...like a fox in a hen house." Grey poured vodka over the ice.

"If you mean, did I notice she's attractive? Yeah. I did. So?"

"Just attractive?" Grey cocked an eyebrow while he poured in tonic water.

"Okay. Yeah, she's hot. I noticed. So what?"

"Getting a bit defensive, aren't you? Did ya kiss her?" Grey stirred the drinks.

Colin could feel the heat travel up his neck. There was nowhere to turn because he knew it would rise all the way to his ears. He'd never been able to fool his brother. Anytime Grey put pressure on Colin, he always 'fessed up.

"So, what if I did?"

Grey laughed out loud.

"Chip off the old block. Didn't waste any time, did you?"

"That's all I did. I kissed her—once."

"Ah, but when an Andrews man kisses a woman, even once, she's spoiled forever for the kiss of another," Grey said, dramatically, as he squeezed a little chunk of lime into each drink.

The two men punched each other in the shoulder and burst into laughter until they could hardly breathe. Carrie returned, tapping her foot until Grey composed himself. He handed her a drink. She kissed him before taking a seat next to Colin at the counter.

"What did I miss?"

"Andrews brothers inside joke." Grey took a sip of his drink.

"Oh?" She raised an eyebrow. "You're asking for trouble."

"Okay, okay," Grey said then he relayed the joke to her.

"I guess I have to agree." She chuckled, shooting a flirtatious look at her fiancé.

"So, you kissed her. Hmm. This is moving pretty quickly. Are you sure you want to take this trip with Leah?" Grey sat down on the other side of Colin.

"What do you mean 'take this trip'?"

Grey coughed. "You know—go the distance—get involved. Or are you simply seeking a one-night stand?"

Carrie sat up straight, a stern look washed over her face. "Colin, you wouldn't, would you?"

"Of course not! Not with Leah. Hell, I'm no saint. I'm not going to tell you I've never had a one-night stand, but Leah is something special."

"She is. You don't know her history." Carrie took a sip of her drink.

"So tell me." Colin raised the beer bottle to his lips.

"Well, Leah's husband, Hank..."

"Grey!" Carrie put her glass down hard. "Don't you think Leah should tell him herself?"

"Maybe, but she hasn't."

"She will."

"Tell me what? Who is Hank? Leah's married?" Colin's eyes grew wide.

"She's a widow," Carrie said.

"Her husband died?" Colin put his bottle on the table.

Carrie nodded.

"How long ago?"

"Five years but you should get this from her."

"She didn't tell me. I have a right to know." Colin finished the last of his beer.

"Do you? Why?" Carrie trained her gaze on him.

"Because I care about her."

"You've known her five minutes, Colin." Carrie took a big gulp of her vodka and tonic.

"We spent the entire day together. I've never known another woman like her. She's amazing. Talented, beautiful, sweet, smart, sexy. She's got it all."

"She doesn't want to get serious about anyone. Not since Hank died." Carrie lowered her voice.

"She hasn't dated anyone seriously since he passed?"

"Oh, she's dated," Grey put in.

"But no one for long," Carrie confirmed.

"Hell, if Delia's men are flavors of the month, Leah's are flavors of the week!" Grey chuckled.

Carrie punched his arm lightly.

"Are you saying she sleeps around?"

"Not exactly. But she's about fun and games, lighthearted, no strings, and hanging with men who agree with her philosophy." Carrie finished her drink.

"I don't want that. I want more."

"I'm not sure she can give you more or wants to now." Carrie put her hand on Colin's arm.

"Then I'll have to change her mind." A frown creased his brow.

"Colin, why don't you listen? I'm sure there'll be some hot chicks at her New Year's party. Find someone there, someone who's looking for a guy like you," Grey put in.

"And you think Leah isn't?"

"I think Leah has some issues and you'd be better off with someone who doesn't. Besides, she's off to Paris. Geographically undesirable." Grey stood up.

"Time for us to dress," Carrie said, taking Grey's hand.

"We'll be down in a few," Grey said, taking Carrie's hand and climbing the stairs.

Carrie stopped halfway up the staircase and turned toward Colin. "Don't forget she has plans. Big plans." Then she continued to the second floor.

Colin plopped down on the sofa. *Maybe she has plans. But plans can change.*

AFTER A SUMPTUOUS DINNER, Colin took Leah home. She invited him in for a nightcap.

He sat carefully on the beautiful sofa. "When can I see you again?"

Leah joined him but kept a cool distance between them. She crossed her legs and folded her hands in her lap. "Hmm. I'm around this week. Have you ever been to the Met?"

"The opera? No. Not much of a fan of opera," he said.

"No, I meant the Metropolitan Museum of Art."

At the revelation of his lack of sophistication, he grew embarrassed. Heat crept up his cheeks.

"No," he said softly.

She reached over and squeezed his hand. "Then it's time you went there. I'd love to take you."

"You would?"

She trained a bright smile his way. "I would."

"When?"

She picked up her phone and checked her schedule. "Tomorrow?"

"Works for me," he said.

"How about the Museum of Natural History?" she asked.

"Not been there, either."

"Okay. Let's add that one on."

They made a second date. After checking his watch, he pushed to his feet and headed for the front door. He didn't want to overstay his welcome and ruin their growing relationship. He brushed his lips against hers in a gentle goodnight kiss, then hopped on the elevator and hurried along Central Park West toward Grey's townhouse, arriving about ten-thirty.

"Nightcap?" Grey asked his brother. "Carrie and I are about to share some very old sherry."

"Sure."

After pouring three small glasses, Grey went to a drawer where he pulled out a piece of lined paper and a pen. He handed these to Carrie and sat down on the sofa next to her.

"What's this for?" she asked.

"Colin's list."

"His list?"

"A dating list. For dating Leah. I assume you asked her out?" Grey raised his eyebrows and then glanced at Colin.

"Yup. We're going to the Metropolitan Museum tomorrow and the Natural History on Wednesday. What's a dating list?"

Grey chuckled. "Jenna made a list for me, a marriage list."

"It's the list that got him engaged to me in the first place."

"Then Carrie made me a love list. Kept me from losing her." Grey slipped his arm around her shoulders.

"We're big believers in lists." Carrie smiled.

"Okay, shoot. What do I need to know to date Leah?" Colin sat back and crossed his legs.

"One, she's sophisticated, knowledgeable. She doesn't want to talk about stupid little stuff."

"That narrows it down perfectly." Colin's sarcasm was not lost on Grey, who feinted a punch at his brother.

"What Grey means is she doesn't care about basketball scores," Carrie said.

"Or car racing results," Grey added.

"Or the size of your last girlfriend's breasts." Carrie laughed.

"Two, she hates bathroom humor," Carrie put in.

Grey pointed at the paper. "Three, be a good listener."

Carrie jotted it down. "That's very important. Women love a guy who listens. It's so rare!" She chuckled.

"Treat her with respect. Open doors, pull out her chair, hold her coat, take her arm on stairs," Grey said.

Carrie was scribbling as fast as she could.

"I'm not a Neanderthal, you know. I already do those things. I've had a few relationships," Colin said.

"Never discuss age. Don't make jokes about age, don't point out she's older or that you're younger," Carrie said.

"Isn't that the same thing?" Colin asked, unable to contain his irritation.

"Don't give phony compliments. Tell the truth, most of the time. Don't call her at the last minute for a date, assuming she's always available," she added, writing as she spoke.

"Most of these are common sense, you know," Colin remarked.

"Do you want to win her or not?" Grey asked.

Colin nodded.

"Then listen, Punk!"

"Don't press her for sex if she doesn't want it," Carrie added.

"If she doesn't want it often enough, move on. If you're an Andrews man—" Grey said.

"Enough! I'm an Andrews but I'm not going any further on that topic." Colin stood up.

"Don't forget the list," Grey said, snatching the paper out of Carrie's hand and stuffing it in Colin's breast pocket.

"Okay, okay. Got it. Geez. Don't you two ever let up?"

"You said you wanted a relationship with a real woman. The list should help."

Grey gave his brother a pat on the shoulder.

"One last thing. Let her tell you about her earlier life when she's ready," Carrie said, squeezing his forearm.

"That'll be the hardest one of all." Colin headed toward the stairs. "Goodnight."

CARRIE PUSHED TO HER feet and stretched her arms above her head. Her gaze swept over Grey's toned body and his sandy hair falling rakishly across his forehead, the sight stirring her desire.

"Time to cash in on that raincheck you promised me, mister," she said, resting her palms on his hard chest.

Grey shot a wicked grin back. She took his hand as they climbed the stairs. In their bedroom, Grey pulled her into his arms for a passionate kiss. Carrie combed her fingers through his hair as she pressed her hips against his. He groaned when her soft flesh came up against him, his hands slid down her back to her rump and squeezed.

Carrie unbuttoned his flannel shirt. After pushing up his T-shirt, her hands moved up, brushing through his chest hair, feeling the muscle underneath. He moved his lips down to her neck while his fingers slipped under the back of her shirt. A quick flip on the bra hooks and her breasts swung free, inviting capture by his hands. She moaned as he massaged her before gently pinching her nipple.

"Oh God, Grey." Carrie closed her eyes and leaned against him.

He broke from her to yank the bedcovers down. After taking his shirt off and ripping his T-shirt over his head, he turned to face her as he tugged his pants down.

"Can I help you?" he asked.

She nodded. His fingers made quick work of the buttons on her shirt and the one at the waist on her pants. Shrugging the shirt and bra off, Carrie stood, stripped to the waist. Her pants hit the floor. Grey shimmied her pink lace panties down her legs. His eyes followed the lingerie then skimmed over her body, as a smile played with his lips.

She loved being naked in front of him as he couldn't take his eyes off her. His gaze jumped from body part to body part. His dick grew. A flutter low in her belly stoked her fire. Her nipples hardened. The hungry look on his handsome face made her long for his touch.

"I love you like this," he whispered, approaching.

She raised her chin for him to take possession of her mouth. His lips came down hard on hers as his arms wound around her, crushing her against him. Carrie softened, yielding to their passion.

"You're beautiful," he muttered between kisses.

Grey inched backward toward the bed. He tumbled down with Carrie on top. She straddled him, giggling. With her hands flat on his chest, she leaned down and kissed his neck. His familiar male scent filled her nostrils sending heat through her veins. Then she licked down his neck to his collarbone. He hissed at the touch of her tongue. His hand directed her peak to his mouth where he played, demanding her surrender. She felt boneless, her body crumpling as the heat of her desire spiraled up and up, out of control.

Finally, she capitulated, easing down next to him on the bed as he rolled over on his side. His hand slid down, stopping to cup her hip, his fingers splayed, skimming over her smooth skin. Then he moved it down until it was at the juncture of her thighs. His fingers glided over her slippery core, stroking and swirling until she moaned. When he slipped a finger inside, her hips pumped to his rhythm.

Carrie tightened her grip on his shoulder with one hand before she closed her fingers around his hard erection with the other.

"Oh God, Carrie."

Grey lowered his head, his hot breath teasing and tickling her. He pressed his lips into the soft flesh at the base of her neck and groaned.

"Stop, stop..." he whispered.

Her hand slid up and down on him until he pulled it away. She bent her leg, coiling it around his hip as he gripped her bottom, pulling her closer.

"Come to me, baby," he muttered.

His hand slid over her backside and down the back of her thigh. He rolled onto his knees, crouching between her legs. Slinging her one leg over his shoulder, he drew her other one up and guided his dick to her entrance. When he thrust into her, she gasped.

"Grey!" She pulled his head down until his lips met hers. Her appetite for him consumed her. She took possession of his mouth while he moved inside her. He lowered himself to his elbows, his fingertips resting lightly on her shoulders, caressing her skin. She released his mouth and stared into his hazel eyes, glowing with desire mixed with love, just inches from hers.

"I love you." Her fingertips dug into his shoulders.

"You're mine, forever, honey," he said.

His whispered affection coupled with his plunging hard and steady into her destroyed any shred of control. Carrie's whimper became a groan.

"Come for me, baby," he whispered in her ear.

His words sent her over the top, and the heat inside her burst into flame. She cried out his name as every muscle in her body clenched. Carrie's hips thrust upward then down. He increased his pace keeping her climax going, her hips moving with his.

"Oh God," Grey muttered.

He drove into her again and again, his arms surrounding her, crushing her breasts to his chest as he buried his face in her neck. A loud moan signaled he had reached his climax. He pushed in one more time before collapsing. Carrie ran her hands over his back through a thin sheen of sweat, then dug her thumbs into his muscles on either side of his spine.

"That feels great."

"Good." She closed her mouth over the soft, fleshy area where his neck met his shoulder. The salty taste of his warm flesh reminded her of the sea, and its power, so like her strong husband. Grey bent back, resting on his haunches as he slid his hands down her chest, followed by his lips.

"You are stunning with lusty eyes," he said.

She laughed.

He moved his fingers across her forehead, tucking stray strands of her blonde hair back off her face.

"Lust only for you," she said. Her palm cupped his cheek.

"Beautiful." He kissed her hand, then her nose, and then brushed his lips against hers.

"Hold me a minute, will you?" Carrie said in a quiet voice.

"What's up?" Grey's brows knitted as he rolled on his back before drawing her into his arms.

Carrie nestled her head into his shoulder, stroked his chest then cleared her throat. "My mother is coming."

"When?" He picked his head up an inch or two off the pillow.

"In a couple of weeks."

"Great! I'll get to meet her. Your dad too?"

"Yeah. They've rented an apartment in the city for a couple of months."

"So they'll be here for the wedding?"

She nodded. A tremor shot through her body. Grey tightened his arms around her slightly, planting a kiss on her hair.

"This isn't good?"

"She wants to take over the wedding planning from Delia."

"Oh. Not good." Grey shook his head slightly.

"Delia's going to be furious."

"Why hasn't your mom stepped forward before?"

"We've never gotten along well. She's very controlling. She and my dad had a catering business. She's convinced Delia and I can't possibly plan the food for the wedding."

"But you can." He rubbed her shoulder with his palm.

"I know that...you know that...and Delia knows that."

"Why does she want to interfere?"

"I think she feels guilty for not spending enough time with me when I was growing up. They were always working. Especially on holidays."

"And she wants to make up for it now?"

"I'm going to get caught in the middle."

"What can I do to help?" He stroked her back.

"You're helping right now." Carrie closed her eyes and cuddled into him. Grey pulled the blanket and quilt up over them both, then she switched out the light.

"It's your wedding, Carrie. Have it the way you want it, honey."

"Right now hopping a plane to Las Vegas with you is looking pretty good."

Chapter Five

C olin climbed the stairs to the second floor, entered the guest bedroom, and closed the door. He toed off his shoes and stretched out his tall frame on the comfortable bed. The guest room was painted teal blue with white trim. The down quilt served as a bedspread and comforter with a teal, pink, and white small flower country pattern. The furniture was antique, stained white. It was a pretty and comfortable room.

The townhouse was old enough to have thick walls so Colin couldn't hear his brother and Carrie making love in the next room. He didn't have to. He knew what they were doing. A touch of envy mixed with his happiness for his brother. Grey had been searching for a long time for the right woman. Colin liked Carrie and considered her the perfect match for Grey. He didn't fool her with his bullshit. She shot it right back at him but with playful affection. He liked to watch the two lovers banter back and forth, always ending with a kiss. The mental image made him smile and gave him hope that someday he, too, could find the right woman with the perfect mix of humor and love.

His family treated Colin like a baby who didn't know his own mind. They had no clue he'd been searching for serious love like Grey and Carrie had. Being around older people twenty-four seven had matured Colin early.

Next step in his life involved finding the right woman and the perfect job. Though his inexperience in teaching college might stand in his way for the Kensington State job, his coaching experience was a plus. If he got that job, the only piece missing from his life would be the love of an amazing woman. A woman like Leah.

His mind wandered to images of her, making him restless. He checked his watch. Already eleven o'clock, was it too late to call? He'd chance it. He picked up his cell.

"I hope you weren't asleep," Colin said.

"At eleven? Not usually. Canceling our plans for tomorrow?"

"Of course not. Just wanted to talk to you."

"Oh? It couldn't wait until tomorrow?" she teased.

"Wanted to hear your voice," Colin said, feeling heat rising to his face.

"That's sweet."

"Leah, tomorrow is a date, right?" Colin closed the door to his room.

She laughed. "Do you want it to be?"

"Absolutely." He lay down on the bed.

"Okay. If you want to go out with an old lady."

"You're not an old lady. I'm twenty-nine and you're—" *Shit, the dating list—don't talk about age!* He smacked his forehead.

"I know how old I am, Colin."

"I don't care about age. I like being with you."

There was silence on the other end of the phone. *You blew it, boy. Damn! Read the list!*

"You're amazing, a special woman."

"No one has said that to me in a long time," she said, her voice almost a whisper.

"Why not?" He rolled over on his side.

"Because."

"Because why? You've been dating, right? You must have a string of guys as long as a city block wanting to take you out. Have you been out breaking hearts?"

She laughed again. "You're good for my ego. I don't have a waiting list of men and I'm not a heartbreaker."

"I didn't mean to imply you're mean. Guys must fall in love with you all the time."

"They don't. Besides, I'm not interested in falling in love."

Silence.

"Colin? Colin? You still there? Damn phone!"

"I'm still here. Why do you say that?" He propped himself up on his elbow.

"Too much to go into tonight. I'm going to see you tomorrow, so—"

"You'll explain then?"

"Maybe. Let's just have fun."

"Sure."

"Good. Until tomorrow then."

"Until tomorrow. Goodnight, sleep well, pretty lady."

"You too, sweetie."

Colin stripped down to his boxers and slipped into bed. After turning out the light, he lay sleepless, trying to figure out what Leah meant when she said she wasn't interested in falling in love. He stared at the ceiling and listened for the grandfather clock in the hall to strike two.

The athlete mentality in Colin reared up. He'd never shrunk from a challenge, be it a wrestling opponent, a football linebacker, or a barbell. When she said she didn't want love, Colin refused to believe her.

"Everyone wants love," he said aloud to himself.

He heard her words but sensed her actions belied her statement. For a woman who wasn't interested in love, she sure could flirt and kiss! She had flirted with him like crazy at the clothing store and over the ice cream. Damn if that wasn't a come-on, what was?

He scratched his stubbly chin. Maybe all Leah wanted was a one-night stand? Colin nodded. Sure, he'd oblige a hot one-nighter, but he

wanted more—much more. He'd have to figure out a way to turn it into something real, something lasting.

Carrie said Leah didn't do one-night stands, but he could swear
that's what she'd been angling for. Maybe after one night, she'd change
her mind and see it his way? And maybe not. Then he'd have to find
a different route to get to her heart. Nothing less would do. Grey had
persevered with Carrie and look at how well it had worked out.

Colin made up his mind to give Leah a full-court press. No way
could she hold out if he turned on the heat and used that list. Yep. The
dating list would be the secret weapon he'd use to win the heart of the
most amazing woman he'd ever met. With his decision made, he rolled
over and drifted off into peaceful sleep.

LEAH STOOD ON THE STEPS of the Metropolitan Museum,
wrapping her arms around her torso to keep out the cold. Despite the
bright sunshine, the air was chilly. Sunglasses hid her eyes, enabling her
to watch the people around her, undetected. A tall figure of a man approached the museum steps. *Colin.* A trickle of warmth entered her
blood as he ascended the steps with the grace of an athlete. His brief
wave signaled he'd spotted her. She flashed him a warm smile and then
enjoyed watching the way he moved up the steep stairs. *Such long legs.*

Colin reached the top quickly. Taking her in his arms, he surprised
her with a sweet kiss, transferring more heat to her body than she expected.

"Ever been here before?" she asked as he engulfed her small hand in
his.

"Nope. I wasn't into art as a kid. We did go to the Natural History
Museum, but that was a long time ago."

"We'll go there tomorrow."

"I used to know that place like the back of my hand."

"You can show me around. This is my museum. I've been coming here every week for six months, studying the clothing in the costume exhibit as well as the art. You can learn so much about the way people used to dress from the old Masters' paintings."

Colin raised his gaze to take in the enormous size of the building. "Good thing you know your way around. This looks like the perfect place to get lost."

"Not with me, babe," she said.

He shot her a dazzling grin as they pushed through the revolving doors into an enormous entryway. Being the holiday season, the museum was crowded.

Colin whipped out his wallet, but Leah stopped him.

"I'm a member and you're my guest."

She picked up a map and handed it to him.

"Where do you want to go first? Egyptian exhibit? Armor? French Impressionist Paintings? Sculpture?"

"You lead. I'll follow."

"Egyptian is right here. Let's go there first."

Leah flashed her membership card and they received two metal buttons required for admission. They walked through the archway and were immediately transported back to ancient times. Colin pointed to a passage to a recreated tomb and steered Leah there. Once inside he commented about the hieroglyphics while he snaked his other arm around her and pulled her close. His lips closed over hers, his tongue pressing lightly, requesting entry. She opened her mouth and Colin's tongue took possession, gently stroking hers, coaxing it out to play. He angled his head, deepening the kiss. Heat coursed through her veins, instinctively, her arms coiled around his neck. All thought left her mind as their tongues danced.

The sound of a throat clearing brought the couple back to reality. Leah pushed against his strong chest and stepped back. Blood rushed to her face as she lowered her eyes.

"Sorry. Don't mean to interrupt," an older woman said.

"Please, I apologize," Colin mumbled, making a sweeping gesture, moving back to make room for the other couple.

"Easy to see why," muttered the man under his breath with a sly grin.

Colin laughed while Leah's face grew hotter. She took his hand and yanked him out of the passage, dragging him behind her. After winding around through exhibit after exhibit on the first floor, they turned the corner, landing in the Arms and Armor exhibit. Leah saw the amused expression on Colin's face dissolve as his eyes focused on the metal figures before him. They were the only ones in the room.

He faced her. "Why not?"

"Why not what?" She raised her eyebrows.

"Last night you said you don't want to fall in love. Why not?" Colin moved closer, forcing her to meet his gaze.

"I thought we were here to see the exhibits," Leah said, taking a step back.

"We are. Can't I ask a question?"

She eased her hand from his.

"That's not just a question."

"I want to know."

"I don't owe you an explanation." She eased toward another metal statue.

Colin grabbed her elbow, halting her attempt to evade him.

"Right, you don't owe me anything. Answer the question. What do you have against love?" He kept eye contact.

"I'm not interested in falling in love, that's all." She cast her gaze to the floor.

"I don't believe you."

Leah snapped her head up. "You don't believe me?"

He shifted his weight. A look of uncertainty replaced a look of bravado.

"It's just that, well, yesterday, when we were shopping and at the ice cream place."

He swung his gaze from her face to the exhibit in front of them.

"Look at me. What about yesterday?" Leah grabbed his arm and planted her feet apart.

"Yesterday you flirted with me."

"So? I flirt with a lot of men. Hell, I flirt with Lance, the doorman. Doesn't mean I want to have his baby." Defiance flashed in her eyes, but it had no effect on Colin, he simply became amused instead of angry.

"Really? Have you kissed Lance or any other men in an Egyptian Tomb?" His eyes twinkled as a smile played with his lips.

"I don't know a lot of men who live in Egyptian tombs." Leah avoided his stare.

"Very funny," he replied, clearly not amused.

"*You* kissed *me*." Leah folded her arms across her chest.

"And you kissed me back." He stepped so close, she could feel the heat from his chest. It warmed her, stirring feelings long dormant. He tipped her chin up and gazed into her eyes. Her arms dropped to her sides. His concerned, loving look blended with a spark of desire, held her gaze. Her guard slipped a notch as she lost herself in his gorgeous hazel eyes.

"What happened to you?"

She tried to move away but his hand closed on her arm before she could. He eased her up against him. Her body relaxed. Lightheaded giddiness, as if she had had too much to drink, shot through her. A tingle rocketed along her nerve endings all the way to her fingertips before she put space between them.

"I still don't want to fall in love," she stammered, worried that the heat from him would dissolve her resolve.

"And I still don't believe you. We have a stalemate."

A group of five people strolled into the room removing the couple's privacy.

"I could use a cup of coffee," Leah said, heading toward the exit. "How about I buy you lunch?" Colin took her hand in his. "Which way to the café?"

COLIN COULDN'T BELIEVE how beautiful Leah looked, shivering on the steps of the museum in her cream-colored sheepskin coat which matched her boots. Her fuzzy pink hat, not exactly as high fashion as the rest of her outfit, looked cute in a little girl way, striking a chord in his heart.

He had taken the cement stairs easily, the lightness in his step matching the breeziness in his heart. While the art museum wasn't his favorite place, it was hers. What Leah thought of this painting or that sculpture now ranked as the most important opinion on Earth as he took another step closer to her world. Colin confessed to a serious lack of knowledge about art. He couldn't tell a modern art painting from a finger painting.

He meant to listen intently, take mental notes. But watching her talk, his eyes focused on her seductive lips with their tantalizing pinkness and shape. *So kissable.* When he realized they were the only people in the tomb, he'd seized the chance to kiss her. The power of that kiss almost knocked him on his butt.

Now he wanted more, needed more. Colin had to find out why she didn't want to fall in love. He followed her into the museum café. Leah led him to the Petite Court and Wine Bar on the first floor.

Colin ordered a sandwich, Leah a salad, and both chose coffee. After they ordered, she opened the conversation.

"I don't want to talk about falling in love."

The waitress brought their beverages. Colin sat back.

"Then let's talk about dreams. Did you always want to go to Paris and design lingerie?"

Leah laughed. Her lips curved up in the most charming way, her eyes sparkled. "I grew up in a small town in Connecticut. Mattan Ridge. I was a change-of-life baby. Mom was forty-seven when she had me. Because I was the last child left at home, I was always close to my parents. They had a wonderful life but died in an accident before I graduated college. My dream was to have a big farmhouse like they did and a couple of kids.

"What happened to that dream?" Colin took a sip of his coffee.

Leah added sugar and milk before answering.

"My last year in college I met Hank Golden. Before we got married, I agreed to stay in the city while Hank pursued his dream of success on Wall Street."

She stopped to take a breath and taste her beverage.

"Go on."

"Chasing success was harder than we thought. It kept being one more year, one more year. Two years turned into ten. While he was building our fortune, I became a buyer at Franklyn's, a women's clothing store, where I met Delia, Carrie's aunt."

She picked up her mug as the waitress arrived with their food.

After the waitress left, Colin asked, "What happened to *your* dream?"

Leah stopped her fork in midair, a small sigh escaped her throat.

"Hank died, taking my dream with him." She paused to chew, lowering her gaze.

Colin placed his hand over hers. She forced a smile.

"Now I have a new dream. Go to Paris and become a famous designer."

Silence fell on the table. Leah focused on eating her salad while Colin's appetite went out the window. Pain stabbed through his stomach in a flash and was gone.

"What about your dreams?" Her gaze connected with his.

Colin took a halfhearted bite of his sandwich before answering.

"Teaching and coaching at Kensington State would be my dream."

"Is that all? No family?" She gave him a flirtatious glance.

"Add a spectacular woman plus a couple of kids to the mix and it's complete." His gaze returned to his sandwich.

"Oh? Spectacular? She has to be spectacular? What mortal female can fulfill that?"

"I'm looking at her." Colin put down his sandwich.

She spit coffee into her cup and started to choke. The waitress rushed over to their table to pound Leah on the back. Colin waved the overzealous woman off while Leah cleared her lungs.

"You hardly know me," she choked out.

"I've known you for several days. I'd like to get to know you better, a whole lot better." His gaze caressed her body.

"I've heard that before." She wiped her mouth with her napkin. Blood rushed to Colin's face.

"Not just like that." He covered his embarrassment by eating.

"What exhibit do you want to see next?"

You, naked, in my bed. "Doesn't matter. I'll follow your lead."

"I love the French Impressionist paintings. Let's go there."

Colin wiped his mouth with his napkin and picked up the check. Leah sat back, grinning at him while he pulled a few bills out of his wallet and dropped them on the table.

"Thank you for lunch. It was delicious," she said.

"You're welcome." He stood up and offered her his hand while his gaze rested on her breasts for a moment.

She led him through the archway toward a huge room filled with beautiful paintings.

"Any favorites?" she asked, turning to face him.

"Don't know enough yet. Which are your favorites?"

"I love Van Gogh, Renoir, and Monet," she said.

"Then I'll start there."

His thumb caressed her hand as they strolled along from canvas to canvas. Leah explained the use of light and shadow, color and texture. Gradually, the great works of art captured him. As he listened to her words, he understood how the works of these artists reached out to her.

After two hours, they took a break, relaxing on a bench.

"Can we go somewhere for coffee?" Colin asked, standing up to hold Leah's coat.

"How about back to Nina and Clint's? They have some fabulous coffee from Zabar's there."

Alone with you in that apartment. Wishes do come true.

"You've twisted my arm. Let's catch a cab."

Leah received a text from Carrie: *Making chili. Come for drinks.*

"Carrie and Grey want us there for chili...cocktail hour starts now."

"Damn! I was looking forward to some alone time with you."

"Perhaps this is safer," Leah said, scanning the traffic on Fifth Avenue for an empty taxi.

Colin spotted one and raised his hand high.

"Safer? Are you afraid of me?" he asked as the cab screeched to a halt in front of them.

"It's not you I'm afraid of," Leah said as Colin opened the door for her.

"Then who?"

She slid across the seat, then he followed.

"Me. I'm afraid of me. Driver, we're going uptown. West Side."

Colin closed the door with a chuckle, then the vehicle sped away from the curb.

CARRIE SAT BY THE WINDOW, looking out at the gray, cold day. She shivered, picked up her phone, and sent a text to Grey at work.

Chili tonight with Leah and Colin.

His response was almost immediate.

Great. Be home at five-thirty.

Carrie sent a text to Leah, then put her phone down. She made the rounds of the refrigerator and cabinets, gathering the ingredients for chili. The phone rang, it was Delia.

"Hi, pumpkin. How are you?"

"Good. What's up?" Carrie opened the door to the fridge.

"I've talked to three caterers. I'd love your input."

"Wedding plans? Can you send me the menus in an email?"

"I'm happy to do the planning but honey, you do have to be in-volved—at least a little bit."

"I promise to look them over tonight," Carrie said.

"I like all three menus, so it's up to you," Delia said.

"Why don't we send them to Mom?" Carrie asked.

"Are you kidding? I'd rather wrestle a tiger than discuss menus with your mother. If you don't want to—"

"I get it. I'll have my answer for you tomorrow morning."

"Hugs, baby."

"Hugs, Delia."

Carrie hung up and chewed her lip while anxiety crept through her body. "It's already beginning," she said aloud to herself.

The rivalry between her mother and Aunt Delia, which had sim-mered for years, looked like it had bubbled over. With Carrie stuck in the middle, joyous wedding planning took on a more ominous tone. How could she have the wedding she wanted if they'd be fighting like two junkyard dogs the whole time?

Before Carrie had much chance to worry, Colin and Leah arrived. Carrie put them to work, pushing her wedding out of her mind and fo-cusing on the evening meal.

While Carrie fussed with the chili and Leah made a salad, Colin mixed drinks at the bar. The click of the lock accompanied by a rush of cold air signaled Grey's arrival. Carrie turned to watch her handsome fiancé. Carrie loved the way he looked when his cheeks were rosy from the cold and his hair windblown. Grey took her in his arms, placing his cold lips on her warm ones.

"No fire?" he asked, glancing at the empty fireplace.

"Only in my heart, dear," Carrie tossed back.

Grey hung up his coat and muffler, greeted Colin and Leah, then headed to the fireplace. Carrie brought him a vodka and tonic and plopped down next to him, watching him crumple newspaper.

News of the day was exchanged at the dinner table. Colin went on at length about the museum, which paintings were his favorite, and how he'd never expected to find an Egyptian tomb fascinating. Leah blushed at his last comment. Carrie and Grey exchanged looks. Had something happened they needed to know about? Grey chewed on his salad before adding his news.

"Got a call from Mom today."

Eyebrows raised around the table.

"Mr. Davenport had a stroke. She doesn't think he's going to last long."

Carrie put down her fork. "Who?"

"Mr. Davenport. He lives next door," Grey explained.

"Yeah with his hot daughter, Giselle, who used to have a thing for Grey," Colin piped up.

"She did not," Grey said, but his blush belied his statement.

"Oh?" Carrie raised an eyebrow in amusement and trained her gaze on Grey.

"They used to play *doctor*," Colin said, laughing.

"Doctor?" Carrie's eyebrow arched a touch higher.

"Uh, not really. She's the girl next door. And in high school, we may have gone out a few times." Grey's blush deepened.

"She was smokin' hot. All the guys were after her."

"Colin, shut up!" Grey raised his voice.

"It's okay," Carrie said, resting her hand on Grey's arm. "I'm not jealous. She had her chance and blew it. Now you're all mine."

"Forever, honey." Grey placed his hand over hers. His warm gaze sent a thrill up Carrie's spine.

Silence settled over the table. Colin stared at Leah who dropped her fork. The clatter of the utensil on the plate drew Grey and Carrie's attention. Carrie stifled a grin as she looked from Colin to Leah and back again. Color rose to Leah's face.

"What are you all looking at?"

Grey cleared his throat. Carrie put down her fork and piped up, "So, what is everyone wearing to the party on Friday night?"

Chapter Six

New Year's Eve, Central Park West and 76th Street

Leah lit the final candle in the apartment, blew out the match, and checked her watch. Eight o'clock. People would arrive soon. After dimming the lights, she surveyed the open living and dining area, which sported dozens upon dozens of candles, strategically placed, creating a soft, romantic glow.

She nodded her satisfaction, spying at least one candle on almost every flat surface. The place had a distinctly romantic feel. What was she doing? Romantic? Leah didn't want romantic, did she? She shook her head and laughed. Aloud to herself, she said, "Colin will meet some dazzling young women tonight and fall madly in love."

That notion brought an unexpected sense of loss, which puzzled her. Of course, it was flattering to have such a gorgeous young man hot on her trail. But it wasn't real, and she had other plans. "No time for romance," she muttered.

Jean Luc, the caterer, came out of the kitchen.

"Everything's ready, madame."

"Excellent. I have to change, only take me a minute."

He returned to the kitchen. His helpers set up a buffet on the sideboard in the dining room. Fontina, cheddar, and Swiss cheese cubes piled high filled half a large platter. The other half offered red grapes and strawberries dipped in chocolate. A platter of smoked salmon on corn blini with wasabi cream followed. And last was a serving dish piled high with prosciutto-wrapped tiny melon slices. At the very end of the table was a slow cooker filled with Swedish meatballs.

In the kitchen, the staff prepared hot hors d'oeuvres to be passed among the guests. The offering was sumptuous, including gruyere cheese puffs, crispy crab cakes with artichoke mustard aioli, sausage stuffed mushroom caps, pear and gorgonzola mini pizzas. They prepared baked brie to round out the food in the dining room.

In the refrigerator, keeping cold were finger-sized chocolate eclairs, napoleons, mini cheesecakes, and pistachio cream puffs.

Champagne cooled in buckets placed on two bars. Crystal flutes sparkled in the candlelight.

Her mouth watered at the delicious aromas from the kitchen wafting through the spacious apartment. How many of these special delights had Colin eaten before? Would he be uncomfortable because he might not know what was being served? In the bedroom, she pulled her lower lip into her mouth as she pulled out her clothes. She unzipped her gold dress and stepped in, then struggled with the zipper. *Damn! It's too long and my arms are too short.* She pulled it up most of the way and wiggled. The gold fringe shimmied around her hips, making her giggle. *I look like a flapper!*

As she applied the last of her makeup, the buzzer rang. She knew Jean Luc would buzz the doorman so she had a minute or two before her guests would be coming through the door. She applied one more layer of coral lipstick, slipped her feet into high-heeled gold sandals, and tossed her hair over her shoulder before greeting her guests.

Grey, Carrie, and Colin were the first to arrive. Carrie wore a long silver dress with a slit up to the hip on one side. Grey looked smashing in his Armani tuxedo. They greeted her with hugs. Hanging back was Grey's brother. Leah directed her gaze to him and gasped at her first sight of the expertly tailored tuxedo.

Colin stood twenty feet away, wearing a Ralph Lauren tuxedo that hugged his form. Leah smiled to herself, thinking about how Stan hadn't missed a detail of Colin's form. The store had done a magnificent job. He looked beyond handsome. The dark suit set off his hazel eyes, which focused on her. The slender lines of the pants and the jacket emphasized Colin's height. He looked taller, slimmer. She could hardly catch her breath.

He approached. "Nice tailoring job. Fits like a glove. I have you to thank," Colin said.

"You have your parents to thank for giving you that body." Leah's hand flew to her mouth. *Open mouth, insert foot, Leah!*

He grinned, then his gaze raked her body from head to toe.

"You look gorgeous. Wow! Gold is your color, like a queen."

"Thank you. Would you mind?" She turned her back to him. "I couldn't reach that last bit."

Colin put one warm hand on her shoulder, bared by the dress, and drew the zip up with the other. The tingle from the touch of his fingertips zinged through her body like a surge of electricity. When she turned around, he leaned down and brushed her lips with his. Leah steadied herself with a hand on his shoulder. Her fingers dug in, feeling the power of his muscles. A flutter in her belly warmed her.

Within a minute, her reverie was broken by the insistent ringing of the buzzer. Guests poured in. Leah expected about seventy-five people. Men dressed in formalwear or dark suits were accompanied by women in all manner of revealing gowns in black or white, magenta, hot pink, or iridescent purple. The rooms filled. People hovered by the breakfront, filling small plates with luscious food. Jean Luc's bartender poured champagne into flutes and placed them on the dining room table almost as fast as guests whisked them away. The sound of voices deep in conversation mixed with the tinkle of laughter and the low murmur of whispers. Old friends greeted each other with hugs while new acquaintances were introduced. Shadows created by the candles danced on the faces of the beautiful people. A holiday scent of cloves permeated the air. The mood was festive. Leah took Colin by the arm.

"Come. I want you to meet some people."

She steered him toward a group of five young women and two men, talking and drinking champagne. The women were dressed to the nines. Their ultra-high-heeled shoes brought them to eye level with Colin. The men in dark suits offered their hands. Leah made introductions and then discreetly faded into the crowd. When she glanced back, she saw the young women close a circle around Colin. They didn't waste any time moving in on him. She couldn't blame them, but realizing he'd probably leave with five new phone numbers and maybe a bed partner for the night, a feeling of emptiness tore at her heart.

Of course it would be better for him to claim one of those young women as his partner than to hope Leah would upend her plans for a life with him. She had done the right thing, relinquishing him to the arms of someone else, putting his happiness above her own. Slowly, a soft smile replaced the look of regret on her face as she turned away to greet other friends.

An older man came up behind her. "Leah, baby!" She turned, and he embraced her.

"Rod, how nice to see you!" she gushed, threading her arm through his and escorting him to the food table.

As the hostess of such a large party, Leah didn't have much time to spend with any one guest. Although Rod tried to corner her, she managed to slip away to speak with someone else and grab another glass of champagne. All the while, she kept an eye on Colin, who'd been caught in the web formed around him by the people nearer to his age.

Just before midnight, one of the waiters escorted a drunken Rod to the door. Relieved to be away from his cloying attitude and groping hands, she breathed a sigh of relief and returned to her other guests.

Grey and Carrie left right after midnight, leaving Colin to make his own way back to the townhouse. After most of the guests left, Jean Luc's staff stayed to clean up.

"Wait, I'll walk you to the corner, make sure you find a taxi." Leah gave tip money to Jean Luc before retrieving her coat.

"I'm not a baby, Leah. I can hail a cab on my own." Colin shrugged his broad shoulders into his coat.

"I know, but on New Year's Eve. Cabs'll be scarce and a woman might have a better chance."

Colin held her ermine coat for her, and they went down the elevator together in silence. When they hit the street, Colin spoke up.

"You're not going to see that guy Rod again, are you?"

"No."

"How many other *friends with benefits* do you have?" His gaze locked on her face.

Heat rose to her cheeks. "I haven't had any for a long time."

"Living the celibate life?" He raised his eyebrows.

The frigid wind on Central Park West barely relieved the growing warmth on her face.

"I've spent a lot of time alone lately." She folded her arms across her chest.

"I'm not judging you, Leah. Just looking for information." His gloved hand turned her chin toward him.

"Why?"

"Because I care about you."

"You've got your life in Pine Grove. I'm moving to Paris...why do you want to start something between us?" Leah stopped. Her heart was beating wildly in her chest.

"You and I have something. Call it chemistry—whatever. I've never been as attracted to a woman as I am to you."

"That's just sex. Like *friends with benefits*?"

"It's more than that. You're like a beautiful onion."

"An onion?" She rested her hands on her hips, frowning.

"Each layer that peels back reveals something wonderful and exciting about you. Something I didn't know before. You're creative, smart, classy." His hands held her shoulders.

When her gaze perused his face, she saw sincerity in his eyes. Words of denial caught in her throat. She reached up to cup his cheek. Their lips met.

"Get a room," a lone man on the street said as he walked by.

Leah moved back, away from Colin.

"You don't have to take me to the corner like a nursemaid."

"It's just—"

"Stop! I'll find a cab. It's freezing. Go back inside, I'll be fine."

He turned her around and gave her a gentle shove toward the apartment.

"You're sure? You'll call me when you get home?"

"Leah!"

"Please?"

"All right, all right. Anything if you'll get out of the cold."

Confused, she headed toward her building. She'd never met a man except Hank, her late husband, who was as sweet as Colin. Why did their timing have to be so rotten? Lost in her own thoughts, she wasn't paying attention to her surroundings. An after-midnight holiday evening quiet blanketed the street. Suddenly, an arm snapped around her waist from behind, gripping her hard.

"Give me your purse and your coat," a hoarse voice whispered.

Leah struggled to get away, but his arm held her in a vise-like grip.

"Colin! Colin!" she screamed with all her strength.

"Shut up!" he spat at her with putrid breath.

The man tightened his grip while he slapped his other hand over her mouth. Fighting for breath, she tried to move his fingers, which seemed glued over her lips and nose.

"Gimme your coat!" he demanded, his hoarse voice louder than before.

Leah shook her head, pushing against his hand, to no avail. Her pulse beat wildly. Fear wrapped an icy hand around her heart. Reason returned.

She nodded vigorously, but the man wouldn't let go. He lifted her up so that her feet dangled off the ground. She tried to kick him but flailed her legs back and forth to no effect. Hope was running out as she felt lightheaded from lack of air.

She heard running feet. As suddenly as he'd grabbed her, he let go. His hands tugged on the lapels of her ermine coat from behind as she gulped air into her lungs. Leah kicked back, but he dodged her foot. He spun her around, pulling at her coat. She threatened him with her small fist. He raised his hand and slapped her hard across the face, knocking her to the ground with a cry. Searing pain rocketed through her brain, paralyzing her for a moment. Her hand flew to her mouth. Something warm and wet dribbled down her chin. She tasted blood. Tears clouded her eyes, but she brushed them away, raising her hand in a defensive move.

He lifted his hand in the air, poised to strike her again when a man's hand locked onto his wrist. The man behind him twisted her assailant's arm until he cried out. Then the newcomer yanked the man's arm back and shoved it up his back, causing him to scream in pain. His other arm closed around the man's neck, subduing him with a choke hold.

"Leah, call 911," Colin said as he held the assailant still.

Her hands shook as she took out her cell phone. Between the cold and her fear, Leah couldn't command her fingers to dial. She started to cry in frustration.

"Leah! Pull yourself together." Colin's voice was calm and steady. The man who'd attacked her gasped and then whimpered.

She took a big breath, feeling a shudder roll through her body before a moment of calm set in. She dialed the number, reporting the assault and giving the exact location. They waited at least five minutes in silence before they heard the sound of distant sirens drawing closer. Her body trembled out of control, whether from fear or the cold, she couldn't tell. Maybe both. A sense of relief washed through her as the black-and-white pulled up, lights flashing. They drew their guns on Colin.

"Let him go, sir," the shorter, darker officer said.

Colin let go of the man and raised his hands. The man started swearing and attempted to take a swing with his good arm, aiming at Colin, who dodged him. The smaller police officer subdued the man and then locked him in handcuffs. Colin rushed to Leah and helped her up.

"What happened, ma'am?" the taller officer asked Leah.

Resting against Colin, she took another deep breath and paused before recounting the assault while the man screamed, "Liar." With trembling hands, she retrieved her driver's license from her small bag lying on the sidewalk and gave the policeman her contact information.

When she was finished, Colin folded her into his arms. She let go, allowing the pent-up fear to surface as she sobbed against his chest. The officer gently pried her away from Colin to snap several pictures of her face while his partner put the hollering man in the back of the squad car.

"You might want to get that lip looked at, lady. Do you intend to press charges?"

"Damn right I do," Leah said in a shaky voice.

"Good, gets that guy off the streets. We'll need you to come down to the station house."

"Can I do it in the morning?"

"Okay. Bring him." The officer indicated Colin, then handed Leah his card.

"I'll be there," Colin said.

The taller officer joined his partner in the squad car. They drove away.

Leah's legs shook like quivering jelly as she leaned against Colin on the short walk back to the apartment. The place was quiet when they entered. Colin led Leah right into the kitchen. He took some ice from the freezer, folded a cloth napkin around it, and placed it on her lip, picking up her hand to hold it there. He drew up a chair and sat her down before he poured a glass of wine for her from the bottle of cabernet on the counter.

Leah's hand shook too much to hold the glass. Colin held it up to her lips and she took a sip. When the alcohol met her cut lip, she hissed from the pain.

"I'm sorry. I tried not to get it there. Do you have straws?"

Leah indicated a drawer and Colin retrieved one. As she sipped, the wine warmed her and she calmed down. Colin carried her into the living room. He sat on the sofa, placing her in his lap. As she cuddled into his shoulder, he held her close and stroked her hair. Leah closed her eyes. Colin hunted up some ibuprofen and presented it to her with a glass of water and a straw.

"This will make you feel better in the morning."

"Please don't leave," Leah asked, closing her fingers around his forearm.

"I'm not going anywhere."

She glanced at him with a questioning look.

"I don't want you to be alone. We can spend the night—as friends," he said.

She tried to smile but the pain in her lip made her wince.

"Do we have to take you to the emergency room?"

"Let me see." She fumbled in her purse, still unable to get her fingers to stop shaking. Finally, she found a compact and opened it to examine the damage to her face in the small mirror. Her lip was swollen to twice its normal size, the cut made by her teeth was mostly on the inside and didn't appear big enough to require stitches.

"I think it will heal on its own," she said to Colin.

"Let me snap a couple more pix of you." He whipped out his phone and took a few close-up shots before she could object.

"I must look horrible." Leah tried to get off his lap, but he pulled her back.

"Stay. I think you'll be okay." He placed the ice pack back on her lip.

She nestled into his shoulder, emitted a big sigh, and relaxed. Colin stroked her back. Her eyes closed. Exhaustion set in.

"Sleep would be the best thing," he whispered.

He stood up with her in his arms as if she weighed as little as a ragdoll, then headed for the bedroom, placing her gently on the bed. She stretched out her arms and legs.

"Thank you for saving me."

"I should have realized that guy was up to no good when we passed him and that it wasn't safe for you to walk even two blocks back to the apartment at that hour. I'm sorry. It's my fault."

She slapped his arm and knitted her brows. "It's not your fault! It's that jerk's fault."

She tried to reach around to undo her dress, but her fingers wouldn't cooperate. Colin turned her around and ran the zip down. He retrieved her bathrobe before peeling off the garment. It was obvious she wasn't wearing a bra, maybe no underwear at all, so he draped her terry robe over her shoulders as he slid her dress down. Would his hands on her shoulders feel her tremble? When he pushed the dress down, his fingers came into contact with her breasts for a second or two. A tingle shot down to her core. She slipped her arms into the sleeves of her robe and drew it around her naked body.

Colin removed pieces of his tuxedo, placing them on the dresser and a nearby chair. He laid them out neatly. Wearing only his boxers, he returned to the bed. Leah had her robe wound around her, her hand held it closed at her chest. His grace and perfect body as he moved across the room aroused her despite her pain. She eyed his chest, longing to touch him.

Her gaze raked his body. Colin pulled the covers down in one motion and gestured for her to get in. She slipped underneath and scooted over.

"Sleeping only. I promise. Even if it kills me," he said.

Colin sat down on the bed and swung his long legs over, then pulled up the covers.

"Come here," he said, motioning.

She cuddled up, putting her head on his chest. Her fingertips brushed through his chest hair and a small smile stretched her swollen lips.

"Ouch! Hurts too much to smile or talk." She gestured toward her mouth.

"That's okay. We don't need to talk."

Colin put one arm around her and inched the covers up over her shoulder with the other.

"My robe, I almost forgot," Leah said, sitting up and sloughing one side off her shoulder, exposing her breast to his gaze.

Colin pulled the robe back onto her shoulder.

"No way. I'm not sleeping here with you if you take that off. I'm only human, Leah. If you're sleeping naked with me, then we're making love."

She fisted the robe and held it to her chest. He opened his arms again, and she fell into them with a long sigh. The ibuprofen kicked in. The warmth from his body thawed her frozen fingers and nerves, and peace flowed through her veins. He leaned over and switched off the lamp on the bedside table. Cuddled together, the would-be lovers fell asleep.

At four o'clock, Leah sat up in bed screaming. Colin woke up and touched her shoulder. She shrank back from him.

"It's me, Colin," he said.

'You're still here." She placed her hand on his chest.

"Did you think I'd run out on you?"

"Didn't know what to think," she murmured.

Shivering, Leah reached out to touch his face. He kissed her fingers.

"Come to me, sweetheart," he whispered.

He folded her in his arms and pulled up the covers. She sighed. The next time she opened her eyes, she was staring at the clock, which read ten a.m.

Chapter Seven

The bright, cold, winter sun flooded in her window and poked Leah. She rolled over expecting to find Colin, but the bed was empty. *A dream?* She touched her lips gingerly. They were still sore and swollen, though less than the night before. A sniff of the air detected a distinct smell. *Bacon?*

As she sat up, the door burst open. Colin entered carrying a tray with two plates piled high with bacon and eggs but only one mug of coffee. He placed the tray down on the bed. His gaze sought hers.

"Half a sugar and milk, right?"

"Breakfast in bed?" She raised her eyebrows.

"Yup. The way you like your coffee?"

She nodded.

"I already had a cup so this is yours. Careful, it's hot." He handed her the mug and then removed a plate with one hand while he gathered the utensils with the other.

Leah took a tiny sip, cringed, and then took another.

"Coffee's good. Bacon may be hard to eat but it's damn tempting. Thank you."

The delightful aroma prompted a rumble in her stomach. Colin took his plate and joined her in bed. He wore his tuxedo pants from the night before and the shirt, unbuttoned. His hair was mussed and hanging over his forehead. He had the beginning of scruff on his face. A completely different appetite grew in her belly.

Her robe gaped open. Colin's gaze on her exposed chest created warmth, like the caress of a hand. Her gaze followed his. She turned away, put her plate down, and secured her covering.

"Nice view," Colin murmured before putting a forkful of eggs in his mouth.

She laughed in spite of her injury.

Once they finished, he took the dishes back to the kitchen.

"We have to get down to the police station."

Leah made a face.

"We have to," he said.

"I know. But I don't have to like it. You're coming, right?" She pushed to her feet.

"Of course. I'd never let you go alone." He tipped her chin up and placed a delicate kiss on her injured lips.

Leah threw herself into his arms, tears streaming down her face. Colin held her, stroking her hair.

"What's this? It's all over. You're safe. I'm here," he said.

She cried for a few more seconds before reining in her emotions.

"I haven't heard those words in a long time," she said, casting her gaze away from his, wiping her eyes with her hands.

"What words? *I'm here?*"

She nodded.

"You've been alone for a long time, haven't you?" His voice was quiet.

Words caught in her throat. She gave one nod, blinking to keep more tears at bay.

"Leah, honey, you're not alone now." He brushed his fingers through her hair and then cupped her cheek.

She rested her head against his shoulder, closing her eyes, drinking in his male scent with a whiff of his piney aftershave. She touched his cheek.

"But you'll go back to Pine Grove and I'll go to Paris."

"I'm staying until tomorrow. I'll be back next month for winter break. In time for Valentine's Day."

"And then?"

"I'll return for spring break in April. Then it's summer and I'm off."

"But."

"Stop thinking so far ahead. Can't we enjoy today and tomorrow?"

She tried to smile. Colin wiped away a stray tear with his thumb.

"Get dressed. We have to go to the police station, then football. Pick your team: Nebraska, Ohio State, or Georgia Tech?"

IN SPITE OF THE COLD, Colin and Leah needed exercise to reduce their stress, so they walked to the police station. Stepping quickly against the winterish wind, Colin remembered he hadn't checked in with his brother since late last night. He'd spoken to Grey briefly after the incident, but he'd woken him up and wasn't sure his brother would even remember their conversation. Grey would probably still be fuzzy about why Colin wasn't home and what had transpired. He called his brother.

"Hey, Grey, I'll be sleeping at your place tonight," Colin said.

Leah shot a questioning glance at Colin.

He put his hand over the speaker on his phone.

"One night of brother-sister in your bed is all I can take. Will you be all right on your own?"

She nodded.

Colin turned back to the phone.

"Late. Yeah. Happy New Year to you too." He put his phone away and then took Leah's hand.

The police asked Leah some questions and she signed some forms. They also talked to Colin since the perpetrator complained about Colin's rough handling. The police declined to press charges against the athlete since he was defending Leah. Leah acknowledged she'd have to appear in court to testify against the robber. She agreed. The would-be lovers returned home an hour and a half later.

"Hungry?" he asked, shedding his heavy coat and hanging it on a hook by the door.

"Starving," she said, hanging her coat in the closet.

"Get comfortable. I'll heat up leftovers," Colin said before he disappeared into the kitchen.

He returned, balancing two platters loaded with assorted hors d'oeuvres left over from the party. Leah had changed into a long, rose-colored velour robe, and lounged on the sofa. The slightly open zipper revealed a decent view of cleavage. Colin's gaze zeroed in on the bit of exposed flesh as he set the dishes down.

"You look beautiful," he said.

"This looks delicious. You're spoiling me." She reached for a cheese puff.

"This is it. Eggs, bacon, and reheating leftovers are my whole repertoire."

She smiled with minimal wincing. Colin touched her lower lip with his fingertip.

"Does it hurt much?"

"No. Just a little," she replied.

"You're healing."

"Yes. And I could eat a horse! I love party leftovers."

When they finished the food, Colin cleaned up the kitchen. At two, they settled onto the sofa to watch the game. She cuddled into his shoulder and he wrapped his arm around her. Colin tried to concentrate on the television, but he kept getting distracted by the subtle scent of Leah's perfume. He caressed her forearm with his fingertips.

"You're not wearing anything under that, are you?" He tried to keep his eyes on the large screen.

"Bare ass nekked."

"Do you have to say that with such enthusiasm?" He frowned.

She chuckled. "You asked."

Hunger grew in his loins until the action on the screen intensified, providing Colin with a welcome shift in focus. Leah watched the closely matched college teams struggle against each other as the lead seesawed back and forth between both universities. When it was over, their team had squeaked out a victory.

"Time for you to get some sleep. I'll shove off." Leaving was the last thing he wanted, but she needed rest.

As if on cue, Leah yawned.

Colin slung his coat over his shoulders. Leah took the lapels and pulled him closer. She tried to kiss him, but it hurt too much. He stroked her head and then headed toward the door.

"Thank you. For everything," she said, padding along behind him.

"Happy I could help."

"You're a great guy."

"Thanks."

She snaked her arms around his middle for a hug. He stroked her hair and kissed the top of her head.

"Take it easy, okay? Rest," he said.

She nodded and opened the door. The elevator came quickly, and he was on the street in the blink of an eye.

THE WINTERISH JANUARY wind teased the back of Colin's neck. He raised the collar of his jacket and walked briskly up the avenue. He needed to think. When he got back to his brother's place, Grey and Carrie would question him. They'd want to know what was going on with Leah. He searched his mind for nebulous answers that would give away nothing but found none. The truth? He had no answers. He wanted her, but beyond that, he had nothing. He needed answers he didn't have. He searched his brain but came up with zero.

Exactly what was going on between Leah and him? He had no clue. Maybe he was falling in love. Could that be possible—so fast? Didn't people talk about love at first sight? And when he saw her at the front door, didn't his heartbeat race, his blood pressure rise? And it wasn't only her looks, but a woman who looked like that could bring an entire football team to a halt. She had something more. What was it? Class? Knowledge? Sophistication? Weren't those all the same thing? There had been a wave, a chemistry that had knocked him speechless. But Leah, whoa, she was way out of his league.

For example, he didn't know what half the hors d'oeuvres served at the party were. Sure, he tried them all, and they were delicious. She knew, she knew everything. Leah had to be the most sophisticated woman he'd ever met. What did he have to offer her? Beating up a mugger? Yeah. Earning big bucks, uh, no. At twenty-nine, he'd considered himself fairly knowledgeable about the world—until he met Leah.

He could offer great sex, loyalty, devotion, and his heart, but would that be enough for a woman like her? Couldn't she have her pick of men? Why would she choose him over some Wall Street guy who could give her the moon? No reason, he got that. Gloom settled on Colin. His spirit hit rock bottom.

The temperature dropped even more, and the wind picked up, penetrating Colin's jacket. He shivered. Was it because of the cold or something else—like setting himself up to get his heart smashed to smithereens? Unable to withstand the harsh wind, Colin sought relief in a taxi.

When he reached Grey's townhouse, he knocked. After a curt New Year's greeting, he hit the stairs, heading for his room. He needed sleep and to lick his wounds a little. He'd be heading home soon. Time to get Leah out of his blood, if that was possible. He took off his fancy duds, stretched out on the bed, and settled into a fitful sleep.

Sunday afternoon, Leah and Carrie stood in the vestibule of Grey's townhouse to say goodbye to Colin. Grey pulled up in front to drive him to the bus. Colin kissed Carrie on the cheek and hugged her.

"Thanks for everything, sis."

She stepped back, making room for Leah.

He could barely quell the longing in his heart. He wanted to scoop her up and take her with him.

She smiled, her gaze connecting with his. He pulled her into his arms and held her tight. Leah softened against him.

"Leah," he murmured, closing his eyes and drinking in her fresh scent. With a sigh, he straightened up and rested his chin on the top of her head.

"You're coming back?" She stepped back.

"For President's Week. Will you go out with me on Valentine's Day?"

"I've never been invited so early before."

"Well?"

"I'd love to spend it with you." She reached up to touch his face.

"Good." He pulled her into an embrace and hoisted her up until their lips met.

He pressed his against hers gently, his touch feather-light. Leah parted hers, admitting his tongue. Colin's arms wrapped firmly around her hips and shoulders holding her fast. She ran her hands up his neck and into his hair.

Carrie cleared her throat. "Uh, get a room, guys. Know what I mean?"

Colin set Leah down slowly. When she stepped back, a rush of cold air engulfed him. He frowned, missing her already. "I'll miss you."

"My knight in shining armor," she whispered. Colin turned and jogged down the front walk, sliding into Grey's Jaguar XK quickly and cleanly. Grey threw his brother's bag in the trunk. Leah raised her hand to wave goodbye then wrapped her arms around her torso to ward off the sudden chill.

FEBRUARY 12, LINCOLN'S *Birthday, New York City*

"Any word?" Leah chewed her lip.

"None yet. I tried Colin's cell phone, but all I got was static," Grey said.

"Come in. Get warm," Carrie said, pulling Grey into the living room.

Leah paced in front of a roaring fire in Grey and Carrie's townhouse. Grey entered, stopping to stomp the snow off his feet on the welcome mat. Carrie joined him, planting a kiss from her warm lips to his icy ones. She brushed the snow off his shoulders as he unzipped his jacket.

"What if the bus skids off the road? What if he's stranded in this subzero wind chill?" Leah resumed pacing, her arms folded across her chest.

"But you don't care for him, do you, Leah?" Grey's eyes twinkled.

"We're friends. That's all. Can't I worry about a friend?"

"Colin's a survivor. He's been in worse storms." Grey unzipped his jacket.

Carrie opened a bottle of brandy and poured three glasses. Grey took one. He closed his fingers over her forearm and tugged her down on the sofa next to him. Leah took a draught from her glass and then returned to pacing. Grey flipped on the TV and switched to the news.

"Worst snowstorm in ten years...stalled cars litter the highways...they're talking blizzard," the TV reporter said.

Leah chewed a fingernail, staring at the TV screen. The film footage of incapacitated cars on the snow-covered roads made her nervous. Her heart thudded against her chest. *If anything happens to him...like Hank...*her stomach knotted, turning queasy.

Carrie put an arm around Leah, startling her.

"Colin'll be okay."

"Do you promise, Carrie?" Leah asked, a little too sharply.

"He's not Hank. Nothing's going to happen to him," Carrie whispered.

"I wish I could believe you. Lightning can strike twice."

Leah took a gulp of her brandy to keep a tremble at bay. The drink warmed her inside. She took another big sip, glanced at the TV then returned to the large, rectangular window facing the street. The heavy snow and dark sky destroyed visibility.

"How late is he?" she asked, peering into the darkness.

"About four hours, but that doesn't mean—"

She put up her hand. Stepping closer to the window, she wiped away the vapor clouding her view with her hand.

"I see something." She wiped the glass again. The image of a tall figure making its way down the street went from hazy to clear.

Grey stood up. Carrie joined Leah at the window.

"Hard to tell, but I think..." Carrie said.

Leah dashed out the door, leaving it wide open. She ran down the street without her coat, slipping and sliding in her high heels on the icy walk until she reached the dark figure.

"Colin!" she cried as she leaped into his outstretched arms.

He hugged her, twirling her around and around. His cold lips joined with hers in a hungry kiss. She wanted to devour him. An inner smile spread heat throughout her body despite the snowy cold. It only lasted a few seconds before sharp wind ripped through her thin sweater chilling her to the bone.

"Where's your coat? You'll freeze. It's snowing, ya know," he said, pulling her in close.

Relief flooded her veins, bringing happy tears. She blinked fiercely until they were under control, refusing to look at him.

"You were worried about me?" His eyebrows shot up.

She couldn't escape his keen gaze.

"I'm starved and you're holding up dinner," she said, averting her eyes.

He burst out laughing. "You're a lousy liar."

Colin opened his coat and pulled Leah in close, draping it around her small body. She hugged his waist. When they reached the house, Grey handed his brother a glass of brandy while Carrie took his coat.

"You look half frozen," Carrie said.

"Took you long enough," Grey mumbled, transferring a heavy pot from the stove to the table.

"I practically had to walk the whole way!" Colin took a swig of the warming liquid.

Leah held her glass up for a toast. "To your safe arrival."

They all clinked glasses.

"Great to have my girl here, waiting for me."

"Your girl?" Leah cocked an eyebrow.

"Oops, I mean my woman."

"What?" Leah placed her hands on her hips.

"Don't deny it," Colin said.

He kissed her, draping one arm around her waist and holding his glass with the other.

"Let's eat. You can tell us the whole story over dinner," Grey said, pulling out a seat for his fiancée.

Colin downed his brandy before holding a chair for Leah.

THE NEXT MORNING

Over breakfast, Colin, Grey, and Carrie ironed out plans for Valentine's Day. Colin caught the sly grins being exchanged by his brother and Carrie across the small table in their kitchen. Their private communications made him a tad uncomfortable and a bit envious. *Maybe someday I'll have that. Maybe with Leah.* He shook his head a little to loosen the thought. His gaze drifted to the calendar on the wall. Time was running out. She'd be leaving for Paris soon.

"Where can I take Leah that will make her fall in love with me?" he blurted out, interrupting.

Grey stopped speaking and stared at his brother. "You can't make a woman fall in love with you on one date."

"It's just that she's so sophisticated. I can't afford a five-hundred-dollar dinner. Besides that'd only be pretentious. She'd see through it. I want to do something different."

"Leah loves to laugh. Take her to a comedy club," Carrie put in.

"Stand Up and Laugh is right in her neighborhood too. Then you might be able to wangle an invite to Nina's place again. The bedroom is where you'll make her fall in love with you. If you're an Andrews man through and through."

Carrie batted Grey playfully.

"I don't want to push her."

"Play it by ear, Colin. You'll know if and when." Carrie slipped her hand under Grey's.

"Had Carrie eating out of my hand after the first time."

"What?" Carrie sat back and glared at her fiancé.

Colin burst out laughing. "Looks like *you're* going to be shelling out for a five-hundred-dollar dinner tonight, brother, to make up for that one."

"Your arrogance is—"

"Honey, sweetheart. I was only kidding. Trying to give my brother a little confidence. I know I was puppy-dogging you the whole time."

Grey leaned in to kiss her, but she moved away for a moment before meeting his lips.

"You're the best thing that's ever happened to him, Carrie. We all know that," Colin said. "Comedy club, eh? Interesting." Colin stroked his chin.

"It'll be different. If you want Leah to see you as a cut above the rest, this might be one way to impress her," Carrie said, lacing her fingers with Grey's.

"She has been squired around town by plenty of rich Wall Street guys. You know, fancy schmancy restaurants and such. None of 'em lasted, though. I don't know what she's looking for but you may be it. What are *you* looking for?" Grey asked.

"Her. She's it. Fancy, rich Wall Street guys, huh?" Colin rubbed the back of his neck.

"Obviously, she doesn't want that, or she'd have found it by now. Trust me, Leah dated a lot last year," Carrie added.

"She'd be lucky to have a guy like you. If you want her, don't give up. I didn't, and now I have the best of the best—for life." Grey beamed a loving look at Carrie.

"What's the number of that comedy club?"

Grey tossed his phone to his brother. "Stand Up and Laugh. Look it up."

Chapter Eight

At five o'clock, Colin came downstairs. He wore a perfectly pressed dark gray suit with a light green shirt that brought out the green flecks in his hazel eyes. He twirled a navy and green rep striped tie in his hand while he whistled.

Carrie stood at the bottom of the stairs with her back to Grey. He zipped up her dress and bent to brush his lips over her shoulder.

"Get a room, guys," Colin said, his eyes dancing with mischief.

"Hilarious," Grey responded. "When you have a woman you can't keep your hands off of, talk to me."

"You look great, Colin," Carrie said.

"Wow! What a dress! Where are you going?" Colin asked.

Carrie blushed. "To dinner."

"Where?"

"La Tour Eiffel."

"I heard that is the most expensive place in New York."

"Close," Grey said, straightening his tie.

"Afterward?" Colin cocked an eyebrow at his brother.

"That's private," Grey said, coloring a little as he fastened the hook at the neckline of Carrie's dress.

"See what Grey gave me for my birthday?" Carrie fingered the solid gold heart pendant around her neck that matched her earrings.

Colin whistled. "You always did have good taste, Grey."

"We'll exchange Valentine's gifts after dinner." Carrie shot a sly smile at her husband, who blushed a brighter red.

"A woman who can make Grey blush, now that's news!" Colin punched his brother in the shoulder.

"We shouldn't wait up?" Grey asked, raising his eyebrows.

Now it was Colin's turn to blush. He shook his head. "Probably not."

"That's pretty bold, pretty confident." Grey stared at his brother.

"Hey, if I get lucky, great. If I don't, I'll sneak in quietly. I hate to disturb noisy lovers."

"Noisy? Really? Do you hear us?" Grey asked.

Colin put his hand up. "It's still so easy to get you," he said with a chuckle.

"What are your plans for dinner?" Carrie asked, deftly changing the subject.

"Leah said she has something planned at the apartment for us. Then the comedy club."

"And I'll bet you have something planned at the apartment for her too," Grey said, wiggling his eyebrows. Colin punched his brother lightly in the shoulder.

"Shut up, Grey," he said.

"Have fun tonight. Happy Valentine's Day," Carrie leaned over to peck her brother-in-law's cheek.

"Thanks, Carrie. Same to you."

With nerves climbing, Colin reached into his pocket for the umpteenth time to check if the small box was still there. He put on his new overcoat and the three of them left the townhouse. The air had warmed up some, melting the snow off the sidewalk and some off the street. They squeezed into Grey's sports car and headed downtown.

Colin got out at 78th Street and walked to Leah's building. He nodded at Lance, who smiled back before calling up to Leah. Nerves climbing made his palms sweat. Again, he fingered the box, wondering when to present it to her. The shirt collar rubbed a little. He wasn't used to dressing up in oxford shirts and suits. His neck preferred the soft comfort of a sweatshirt to the stiff collar and the tie a bit too snug around his neck. He took a deep breath. Damn, he needed to calm down. He wasn't sixteen anymore and this wasn't a first date. But come to think of it, maybe it was?

He cracked a rueful smile at his silly nerves. Already in his life he'd faced down two-hundred-fifty-pound gorillas on the football field and aggressive men in the wrestling ring, and never flinched. Colin had been a ruthless competitor, a winner-take-all champion in sports since his early days on the soccer field as a kid. And now he found himself reduced to a mass of quivering jelly by the penetrating stare and confident attitude of a petite woman who probably weighed about a hundred ten pounds. Where was his grit? His determination? His confidence? Flown out the window, he feared. Outclassed by a mile, Colin refused to quit, though the odds of victory were not in his favor. He'd found the woman he wanted and nothing less would do.

As ready as he could be, Colin took a deep breath and strode to the elevator.

HE STEPPED OUT OF THE elevator and turned to find Leah waiting at the open door. She wore a winter white wool dress, trimmed in ornate gold ribbon. The neckline was low enough to pull his gaze. The short hemline drew his sight down to her shapely legs.

"You look gorgeous," he said, leaning down to kiss her.

"So do you."

She took his arm and guided him into the apartment. Colin looked around, amazed to see what must have been twenty candles of all sizes and shapes blazing. Places were set on the coffee table and a mouth-watering aroma wafted in from the kitchen.

"Veal stew, one of my favorites," she said. "Please open the wine. I'll be right back with the food. I know we have an eight o'clock show. Will you tell me now where we're going?"

"Nope. After dinner."

She grinned. "I love surprises!"

Leah disappeared into the kitchen. He attacked the bottle of chablis, easily removing the cork, and poured two glasses before placing the small box that was in his pocket next to Leah's plate. She returned carrying a tray with two steaming bowls of veal stew resting on a bed of brown rice. Colin helped her place the bowls on the plates as a low rumble tiptoed through his belly. Suddenly starving, he eyed the stew with a hungry smile.

"What's that?" she asked, referring to the box.

"Just a little something for Valentine's Day," he said.

She picked it up. After removing the top, she uncovered a beautiful solid gold heart pendant on a gold chain. Her sudden intake of breath and big smile warmed him.

"It's beautiful! You shouldn't have."

"I'm giving you my heart."

Leah shot him a stern glance, accompanied by a frown. "Don't go there."

"Put it on." Colin ignored the painful twinge in his heart.

She turned her back so he could fasten the delicate chain. The heart nestled at the cleft of her breasts, near her own heart.

"I love it," she said leaning toward him to plant a kiss on his lips.

"Good. Let's eat," he said.

They tucked into their food leaving unspoken thoughts hanging. Leah's negative reception of his declaration kept him from saying the "L" word, though it was on the tip of his tongue. Though the food filled his stomach and nourished his body, his heart needed mending.

"The stew was excellent," he said, refilling their glasses.

"Thanks. So *now* can you tell me where we're going?" Leah put her glass on the table.

"Stand Up and Laugh. It's a comedy club around the corner."

"Oh my God!" She covered her mouth with her hands and leapt up from the sofa.

"Is that good?"

"I've been wanting to go there for ages. I'm dying to go there! I love comedy clubs. How did you know?"

Colin beamed. "Lucky guess."

She hugged him. "I almost forgot!" Leah opened a drawer in the coffee table and pulled out an envelope. She extended it to him. "Happy Valentine's Day," she said, grinning.

Colin opened the envelope and found two tickets to a Knicks game the day after tomorrow.

"Wow! How did you know I like the Knicks?"

"A little birdy told me."

"Thank you," he said as he bent down to kiss her. "You're coming with me, right?"

"Unless there's some other woman you'd rather take."

"Get serious. What time shall I pick you up?"

They agreed upon a time and then threw on their coats as the comedy show was scheduled to begin in ten minutes. At ten, they staggered out into the cold still laughing from the last joke. Leah took his hand, leading him back to the apartment.

"Dessert. We didn't have time for dessert," she said, taking a deep breath of frigid air.

They walked home laughing and talking about the show. When they reached the building, Lance, the doorman tipped his hat.

"Happy Valentine's Day, Lance," Leah said.

"Same to you, Missy. Looks like you got a winner this time," he said, nodding at Colin.

Leah's cheeks pinked. With her head tucked down, she ushered Colin through the door and into the waiting elevator. Colin draped his arm over Leah's shoulders as they rode.

"At least Lance likes me." He chuckled.

Colin took their coats, freeing her to escape into the kitchen. When she joined him in the living room, he was on the sofa. She put a bottle of cabernet sauvignon on the table.

"I know, I know, open it, right?" he asked.

She nodded with a chuckle and left the room. While he was pouring the dark red liquid into two glasses, Leah returned carrying dessert. A small flat dark chocolate cake with a squiggle of whipped cream on top graced each plate.

"Molten chocolate cake," she said, placing a plate on the table in front of Colin.

When she finished, he took her hand and pulled her into an embrace.

"You're the only dessert I want."

His lips sought hers. His tongue pressed for admittance so she parted. The comfort of his strong arms brought her peace and safety. She relaxed into him, raising her tongue to meet his as sparks ignited between them. Colin held her tighter, crushing her breasts against his chest, his mouth insistent. Her arms slid over his shoulders, and her fingers gripped his muscles. Passion sucked her breath away, making her almost lightheaded.

Leah forced herself away from him slowly. She stood up, averting her gaze to avoid the questioning look in his eyes.

"Why are you running away from me?"

"I'm not running. I'm trying to keep this light." She walked over to the window.

"Why? Is it because I don't have a ton of money like the Wall Street guys you usually go out with?"

Leah's head snapped back as if he had slapped her. "Of course not! Who told you I go out with Wall Street guys?"

"Come on, Leah. What's going on?"

Colin sat back and sipped his wine. His penetrating gaze never left her face.

"I don't know what you mean."

"Yes, you do. You keep pushing me away, but not completely. You come just close enough to tempt me, then you pull back." He got up and moved next to her at the window. "And I want to know why."

His warm breath caressed her neck. For a second, she closed her eyes, letting her senses take over.

"It's just that I don't feel...we're too far apart...you're here, and I'm going to Paris. There are too many things against us, Colin. I don't want to hurt you and I don't want to get hurt."

She raised her head to look straight into his eyes. Smoldering desire burned there behind a flash of anger.

"Why don't you give us a chance? You went out with those rich guys. Give a poor guy a chance."

"Those rich guys? They're not so great. Do you want to know about my life before?"

"I do. Take your time."

"Maybe that'll help you understand," she said, retrieving her glass and leaning against the wall.

"I'm listening."

"Sure, I went out with Wall Street men. Looking for a man like Hank. I thought I could find my dream with one of them. But I was wrong. They wanted a pretty companion on their arm, in their bed, but no more. They were committed to their careers with no place for a commitment to me. So, after having my heart broken a few times, I figured out the game. I learned how to play but on my terms. I took what I wanted from them, and then moved on before they did."

Colin sat quietly, listening. He took a mouthful of wine, averting his gaze to his glass for a moment before facing her. She looked at him expectantly. "You're not doing that with me," he said.

"You noticed?" She laughed. "You're different."

He frowned. "Oh?" Then cocked an eyebrow.

"In a good way."

His frown softened. "What do you want from me?"

She turned to face the wall. "Friendship."

"Ouch! No one who kisses like you is looking for only friendship. You don't want me at all?" he asked.

Leah heard the hurt and disbelief in his voice.

"You're confusing me...I didn't say that I...I..." she stammered.

"I don't believe you. What happened to Hank? What happened to your dream?" Colin sipped his wine while watching her.

"I guess you have a right to know." She slumped down on the plush bench near the window.

Colin sat forward, listening.

Silence.

"Hmm, the dream, remember?" he reminded her.

"We were living on Park Avenue South in a beautiful apartment overlooking the avenue. Hank had been made vice president. It was my turn, time for my dream. We found a house in Connecticut, not far from Delia, Carrie's aunt. We put down a deposit and signed a contract, then threw away my birth control pills. I'd never been happier. Hank went for his usual run. I secretly suspected I was pregnant, so when he left, I did a home pregnancy test."

She took a deep breath then a gulp of wine. Tears stung at the backs of her eyes. Colin moved to her side, placing his hand on her shoulder.

"Sure enough, I was pregnant. I was so excited that I went to the window to wave. That's when it happened." Her voice cracked, and a shudder rocketed through her. Colin squeezed her shoulder.

"Take your time," he whispered.

"When I was at the window, I saw a taxi coming up Park Avenue too fast, then an idiot trying to zip across 38th Street. There was a crash as the cab hit the front of the car and spun up the sidewalk, right toward Hank. The taxi uprooted a tree and flung it plus a metal garbage can up the sidewalk so fast Hank couldn't get out of the way in time.

I saw the garbage can knock him flat." She paused, her breathing unsteady.

Colin snaked his arm around her shoulders and pulled her into his embrace. Her hands shook as she tried to compose herself.

"Then the cab came sliding up the sidewalk sideways, fast—so fast—right over him, crushing him. It was horrible." Tears cascaded down her cheeks as she struggled to catch her breath. Colin pulled her closer, wrapping his other arm around her.

"And you saw all this?"

She nodded.

He held her close as she buried her face in his shirt.

"My God," he murmured.

Leah closed her arms around his middle and sobbed into his chest. He offered her his handkerchief.

She wiped her eyes and nose, then took a deep breath. "I know it's been a long time, but I still dream about it."

"You can't expect to forget an experience like that." Colin smoothed her hair down.

After a moment of silence, she spoke. "Two weeks later, I miscarried."

"Shit!" Colin's head snapped up.

"That was my dream. Since I can't have that dream, I have a new one. To be a Paris clothing designer."

She let out a breath before she leaned against him.

"I'm off to Paris. I don't know how long I'll be there," she said.

He held her.

"Even if we could ignore our age difference," she said.

"I don't care about any age difference between us," he blurted out.

"I don't see a future for us. That's what you want, a future, and I can't promise one."

Silence fell over them like a soft blanket. Leah moved up against his chest as he rested his cheek on her hair. She fisted his shirt. Absorbing strength from him calmed her. The loving protection of Colin's embrace healed a piece of her broken heart.

"I want you any way I can have you. For however long. I'm willing to risk it. If you leave me because you're following your dream, it won't be as bad as not having you at all, not being together at least for a little while," Colin said. "Women like you don't come along every day."

His hard chest invited her touch. Her fingers wrapped around his bicep. She listened to his heartbeat, smelling the aroma of his spicy aftershave mixed with his masculine scent and the clean smell of his freshly ironed shirt—it was a heady combination. Need, want, and trust came together to break down her resistance. She felt tingly all over.

"If you don't want me, I'll leave now and not bother you again." Colin sat back, releasing her.

"How could I not want you? You're amazing. Gorgeous, sexy, smart, sweet."

He brought his mouth down on hers in a hungry kiss. Leah opened. His tongue coaxed, teasing, and seducing her. Heat ran through her veins. Leah pushed to her feet, putting a few steps between them. Colin came up behind her. He wrapped his arms around her waist and bent down to whisper in her ear.

"I want you. Let me touch you, let me love you."

All resistance gone, Leah let her head fall back on his shoulder. With eyes closed, she muttered her assent. Colin's lips trailed up and down the column of her neck as his hands moved up slowly to close over her breasts. At his touch, she groaned.

"I want you. God, Colin. Make love to me," she breathed.

He picked her up and carried her into the bedroom, laying her down gently. She rolled over on her stomach and shot him a sexy look. Colin ripped his tie off and unbuttoned his shirt before leaning over to unzip her dress. Leah sat up when he joined her on the bed. Before sliding her dress down, she pushed the shirt off his shoulders. He ripped his T-shirt over his head and tossed it on a chair.

A small noise escaped his throat when he eased her dress down, exposing her black lace demi-bra. The heat of his gaze warmed her bared flesh. He reached around and unsnapped the bra. The garment fell. Her hands brushed through the hair on his chest while his hands found her breasts.

"You are so beautiful." As he stared, fire flickered in his light eyes.

Warmed by his words as well as his hands, Leah pulled him down for a kiss. She fell back, and he landed on top of her, bracing himself with his hands. He bent his head to kiss her breasts while her fingers unbuckled his belt. When she unzipped his pants, he pushed away from her, quickly shedding his pants and boxers. Turning back to the bed, his jaw dropped when he saw that she had shed her dress and all she was wearing was a skimpy pair of black lace bikini panties.

"May I?" he asked, reaching down.

She nodded. He hooked his fingers into the sides of the panties and slid them down slowly, following their path with his eyes. When she pushed them off, he knelt on the bed and murmured.

"Wow!"

Heat crept up her neck into her cheeks. Her gaze roamed over his body.

"I agree."

He looked up, bewildered for a second until he realized she was referring to him. A blush reddened his chest and neck. She put her hands on his shoulders and dragged her fingernails down over his chest, stopping to play for a moment in his chest hair while their eyes locked. Colin lowered his mouth to hers in a hungry kiss. His tongue explored, teasing hers while his hands cupped her breasts. Then he kissed his way to her peak.

Leah closed her eyes, letting heat from his lips travel through her. Her fingers dug into his shoulder muscles, eliciting a groan. His fingers caressed her skin moving to her side as they worked their way down. He palmed her bottom, squeezing as she wrapped her leg around his waist. His hand slid up her thigh, then down again as his fingers found her damp center, probing, seeking her hot spots. She moaned, moving her hand down to close around his shaft.

"Wow," she muttered, opening her eyes to stare directly into his.

He blushed again.

"Like steel."

"You do that to me," he whispered before planting kisses on her neck.

When his fingers found her clit, she groaned loudly. He chuckled, intensifying the pressure for a moment before pulling back. He lowered his head, replacing his fingers with his tongue.

"Don't stop."

Colin gently removed her hand.

"Gotta slow this down a little."

He lifted his head to stare into her eyes.

"Colin. Take me. I'm ready, please."

"What's the rush?"

She moved her hand to his side, then his butt, pulling him to her. "If you don't...I'll..."

"Go ahead." He thrust two fingers into her wet core.

She threw her head back as want became need, spiraling up almost out of control. Her hips arched against him, but he kept up the pressure while lowering his lips to her breast. When he sucked on it, she emitted a small gasp.

"Come for me," he whispered.

At his words, her muscles tightened, held, then shot pleasure tumbling through her veins. The hot bliss raced all the way to her fingers and toes. Her hips shot up off the bed.

"Condom?" he asked in a strangled voice.

"On the pill."

Colin nudged her legs wider apart. He knelt between them and eased into her. With her leg resting on his shoulder, she gasped loudly as he filled her.

"Ahhhhhh, Leah," he muttered, burying his face in her neck.

"So good. So good." She lost her fingers in his hair.

He withdrew and then plunged in again hard, making her groan. His hips thrust in and pulled back in rhythm. Bearing most of his weight on his elbows freed up his fingers to tangle in her hair. Starting slowly, he stopped occasionally, making her cry out for him to continue. A sexy smile crossed his lips as his gaze connected with hers.

"Makin' it better," he whispered.

"Torture!"

He chuckled before picking up the pace. Leah opened her eyes to see his lips descend to hers as his hips moved faster and faster. Smoothing her hands down his back through a fine coating of sweat, a powerful orgasm captured her body, causing her hips to pump with his.

"Colin!"

She opened her eyes in time to see him close his and an expression of sheer bliss cross his face. Sweat beaded on his forehead as he moaned her name while giving three hard thrusts then collapsing. Leah hugged him to her, resting her head on his damp shoulder, her lips delivering soft kisses to his neck. Two fingers brushed her hair out of her eyes. Leah hadn't seen such a loving expression on a man's face since her last time making love with Hank.

"I love you," popped out of his mouth, causing her to raise her eyebrows.

"You don't know me very well."

"I know enough. That was amazing."

"It was sex. Great sex, but only sex."

"There couldn't be *only sex* with you."

She chuckled at his innocence but basked in his adoration. She swept his hair off his forehead, then rested her hand on the back of his neck. He kissed her nose before rolling off to the side.

"Come here." Colin pulled her into his arms.

Leah curled up, her head on his chest, listening to the steady beat of his heart. He covered them with the comforter and switched out the light. A sense of well-being washed over her as a sigh of contentment left her lips.

"Fabulous," she whispered.

He answered her with a kiss on the forehead and a tightening of his arm around her. Sleep engulfed the exhausted lovers.

Chapter Nine

Across town, Grey and Carrie had finished their meal and headed for the car. They held hands at the red lights on the drive home.

"My present awaits you, my queen," Grey joked.

"Mine too." Carrie wiggled her eyebrows.

Once in the house, Grey lit the fire in the fireplace and spread a lambskin on the floor while Carrie opened a bottle of cabernet. The fire crackled, hissing and spitting, casting a warm glow on the faces of the lovers. Carrie handed him a glass of wine and joined him.

"To us." Grey held up his glass.

"To love and fidelity forever." Carrie clinked her glass to his.

When she put hers down, Grey reached into his pocket and pulled out a small velvet box.

"To the love of my life, Happy Valentine's Day."

Carrie opened the box to find a pair of exquisite diamond earrings. She gasped.

"Oh my God! Designed by Monsieur Gris. They are the most gorgeous." She held them up to her ears.

"Put them on."

Carrie popped up to get to the nearest mirror. The earrings each had a chain of three tiny diamonds ending in one larger one. She turned her head this way and that.

"They're fabulous, Grey. I love them!"

He grinned. "Surprised?"

"Absolutely. Thank you, darling."

Carrie leaned over to kiss him. He took the opportunity to pull her into his arms, his hand claiming her breast. She melted against him, moving closer, her hands anchored on his wide shoulders. When they broke, she had to catch her breath.

"Your gift is upstairs."

He shot her an amorous look.

"I was hoping you'd say that."

"Give me a few minutes."

Carrie slipped upstairs. In five minutes, she called down.

"Come up for your present!"

Grey bounded up the stairs. Eager for his arrival, Carrie cracked the bedroom door and peeked out. When he reached the top of the stairs, she threw open the door and raised her arms.

"Do you like it?"

Grey's mouth hung open. Carrie wore a saloon gal outfit that only went as far down as her bottom. The top had straps of magenta satin trimmed in black lace. The bodice was low cut, trimmed in the same black lace. Magenta satin made up most of the bodice with black onyx gems sewn on. Black lace combined with the satin to make vertical stripes that ended in a handkerchief hem only halfway down her thighs.

"I've never seen anything like this. I've been to all the best stores. Trust me, if I'd seen this before, you'd have it in every color." He stood frozen, staring, his gaze running up and down her body.

"It's one of Leah's creations. She made it up just for me."

"You mean, for me, don't you?" He chuckled.

Grey was practically drooling. His eyes were as wide as saucers.

"Do you like it?"

"Are you kidding? I love it. It's amazing. Are you wearing anything underneath?"

She shook her head, a sly grin stealing across her face.

"Oh my God, then you don't need to take it off when we..."

"Nope. That's the idea."

"Wow, Carrie. That's all I can say. Wow," he muttered, yanking at his tie, then unbuttoning his shirt.

"Let me help with that." She walked over and unbuckled his belt while he finished with the buttons. The shirt fell off his shoulders to the floor along with his pants. Grey toed off his shoes, ripped his T-shirt over his head, and grabbed her. Carrie tried to stifle a giggle but was unsuccessful. He shot her a quizzical look.

"Socks," she said, pointing to the floor.

He was stark naked except for his black socks. He chuckled as he pulled each one off and left it where it lay. Gathering her in his arms, Grey kissed her hard. Carrie jumped up and wrapped her legs around him. He walked them to the bed, flopping down on the mattress. She stretched out underneath him, watching his liquid gold eyes glisten with desire. He slid his hands down her chest, first pushing the wide straps down over her shoulders, then slipping his fingers under the lace. His thumbs found her peaks and rubbed them while he bent over and nuzzled her neck. Withdrawing his hands, he cupped them over the garment and caressed her through the satin and lace.

The touch of his fingers, gentle but insistent, ignited the fires always smoldering inside her for Grey. Her fingertips rubbed the light scruff on his face, a sensation that always turned her on. He pinched her lightly through the cloth.

"Is this silk? Will I ruin it if I get saliva on it?" He stared at the erect nipple showing through the delicate fabric.

"It *is* silk and if saliva drips a little because you're drooling it's not a problem." She laughed. "But your full mouth would wreck it."

"Damn!"

Carrie ran her hand down his back as he lay crouched between her legs while his hands glided over the smooth fabric. The piney scent of his aftershave aroused her senses almost as much as the rasp of his chin on her skin.

"Do you have to take it off?"

"I don't intend to."

His grin widened as he slipped his fingers under the hem, closing them around her hips. As she raised her legs, she felt his thumbs at her core. As his erotic massage made her wild, she closed her eyes and let a groan escape her lips. Her hips squirmed under his touch while her hand searched for his shaft.

"Looking for something?" A devilish gleam shone in his eyes.

Her hand closed around him.

"Gotcha!"

"That's what you think. I'm not done with you yet," he said, dislodging her hand.

"Grey, you're making me crazy, please."

"Sweet torture, honey."

He secured her hands with his, raising them above her head, and then lowered his mouth to hers. When he was done kissing her, his lips and tongue blazed a trail across her jaw to her ear lobe then down her neck and chest. Carrie panted, her hips pressed against him in a silent plea. His touch felt like tiny flames dancing across her skin. Lust for him coursed through her veins as the ache inside her threatened to take over. The intensity of their passion wiped her mind of any thoughts except Grey, wanting him, needing him.

As quickly as he took her hands, he released them. His hands pushed the skirt up. He stared for a bit before lowering his lips to her belly and kissing down. When he got to the juncture of her thighs, he swiped her with his tongue several times. She gasped and squirmed under his loving attention.

"Oh God, Grey. Please, please."

"My pleasure."

He raised his head as his hands grabbed her bottom, squeezing it, and then raised her hips. He positioned himself and thrust into her, causing her to arch, throw her head back, and cry out. He chuckled, watching her, then made love to her in earnest, his hips beginning a rhythm she followed.

"You want me, honey?" he whispered.

"I do."

"Say it."

"I want you. I want you with all my heart and soul."

"Carrie. Love you, honey."

The conversation stopped as he moved inside her. The slap of flesh on flesh, grunting, moans of pleasure, and finally cries of release thickened the bedroom air with desire.

Carrie opened her eyes to see the loving look on Grey's face—the look he always had after they made love. His face softened, and his gaze became tender. His love surrounded her like a fleece blanket, caressing her, warming her, shutting out the cares of the world. He spun an emotional cocoon around her, protecting her, keeping her safe. Her fingertips caressed his cheek until he bent his head to kiss her palm.

Reluctantly, he pushed up on his hands. As cool air replaced his body heat, Carrie sighed. His gaze roamed over her one more time.

"Can you iron this thing?"

She laughed.

"Hope so."

Carrie took off Leah's gorgeous creation and hung it in the closet. They washed up, then slipped into bed, naked. Wearing her new diamond earrings, Carrie cuddled up to Grey and closed her eyes. He spooned her, slinging an arm around her waist, then turned out the light.

"Best Valentine's Day present ever," he mumbled.

"Good night, my prince."

"Good night, my lady."

THE SUN STABBED COLIN in the eyes at six o'clock. Disoriented for a moment, he rolled over and bumped into Leah. She muttered something, then pulled the covers over her exposed chest before going back to sleep.

Colin touched her shoulder to make sure she was real. He grinned, realizing the night before had not been a dream. He was in Leah's bed, a place he had longed to be. Tucking one arm under his pillow, the other around her middle, he snuggled up to her and drifted back to sleep.

By nine o'clock, he was wide awake. The sweet scent of sleeping Leah woke him up. His hand rested on her breast and try as he might, he couldn't resist moving his fingers to caress her soft flesh though she was still asleep. She moaned, tossed, rolled over then laid her hand on top of his.

"Good morning," he whispered into her ear.

"Ummm."

He nuzzled the soft spot under her ear. She giggled and swatted at him as if he were a fly.

"Come on, lazy bones, time to wake up." He planted a soft kiss on her lips.

She rolled over, facing him. One small hand rested on his chest, teasing him. The sight of her so close, her scent so alluring, her body so inviting made him hard.

"How do you feel about making love in the morning?" he whispered, bending over her chest, letting his lips explore her silky skin.

"Thought you'd never ask."

After lovemaking, a shower together, and breakfast, the lovers ventured outside. Bundled up against the cold, Colin and Leah braved the icy winds whipping up and down the avenues of the west side of Manhattan to visit the American Museum of Natural History. With her leather-gloved hand tucked into the crook of his arm, joy took over his heart. Making love to Leah had exceeded his expectations. He simply couldn't stop smiling.

"After this, we could go ice skating and have hot chocolate in Rockefeller Center. Then maybe window shopping on Fifth Avenue?"

"A man suggesting shopping of any kind, do you feel okay?" She reached up with her hand to feel his forehead. "No fever."

He laughed. "Things you might want to do."

"Isn't there a basketball game on this afternoon?" she asked.

"Basketball? You want to watch basketball?"

"I happen to like basketball. Cuddling up with you, a bowl of chili and the game sounds like fun. I'm not a winter girl. I prefer indoor sports when it's cold outside."

She shot him a sly smile.

"I hit the jackpot, didn't I? A woman who likes indoor sports."

Though he tried to hide his embarrassment, her chuckle, plus the knowing look in her eye, told him he hadn't fooled her.

"I have all the ingredients for chili. But it will take a little time to cook."

"What are we waiting for? It's damn cold out here."

"The museum will be there tomorrow and it's supposed to be warmer."

The couple turned around and headed back to the apartment. After hanging up their coats, Leah headed for the kitchen with Colin close behind.

"Can I help?"

"Ever made chili before?" she asked.

He shook his head.

"Always a first time. Apron over there."

"First I have to learn how to keep my hands off you," he said, closing his arms around her.

Leah extricated herself gently. "Later, Romeo. First, kidney beans and onions."

"Aye, aye." Colin slipped the apron loop over his head.

Leah came up behind him to tie it but instead slipped her arms around him.

"Last night was the best Valentine's Day I've had in years," she whispered.

"Me too." Colin placed his hands over hers.

"While the chili's cooking, why don't you run up to Grey's and get your stuff? You can stay the rest of the vacation here with me."

He turned to look in her eyes.

"Really?" He raised his eyebrows.

She nodded. Colin picked her up, twirled her around the kitchen then crushed her to him.

"A dream come true. Wait here." He whipped the apron over his head. "I'll be back soon."

"Hurry, darling." She blew him a kiss.

"What did you call me?" He stopped short, almost falling over.

Color flooded Leah's face.

"Never mind. Hurry. Game starts in an hour."

She tried to shove him out the door but wasn't strong enough. After a quick kiss, he bolted, laughing all the way down the hall.

UPTOWN, THICK DRAPERIES kept the sun from waking Grey. Carrie bounded out of bed at seven, as usual. She stood up and stretched her arms high. She felt good, great, better than better. She smiled at her sleeping fiancé. She bent down to plant a kiss on his lips. He stirred.

"Not time yet, babe." She ruffled his hair lightly, donned a long flannel robe, and padded downstairs.

Carrie pulled out the ingredients for his favorite, German apple pancakes. The slight brush of the earrings against her neck was a constant reminder of his gift. Switching the radio on, one of her favorite songs came up next "Just Haven't Met You Yet." She sang along, moving her hips to the music. When he came up behind her, placing his hands on her waist, he startled her. Carrie jumped slightly then turned and laughed. He wore nothing but his blue plaid robe, and his hair hung over his forehead. When he sported that sexy, knowing grin, she wanted to kiss it off his face.

"Something smells good," he said, folding her into his embrace.

"Hungry?"

"Starved!"

"One appetite then the other."

He laughed before kissing her. Grey went to the drawer and took out silverware.

"Working at home today?" she asked, pouring the batter onto the griddle.

"Always take off after Valentine's Day. Usually need a day to recover. I have some business plans to look over tomorrow, though."

"Today we can play. Two plates or three? Did Colin come home?" She hesitated.

"I checked his room on my way down. Bed's not been slept in," he said, a smug grin spread across his face.

"And you're proud of him, aren't you?" She put her hands on her hips.

"Damn right I am. Another score for an Andrews man." He pumped his fist.

"Score? You think Leah's a score?" She raised her eyebrows as she plucked two plates off the top of the stack.

"Not really, but he wanted her, now he's had her."

She softened at the sheepish look on his face. "He's in love with her," she said.

"Love? I thought it was simply lust, advanced lust maybe, but just lust."

Carrie pulled the large pancake from the oven and turned it over on a small platter.

As Grey reached to pinch off a small piece, she pushed his hand away. "It's hot. Give it a minute to cool."

"Okay, okay," he said, pulling his hand back.

To allow the pancake to cool fast, she cut it into generous wedges.

"I don't think it's just lust," she said. "Not this time. He's a goner." She put one wedge on each plate, handed one to Grey, took hers, and joined him at the table.

"But she's going to Paris. Wanna talk geographically undesirable! My little brother's gonna get his heart stomped." Grey filled his fork.

"Sometimes you don't have a choice."

"What does he know? He's a baby." Grey stuck a piece of pancake in his mouth.

"He's almost thirty. She's only four, maybe five years older. So what? He loves her, right?"

"This is delicious, babe." Grey finished chewing. "Colin doesn't know a thing about women."

"I disagree. He must know something, he's seduced one of the most glamorous, sought-after women I know. I don't think Leah's had a date-less weekend in over a year."

"Chip off the old block." He beamed.

"The old block better hang up his seducing talents right now!" Carrie cut her pancake with her fork.

"I've seduced my last woman. Saved the best for last." He laced his fingers with hers.

"You seduced me? I thought I seduced you!" She chuckled while he raised her hand to his lips.

"Just looking at you seduced me."

Carrie finished her last bite and then slipped into his lap.

He snaked his arm around her waist, pulling her closer. "Looks like you're doing it again." His lips sought her neck.

When the phone rang, she made a move to get up.

"Let it ring," Grey said.

"You never know. Maybe it's Colin calling you for advice." She burst out laughing. "Funnier things have happened, you know."

He wagged his finger.

Carrie handed the phone to Grey.

"Your mom."

Grey put the phone to his ear. "Mom? What? Oh, that's too bad. Yes, I'm working this week. What? No, Saturday's fine. Colin? You want to speak to Colin? Uh, uh," He looked at Carrie, his face reddening.

"Remember? I sent him out for the paper," Carrie said loud enough for Grey's mom to hear.

He gave her a thumbs up. "Okay, Mom. Yeah. Yup. See you Saturday."

Carrie gave him a questioning look when he hung up the phone.

"Angus Davenport, our neighbor, died. Family visiting hours are this coming weekend. Would you want to go up there with me on Saturday?"

"And meet the gorgeous, the infamous, Giselle Davenport? You bet I would."

"Honey, she's got nothing on you."

"I'll be the judge of that."

She fell into his arms for a delicious kiss.

"Ohhh, you're sexy when you're jealous." He chuckled.

Grey had his face buried in her neck when the doorbell rang.

Chapter Ten

"Surprise! Did I interrupt anything? Hope so." Colin wiggled his eyebrows before stepping inside their warm house. "Happy Valentine's Day, Carrie, Grey."

"Where the hell have you been, little brother?" Grey closed the door behind Colin.

"I'm staying at Leah's. Just came back to get my stuff."

"Oh?" Grey arched an eyebrow.

"Yeah. You got a problem with that?"

Grey shook his head. "Guess not."

"What's that supposed to mean?"

"Mom called and wanted to talk to you. We made up a story about you being out to get the paper."

"Why hide it? I'm almost thirty. Geez."

"Do I have to be the one to shove it in Mom's face her baby boy is getting laid?"

Grey refilled Carrie's coffee then his own. Colin grabbed a mug and took the pot from Grey.

"Okay, okay, guys. Enough. Here's a stupid question, Colin. Have a good time?" Carrie patted Grey's hand.

"Best Valentine's Day ever."

"I'll bet." Grey snickered.

Colin punched him in the shoulder.

"She gave me Knicks tickets. We're going tomorrow night. Today we're watching basketball, then a chick flick. Leah's making chili. Suppose it would be nice to invite you two, but not gonna. I don't have much time alone with her and I don't want to share."

"We understand." Carrie smiled.

"Yeah. I get it." Grey pumped his fist in the air.

"Hey!" Colin shouted.

"Another Andrews man scores." Grey laughed.

"Another Andrews man bites the dust," Carrie said, under her breath, stifling a smile.

At the front desk of Leah's building, Colin stopped to chat with the doorman. "Who are you rooting for tomorrow night, Lance?" Colin asked.

"The Knicks, of course. You?"

"Same here. It's too bad you have to miss the game."

Lance gestured to a tiny TV hidden behind the podium in the lobby.

"Oh, I see."

The doorman smiled as he pressed the button to the apartment.

"You can go right up, Mr. Andrews."

"Colin, Lance."

The doorman nodded.

The aroma of Leah's chili greeted Colin's nose when the elevator doors opened. It got stronger as he neared the front door. Leah greeted him on tiptoe for a kiss. He lowered his lips to hers, his tongue tasting the richness of the meat and tomato. His hands held her close enough to feel her breasts pressed against his chest. Desire stirred in his loins.

Leah stepped back and took his arm. Set up on the coffee table, facing the huge flat screen TV was a tray with guacamole, chips, and cheese cubes. Two bottles of beer accompanied the snacks. Frozen on the screen was the starting lineup for the game.

He shed his shoes and followed Leah. They curled up together on the sofa. Colin stretched his legs, resting his feet on a nearby ottoman while Leah cuddled into his shoulder, her hand on his chest. He hit play. The Knicks got off to a good start, leading by ten at halftime. Colin gobbled up the chili.

"This is the best chili ever," he said, getting up to help himself to more.

"My aunt's recipe," she said, putting the game on pause again.

With his bowl refilled, Colin retrieved an envelope from his pants pocket before sitting down.

"I have the second half of my Valentine's Day present for you."

She cocked an eyebrow when he handed her the envelope.

"What is this?"

"A round-trip bus ticket to Pine Grove."

She raised her eyebrows.

"I want you to stay with me, next weekend, the weekend after, as soon as you can."

"You were debating giving this to me?"

"If you didn't want to sleep with me, it would've been a waste to give you the ticket. I only have one bed. So, when I didn't know what was going to happen—"

"You waited. Smart. You're right. If I didn't want to sleep with you, I would've returned this gift. But since I have, I'm accepting it. It's a wonderful present." She kissed him.

"I want to show you around my town. Take care of you at my place."

"I'd love to. Let me check my calendar, we can make a date now." She reached for her phone.

The afternoon passed quickly. The Knicks squeaked out a win by three points. Leah brought out brownies and coffee.

"This is my favorite chick flick," Leah said, changing channels.

"What is it?"

"*While You Were Sleeping*. The best!" She took a brownie and sat back.

Colin helped himself to food and drink, then moved closer to Leah to watch the movie. Within ten minutes, he was totally engrossed in the story.

"I don't usually watch chick flicks, but that one was good," he said, wiping his mouth with a napkin.

"I know, right? The best."

After they cleaned up, Colin took her out for dinner to a small, romantic restaurant only three blocks away. When they returned, he scooped her into his arms and headed for the bedroom, tapping the door shut with his foot.

The next morning, when the sun crept in between the curtains, coaxing his eyes open, Colin rolled over to escape the sharp light and linger longer in his dream. *Leah—a farmhouse in the country—professorship.* Leah's warm scent enticed him, drawing him closer. He spooned her from behind, slipping his arm around her waist and closing his fingers around her breast. Her firm bare behind pressed gently against his groin and stirred his dick. Now he was wide awake. She stretched her arms above her head and murmured something he couldn't understand. His fingers caressed her warm flesh, arousing a response.

"Again? Three times last night didn't wear you out?"

"I'll never get enough of you," he whispered.

"I'm not sure I'll be able to walk if we make love again."

"I'll be gentle."

She rolled over to face him with a saucy smile spread across her face.

"I can be convinced," she said, her voice low and sultry.

"I'll do the work, lie back, relax." His lips closed over her peak.

She slid her hand down his body.

"Your motor's already running." She closed her fingers around him.

"Being near you keeps it revved up."

"I'll bet you say that to all your girls."

"No more girls. Only women, one woman, you."

He leaned over to kiss her neck while his hands cupped her behind. "Oh my God, you're amazing," she breathed into his ear.

THE WEEK PASSED QUICKLY. Colin and Leah were inseparable. Grey and Carrie headed upstate to make the condolence call. They arrived at the Andrews family home in Pine Grove on Saturday about three o'clock. Fran Andrews, Grey's mother, greeted them warmly at the door while Buster and Daisy, their two fawn pugs, danced around, barking and panting. After planting a kiss on his mother's cheek, Grey bent to pet the pooches.

John Andrews, his father, followed the dogs into the foyer. After hugs were shared, they were ushered into the living room. Tea and homemade scones awaited them in front of the huge fireplace. Daisy and Buster flopped down on their beds near the warmth of the fire to catch some shuteye.

"What happened to Angus Davenport? I thought he was a hearty old guy," Grey asked.

"Brain aneurysm," John said.

"He went suddenly. Giselle is still stunned. We all are," Fran chimed in.

"I'm looking forward to meeting her. I understand she was one of Grey's girlfriends."

"We were friends," Grey interrupted.

"They were friends when they were little but by high school..."

"Friends, Mom. Friends," Grey said.

"She didn't speak to you for a year. That doesn't seem very friendly to me. Would you like one of these, Carrie? They're chocolate chip." Fran offered her a scone.

"Thanks, Fran. They look delicious."

"Fran makes the best scones in the county," John said.

She blushed under his praise but then made a dismissive motion, but Carrie could see the pride underneath.

"We're going over after dinner to bring her some food. Grey, I hope you can find time to chop some wood for Giselle tomorrow. I'm working on a nice casserole. When we finish here, maybe Carrie can give me a hand."

"Barb and Jenna coming?" Grey asked.

"Nope. Barbara's on a business trip and Jenna's skiing," John said.

"Colin's coming tomorrow for dinner with his new girlfriend."

Grey and Carrie looked at each other.

"You met her?" John asked.

"I've known Leah for a long time. She's like family," Carrie replied.

Fran smiled. "Well, if she's anything like you, I'll be pleased to meet her." She patted Carrie's hand.

"She's a lot like Carrie. Quite a dresser too," Grey added.

"Bet she's pretty. Colin always had an eye for good-lookin' girls," John said.

"Grey too. Look at our Carrie." Fran beamed.

When she realized that Colin's parents had no idea how old Leah was or that she was about to move to Paris, Carrie's nerves kicked up. They were in for a shock. She looked down at her hands, then at Grey. She gulped down the rest of her tea and polished off her scone.

"Why don't we get on that casserole, Fran?" Carrie said, pushing to her feet.

"If you don't mind, dear? Grey, please take the bags upstairs."

Fran and John stood up. John carried the tea tray. Grey shot Carrie a look of relief behind his parents' backs before he headed for the stairs.

Dinner was a pleasant affair, as it always was, with Grey's parents. Carrie grew closer and closer to them as time passed. Most of the meal was spent discussing the location for the rehearsal dinner and how many people they expected to show up.

"When are we going to meet your parents, Carrie?" Fran asked as she carried in an apple cobbler for dessert.

"I don't know when they're coming, exactly. They'll be renting an apartment in the city for a month or two." She shifted in her seat.

"Ya don't know? Don't ya talk to your own parents?"

"John!" Fran raised her hand.

He turned his attention to the dessert on his plate.

"Janice and Harv travel a lot," Grey said, picking up his fork.

"Hmm. Jan and Harv, eh? Met them yet, Grey?" John asked.

"Not exactly. I've talked to Janice on the phone, though."

"I've got four kids, and we talk to 'em seems like every day. 'Specially when I get the phone bill!" John chuckled. "Your folks only have two."

"We've never been very close. Delia is more like a mother to me," Carrie said.

Embarrassment stained her cheeks.

"Delia Tucker? We love her! She's a real hoot. A dear, dear lady," Fran said, patting Carrie's hand.

"She did a fine job raising you, I'd say," John said, a smile creasing his face.

"Thanks." Carrie turned her gaze to her food.

Grey took her hand under the table and gave it a squeeze. She turned grateful eyes to him.

"When are we going over to the Davenports?" Grey asked.

"As soon as I finish this last forkful of cobbler. Fran, you make the best cobbler in the county," John announced.

After winter coats were distributed and the casserole bundled up, they trekked through the well-worn shortcut path to the gloomy old Victorian next door. Carrie looked up at the house. She could see signs that it had once been grand, like the Andrews' house. But now, in places, the white paint on the wood trim had peeled. The light lavender on the house was faded so much it looked almost like a dirty gray.

Weeds grew up between the bricks of the front walk. Shrubs sorely in need of trimming lined the front of the house, blocking some of the large windows. The low white picket fence was missing a slat or two here and there, and the gate in the fence had rusted open. One hinge had come undone.

"Wow, their house sure has gone to the dogs since Martha died," Grey said.

"Shhh! Not so loud. Giselle will hear you. She's tried but keeping up a house like this by herself isn't easy."

"She needs a good man to help her," John said.

Carrie managed a tight smile as they paraded single file through the old gate.

"She's not married? I'm surprised," Grey said. "Thought she was involved with Cal Morrison?"

"She's been living in Europe most of the time. Just come back for a couple of visits in the last year since Martha died," John said.

"What about Colin?" Carrie asked.

"She's Grey's age, too old for Colin," Fran responded. "She and Cal broke up a while ago."

Grey shot his fiancée a panicked look. Carrie shrugged and gripped his arm tighter as she navigated the icy walk carrying a plate of Fran's homemade cookies. He steadied her up the walk. Carrie looked up in time to see a beautiful, slender woman with short dark hair and big gray eyes open the door. A smile lit her sad face as she greeted the Andrews clan. Carrie noted Giselle's greeting of each Andrews family member, especially Grey. Each received a hug, but Grey also got a peck on the cheek. Carrie smiled.

"You must be Carrie. I've heard so much about you." Giselle gave her a warm smile and extended her hand.

Carrie shook it and smiled back. Curiosity mixed with jealousy in Carrie's heart. Was Giselle someone to worry about?

"Please come in." Giselle stepped back, allowing Carrie to pass.

"What a grand old house," Carrie remarked, her gaze traveling from walls to ceiling, from bookcase to rolltop desk to a door with a glass transom.

"It was when Mom was alive. But between taking care of Dad and upkeep on the house, well, I haven't had time to do a good job."

Carrie moved through the entryway into the living room. Grey joined her.

"I see Grey still has great taste in women," Giselle said. "Congratulations on your engagement. He's a lucky guy."

Carrie beamed as she slipped her arm through his. "That luck runs both ways."

The chime of her cell phone stopped Carrie. "Mom?" Carrie stepped back into the entryway for privacy.

"Carrie! Darling!"

"Where are you?"

"In New York, sweetheart. Where are you?"

"I'm upstate."

"Well, come home, dear. We have so much work to do."

"I'm at Grey's parent's house."

"Those country people? Boring. Please, Carrie. Home tomorrow. First thing."

"Where are you staying?"

"The Devon Apartments. We got a cozy place, a studio. It's tight but since your guest room is still under renovation, what can we do? I want to meet that man of yours. Make sure he's good enough to become part of the Tucker family."

Carrie frowned. *Oh God.*

"Carrie? You still there? This damn phone."

"I'm still here. I'll be home tomorrow, Mom."

She put her phone away. Grey faced her.

"Your mom and dad are in the city?"

She nodded.

"Great! We'll get an early start tomorrow. I want to meet them."

"They want to meet you too." Carrie's stomach lurched.

Quietly watching everyone, listening to the conversation, she smiled and nodded but her mind was elsewhere. Her senses picked up that there was no heat between Grey and Giselle. When Grey glanced at his watch, she knew his signal for time to leave.

"I'm sorry for your loss," Carrie said to Giselle as the Andrews clan filed out.

Goodbyes were murmured with Fran and John, promising to return the next day. Grey stretched and yawned, perhaps too obviously, making Carrie hide her smile. It was only nine-thirty, but he was ready for bed, though maybe not for sleep.

Once in their room with the door closed, Grey took her in his arms. Carrie rested her head on his shoulder.

"Could we have a cuddle night tonight?"

"Not up for hot sex?" he teased.

"I have a lot on my mind."

Grey sat down on the bed, pulling her onto his lap. He kissed her hair and stroked her back. "Want to talk about it?"

"It's nothing, yet. Just a feeling I have."

"What kind of feeling?"

"That things are going to be difficult."

"How so?"

"My parents. They always make things hard for me. My mother doesn't get along with Delia. The wedding plans have started. Already she's objected."

"Wait!" He put his hand up.

Carrie sat up.

"Nothing would make me happier than to watch you stroll down the aisle in a white dress, but if this wedding business is going to make you unhappy, we can elope to Las Vegas."

"But this is your first."

"All I care about is marrying you. The rest is icing on the cake. I can easily do without it. As long as we're hitched, I'm happy. Don't make yourself crazy. Say the word and we're on a plane."

Carrie smiled. "You're the best. I love you so much."

He grinned. "Love you too, honey."

Carrie stood up to stretch. Feeling Grey's eyes on her body, she slowly eased her sweater up over her rib cage, humming the beginning of the song "The Stripper". Glancing at him over her shoulder, she noticed his eyes grow wide.

"If only this house had a carriage house. Some place we could be really alone," she said.

"So when I make you scream with passion, no one hears us?" He snickered.

"Right."

"We've only mastered quiet loving once, right?"

"Let's practice now," she said, unfastening her bra and letting it fall to the floor.

Chapter Eleven

The February sun melted the thin coating of ice on the trees on the Palisades Parkway as Grey's Jaguar cut through the smattering of cars returning to New York City. Carrie held the cell phone to her ear, making faces as she spoke with her mother.

"We're on the way, Mom. What? As fast as we can." She turned her wrist to glance at her watch.

"How about coming to dinner tonight? Good. You have the address? See you at six."

"Dinner with Janice and Harvey Tucker, eh? What do you plan to make, arsenic stew?"

"Don't think it hasn't crossed my mind. Oh, don't forget our guest room is still under construction."

"You finished that weeks ago."

"I know."

"Colin has been staying there."

"I know. But if I told my mother it was ready, they'd be camping out there for the next three months."

"Oh my God. No way."

"Yes, way. They would."

"We need our privacy."

"How about a rule on how long guests can stay?"

"How does fifteen minutes sound?" He grinned.

She laughed.

"Seriously. How about five days?"

"Too long."

"Three days?

"Still too long."

"Grey!"

"Okay, okay. Five days and not one minute, not one second more. Can I help it if I want to be able to chase you around the house naked?"

"Who's naked, me?"

"And me. More fun that way."

"Get this out of your system now because when my parents arrive."

"I'll be as straight-laced as a banker with no balls."

Carrie burst out laughing. He grinned as he maneuvered the car deftly around the curves.

They arrived home early enough for Carrie to get dinner going. By five o'clock, beef stew was simmering on the stove. Grey popped the cork on a large bottle of cabernet sauvignon. Wearing a frown with her long teal velour dress, Carrie ran down the stairs. She stopped on the bottom step to insert an earring.

"You look gorgeous," he said, bending down to kiss her. "Smell great too."

Before she could reply, the doorbell rang.

Carrie gave herself a shake. After a deep breath, she turned the knob.

A slim woman in navy wool pants and a fur jacket stepped into the house, immediately grabbing Carrie for a huge hug. Janice Tucker's silvery blonde hair was cut fashionably short, and her makeup was perfect. She was followed by a tall, stout man wearing gray slacks, a sheepskin coat, and a big grin.

Carrie introduced Grey. He kissed Janice's hand and shook Harvey's. Carrie seated them by the blazing fire while Grey poured the wine.

"Nice place here. This all yours?" Harvey asked.

"I bought it a while ago. Carrie's been fixing it up."

She shot him a panicked look. He continued.

"It's slow going. Hard to find a reliable contractor. She's finished the first floor, but upstairs is still under construction."

"Must cost you a pretty penny to run this place," Harvey continued.

"I can afford it." Grey wandered over to the back window, accompanied by his future father-in-law.

Janice wasn't shy about looking Grey up and down, then casting her gaze around. She smiled at her daughter.

"It's beautiful. Very tasteful, Carrie. Good job, dear, and he's a hunk."

"Mom!" Carrie could feel the blood rush to her cheeks.

Fortunately, when her mother dropped that comment about him, Grey had been engrossed in conversation with Harvey.

When Janice stopped speaking, the men's voices carried to the fireplace where the women sat.

"Nonprofit, eh? How can you make money if it's a 'nonprofit'—pun intended!"

Grey chuckled but shot a look at Carrie. She shrugged.

"We manage. I have good investments, and I own several townhouses like this one that I rent out. You don't have to worry, Harvey. Carrie will be well provided for, always. She'll never want for anything."

"Glad to hear that. Good to know my little girl's gonna have it easy. She's worked pretty hard in her life." Harvey rejoined the women by the fire and took a sip of his wine.

"We're no strangers to hard work, Grey," Janice put in. "Harvey and I worked seven days a week and always on holidays when Carrie was growing up. I know it was hard on her. But the money we made went to pay for her college education and a comfortable apartment."

"She's often spoken with pride about your work. Think she's modeled herself after you," Grey said. "She works harder than I do."

Carrie could tell by the expression on her mother's face, she was looking for something to criticize Grey about but he was being his most charming self. Janice was left without ammunition. Carrie blew out a breath as a smile crept across her face.

When the stew, made with her parent's recipe, was served, they showed proper appreciation.

"How are the plans for the wedding coming?" Janice asked.

"Fine. We're having it at Delia's house. She's taking care of most of the planning. I'm on deadline with a new book, so I've left things to her."

"You can't do that! Delia's not even a real Tucker now that she's a widow. Besides, she'll have pigs in blankets and other low-class food if you don't take control. Good thing I'm here."

"Janice was the creative one. The foodie. I handled the business side of our catering company. I always left food decisions up to her, she's uncanny!" Harvey said, stabbing a carrot with his fork.

"What about a dress?" Janice asked before putting a piece of beef in her mouth.

"Delia and I found one At Bonnie's Bridal—"

"That awful place! Only second-rate stuff there. You need to go to Luigi's Bridal Shop. He has the best gowns, hand-beaded in Italy—"

"I don't want a beaded gown, Mom. We talked about it."

"You talked about it with Delia, but I'm your mother. I should be having a hand in this."

A blanket of silence fell on the four at the table. The only sound was the clinking and scraping of knives and forks.

"At least could you come to Luigi's with me and look. Dad and I will pay for it."

"It's not a question of money."

"Humor your mother, Carrie. This is the only wedding she'll get to plan. After your elopement to that loser."

Carrie threw down her napkin and pushed away from the table. Tears clouded her eyes, her mouth set in a grim line as she stood up, marched upstairs and slammed the bedroom door.

Her parents sat with their mouths open.

"What did we say?" Janice asked.

Grey flashed his palm and followed his fiancée. He knocked softly on the door.

"GO AWAY," CAME THE tearful reply.

"It's me, honey," Grey said, turning the knob slowly.

He walked in to find her sitting on the bed, crying. He took her in his arms and let her sob against his chest. Within a few seconds, she pushed away to reach for a tissue.

"They always do this. Dad has never let me forget about my first marriage and Mom wants to voice her opinion even when I don't want it. And she's never here when I might need her to help. Nothing I do is good enough."

Grey stroked her back then her hair. She nestled her head into his shoulder.

"You need to tell *them*, not me, honey. In a nice way..."

She nodded, wiping her face and blowing her nose. He took her hand and led her downstairs.

"I'm sorry if I upset you, Carrie," Janice said, squeezing her daughter's hand.

"Me too. I'm always putting my foot in it. That's what your mother says, anyway."

"Can we not talk about wedding plans now? It's our first night together in a long time."

"Did you buy the dress already?"

Carrie nodded, casting her gaze down to her plate.

"Well then, that's settled. Score one for Delia, zero for Janice."

Carrie snapped her head up. "It's not a competition, Mom. Delia is here. You're not. It's that simple."

"Couldn't you have waited for me?"

"Not and get it altered and ready in time. We bought it three weeks ago."

"Oh. What about the food? You know I'm an expert."

"Can we talk about this after dinner? Like, maybe tomorrow?"

"Sure, sure, baby." Janice patted Carrie's hand.

"This one looks like a winner to me," Harvey said, beaming at Grey. The blood rushed out of Carrie's face.

"Dad."

Grey laughed. "Thanks, Harvey. Nice to have your blessing."

"Call me Harv. All my friends do." Harvey slapped Grey on the back.

Carrie covered her face with her hands for a moment, hoping this was a bad dream.

"Okay, Harv. Since we're friends now, do me a favor."

"Sure. Anything, Grey. Name it."

"Please stop bringing up Carrie's first marriage, including the man she was married to."

"Oh." Harvey's face turned red. "Sure, sure, sorry about that, Bunny. Won't do it again."

"Bunny?" Grey's eyes got wide.

"That's my little nickname for her. Cute as a bunny when she was little."

Grey couldn't hold in a guffaw, though he did cover his mouth. Carrie glared.

"Don't egg him on, Grey. He doesn't need any encouragement," Janice said.

"I don't see anything wrong with that nickname." Harvey sat up straighter.

"We're taking a cruise in March," Janice said, putting down her fork.

"What?"

"Your mother's convinced me to go through Italy by boat, then Spain and Greece. We'll be gone a month."

"A month? And you want to help with the wedding?"

"We have two weeks until we leave. Then we're back in May. Plenty of time to help you make the important decisions."

"You think so?"

"I do. What color are the bridesmaids wearing?" Janice picked up her plate plus Harvey's and carried them to the kitchen.

"You servin' dessert, Bunny?"

"Dad, I think you'd better stop calling me that."

Carrie eyed Grey, who smirked behind his hand, unable to contain his laughter.

"I've been callin' you that all your life. Not stopping now," Harvey said, getting out of his chair.

"Oohh, look at what I found! Apple cake. Is this my recipe?" Janice turned to look at Carrie.

"Sure is." Carrie joined her mother.

"Why don't we sit by the fire? Harv, Janice, would you like a brandy?" Grey asked.

"Why not? What have you got?" Harvey joined Grey at the bar.

"How about some Courvoisier? I've got VSOP too."

"Brandy sounds good."

Grey placed the bottle plus four glasses on a tray and carried them to the fireplace.

While Grey poured, Carrie and Janice cut up the cake and put it on plates.

"I know I wasn't around much when you were growing up. Delia took you under her wing when you were twelve. But I'm still your mother and I love you. I only want the best for you, Carrie. The best wedding. The finest food."

"I know, Mom. It's a bit of an adjustment having you around to help with decisions. But I already have the best, the finest man, so the rest doesn't matter that much."

"He does seem to be a fine man, but what do you really know about him?"

"Plenty. He's amazing, and he loves me. You have no idea how happy he makes me."

"We'll see. On the surface, he looks pretty good, but time will tell."

Carrie turned her mother to face her and dropped her sweet façade.

"If you screw this up, Mom, I'll never forgive you," Carrie said with an edge to her voice.

"Those are harsh words for someone who only has your best interests at heart."

"Grey has my best interests at heart, Mom. I meant what I said. Stay out of my relationship and away from Grey."

"I wouldn't dream of interfering. Simply looking out for my daughter."

Janice patted her daughter on the shoulder, picked up two plates with cake, and walked over to join the men. With narrowed eyes, Carrie watched her mother walk away. She sighed, picked up the remaining two plates, and joined the others at the fire.

SATURDAY NIGHT, FEBRUARY, Colin's rental—the Dailey Apartment in Pine Grove, NY

"You expected something wild on a Saturday night in Pine Grove?" Colin chuckled as he toweled himself off.

Leah had to roll up the sleeves on his bathrobe before she rubbed her thick hair dry.

"I didn't expect to be meeting your parents. Geez. This sounds serious."

"Naw. A casual dinner at their house. No big deal."

"Seems like a big deal to me. I don't know what to wear."

"You'll look great in anything, or nothing." He snickered, snaking an arm around her waist.

"Can't believe you're still horny after last night, then this morning." Leah pulled out two tops and held them up to the mirror.

"Can I help it if I can't get enough of you?" Colin watched her while he slipped on his boxers.

"This one is too low cut," she said, putting it back in her suitcase.

"Damn! I was hoping for that one. Love to look at those across the table."

He cupped her breasts from behind. Leah eased her head back, baring her throat. Her skin tingled as his lips kissed up and down her neck. His fresh scent intoxicated her. She drew a deep breath.

"You smell good," she said. "Before we get carried away, let's get dressed and get this dinner over with," she said.

"Over with? It'll be fine. You'll like my parents, you'll see."

"But will they like me?"

"Are you kidding? What's not to like?"

He let her go while he retrieved his clothes and flipped on the radio. "Bad Romance" came on. Leah danced as she dressed. Colin watched her in the mirror. Feeling his stare, she became self-conscious and stopped.

"Why'd you stop?"

"Because you're staring at me."

"I like to watch you dress, watch you move." He stepped closer, bending his head to capture her lips with his in a sensuous kiss.

Pleasure brought color to her cheeks. She smiled shyly. Colin buttoned up his brown and gold plaid flannel shirt and stepped into his pants.

"Casual?" she asked.

He nodded. Leah pulled out a pair of dark blue narrow-wale corduroy pants and a white cashmere sweater, simple and elegant. When they were both dressed, she finished drying her hair. Colin held her fur coat for her then threw on a down jacket before they headed for the car.

He pulled his four-wheel-drive SUV into the driveway of the big, elegant Victorian house which started a cacophony of barking from inside. By the time they started up the walk, they were assaulted by the two Andrews family pugs, jumping up to plant wet kisses on unsuspecting faces. Leah laughed as the male leapt up to lick her. Colin tried to pull him down but the persistent pug made another attempt and connected.

"I'm sorry. I forgot to warn you about the dogs. That's Buster and this one is Daisy."

"They're adorable!" Leah laughed as she wiped her cheek with her hand. The dogs ran to the front door and back to Colin and Leah.

When the door opened, Leah caught her first glimpse of Colin's parents. Fran, an attractive brunette, wearing an apron had her arms wrapped around her torso. John, tall with thick silver hair, wore a dark plaid flannel shirt and held an unlit pipe in one hand and the doorknob in the other.

Fran engulfed her son in a quick hug while her husband motioned them inside. Colin took Leah's hand and led her into the warmth of the entryway. After introductions were made, John took coats and ushered the lovers to the blazing fire.

"What's your poison?" John asked. "I've got the hard stuff, red wine, white wine..."

"A glass of red wine would be great."

Fran took off her apron, folded it then laid it on the arm of the sofa while she sat down. She picked up her glass of white wine and took a sip as her eyes examined Leah. After John handed out drinks, he sat down.

"So, tell me, Leah, what do you do?" John asked, sitting back against the sofa.

"I'm a clothing designer."

"Who do you work for?"

"I'm going to be working for Madame Jeanne."

"Never heard of her. You, Fran?"

"I think she has a line of very expensive lingerie, right?"

Leah nodded. John blushed.

"Undies, huh? Live in Manhattan?" John asked, changing the subject.

"Actually, I'm staying with a friend in Connecticut right now. But I do apartment sit in Manhattan for a friend when she comes up here. You might know her, Nina Wells. She and her husband, Clint Hayworth, have a weekend house somewhere in Pine Grove."

"Oh, that short actress lady and the tall fella she lives with?"

"He's her husband, John," Fran corrected.

"That's them." Leah grinned before taking another sip of wine.

"So you don't have your own place?" Fran asked.

"Not right now. I'm going—"

"What's for dinner?" Colin interrupted.

"All your favorites: roast beef, scalloped potatoes, and green beans almondine." Fran grinned at her son.

"Great. I'm starved."

"Have a piece of cheese. I thought we could take a little time to get to know Leah first."

Fran picked up the small platter and handed it to him.

"Are you from New York?"

"Born and bred. I've lived there all my life."

"Breathe a little clean country air while you're here, might put some meat on your bones," John said.

Color flooded Leah's face as she sensed John's disapproval.

"Leah's bones are just fine...better than fine, in fact," Colin said.

"Are you working on any special designs now?" Fran asked.

"I am. I'm taking costumes from the Old West and—"

"Are you sure we can't eat now?" Colin asked, butting into the conversation again.

Frustrated by Colin cutting her off, Leah wondered what was going on. If she can't talk about what she designs and she can't talk about going to Paris, what could she talk about? Why wouldn't Colin let her speak?

"Colin! Don't interrupt," Fran said.

"Have you lived here all your life, John?"

"Yup. Don't get me wrong. I enjoy visiting the city but I'm always glad to get back to the peace and good air up here."

"I haven't seen much, but the little I've seen is beautiful. Colin's cabin is lovely. Nicer than I expected," Leah said.

"He makes decent money at the school." Fran stiffened slightly.

"No, no, I meant, you know, guys sometimes have messy places, sort of thrown together. Or just a lounger, a TV, and a beer fridge." Embarrassment tinged her cheeks again.

"The apartment in the Dailey's house is quite nice. Laura's a talented seamstress. I believe she made the bedcovers and curtains," Fran said.

"Hell, Barney can fix anything. So can their nephew, Gavin, for that matter," John added.

A heavy silence hung in the air like a rain cloud. Leah fidgeted with the hem of her sweater. Colin wiped his palms on a napkin while Fran and John continued to look Leah over.

"Do you want children?" popped out of Fran's mouth. She slapped her hand over her lips, but it was too late.

Leah stared as her eyes filled. Colin stood up.

"Mom!"

"Excuse me," Leah said, reaching for her handbag, blinking furiously. "Where's the bathroom?"

Colin took her by the hand and led her down the hall. Leah closed and locked the door. She rested her forehead against the mirror over the sink then took several deep breaths.

She doesn't know you, Leah. Calm down. Breathe.

Leah stayed in the bathroom for a few more minutes. Once she had composed herself, she returned to the living room. Fran got up and put an arm around her.

"I'm sorry if my rude question upset you. Please forgive me."

Leah stayed in the woman's embrace for a moment.

"It's okay. Doesn't have anything to do with you all or Colin."

"Fran, I think it's time to go in to dinner," John said, rising from the sofa and picking up the cheese tray.

Colin took Leah by the hand, sitting her next to him at the table. John carved the meat while Fran passed around the vegetables. More wine was poured and a toast was made.

"To Colin's new friend, Leah. Long and healthy life," John said, raising his glass.

Conversation turned to the death of Angus Davenport and news of their friends in town.

Colin rested his hand on top of Leah's between courses. She spied his parents each steal a glance at their coupled hands. A million questions swirled through her mind. Did she pass inspection? Do they approve or disapprove of her? She wasn't sure about his father. He appeared a bit defensive. Or was she reading into his gruff demeanor? Did it matter if they liked her or not? She'd be gone soon enough anyway, out of their lives and their son's too. She cast a wistful eye at Colin but turned away quickly. *This might be harder than I thought. Harder to leave him.*

Directing her attention to her plate filled with delicious food, Leah decided to focus on the meal and stop worrying about the future. She put a succulent piece of roast beef in her mouth and savored the delectable flavor. Colin entertained his parents with stories of their time together in New York City. He was careful to avoid any controversial topics, like where he slept. Fran and John appeared content to listen and ask questions. After dessert, Colin stretched his arms and made up an excuse to leave.

Chapter Twelve

Leah was grateful to get in the car. They entered through the private entrance instead of going through Laura and Barney Dailey's house. Once Leah shed her coat, Colin swept her into his arms for a passionate kiss.

"You look so adorable. I've been dying to kiss you all night."

"Why didn't you?"

"Kiss you in front of my parents? Don't think so. They'd have us engaged."

"Didn't you ever bring a girl home?"

"Sure, plenty of times but nothing serious."

"Never kissed a girl, even a peck, with them in the room?"

"Nope. Don't plan to start now. What they don't know will save me grief."

"You think they don't know we're sleeping together?"

"Haven't thought about it. Don't care to."

She laughed. "You are naïve. How do you think you got here?"

"Don't want to probe that question, either. Come over here. Let's not waste time." Colin had his shirt half unbuttoned, and a gleam of lust shone in his eye.

"Let me finish that for you," she said, grinning.

After some energetic lovemaking, the couple settled down for the night. Leah slept soundly, wrapped in Colin's embrace and a big, ole country down comforter. The silence and the darkness provided the perfect backdrop for deep, soul-refreshing slumber.

The next day, Colin and Leah stopped at Homer's for an early dinner. She planned to make a seven o'clock bus back to New York. As they drank their coffee, a reluctance to leave swept over Leah.

"You have a nice life up here," she said, taking a bite of chocolate cake.

"Can I ask you a question?" he said.

"Sure," she replied.

"Your dream, before the Paris designing one—the one about a house and family—can we talk about that?"

She nodded.

"Was it kind of like what my parents have?"

"Sort of. Except the house was a simple farmhouse, not a grand Victorian. Don't get me wrong. I love Victorian houses and your parents' place is fabulous, but you asked about the dream and the farmhouse was the dream. Big old-fashioned black stove, maybe wood burning stove too. Real acreage, not less than, oh...say, ten acres?"

"How many kids?"

"Two? Three? I didn't have any definite plan there."

They drank their coffee in silence. Colin sliced into his piece of cake with his fork.

"Why do you ask?" She cocked her head slightly.

"No reason. Just curious." He shoveled a piece into his mouth, his eyes avoiding hers.

"You're not a 'no reason' kinda guy, Colin. Give."

They sat quietly while he chewed. Leah sat back against the booth and nodded when the waitress asked if she wanted more coffee.

"Don't we have to get to the bus?" Colin asked.

"Plenty of time. Give."

He dropped his gaze while he played with cake crumbs on his plate with his fork. Leah added milk and sugar to her coffee, keeping her eyes trained on him.

"I guess I was wondering if you'd consider that dream again. If something happened to this dream. Not that I'm hoping for that or expecting it! I expect you'll be a big success. Just saying, if you were to change your mind about Paris or something, would you consider that again?"

"Haven't thought about it. If something happens to Paris, I'd have to start all over again. Who knows what dream I might be pursuing then?"

Colin placed his hand over hers.

"If that should happen, God forbid, I hope your new dream would include me."

A lump formed in Leah's throat. She swallowed twice before she could speak.

"Let's not go there. One dream at a time." She pushed out of the booth, stood up, and grabbed her coat.

They drove to the bus station in silence. Leah fished the return ticket out of her pocket.

"Come back next weekend," he said.

"What?"

"You heard me. Come back next weekend, and the weekend after...every weekend until I come to New York for spring break. This is a ten-ride ticket."

Leah stared.

"I want to be with you every minute you're not working," he said.

Pulling her into his arms, he gave her a long, passionate kiss. Applause broke out when they parted. Leah's pulse raced, and she felt lightheaded. Leaning against him for support, she concentrated on bringing her breathing back to normal.

"Say you'll come," he whispered.

She stepped back, her gaze connecting with his, and nodded.

"If you want me."

He grinned, pulling her into his arms for a hug.

"Last call for the seven o'clock to New York," the driver announced.

Leah broke, kissed him quickly then ran to the bus. As the vehicle rolled out of the station heading for the highway, she waved to Colin and touched her finger to her lips. Every weekend. She smiled. *Pine Grove does have its charm.* As she rolled along, Leah sat back, closed her eyes, and lost herself in a dream.

END OF MARCH, NEW YORK City

As Carrie laid out silverware for dinner, Grey entered from the den, putting down his phone. He eyed the table.

"Dinner for four...Janice and Harv, again?"

"Yup. Sorry."

"No apology necessary." He kissed her quickly. "I've got to go out of town for a day or two tomorrow."

"Oh?" She cocked an eyebrow.

"Business." He paced for a moment before plucking a bottle of red wine from the wine rack.

"Perfect. Meatloaf tonight." She folded napkins.

"Hmm, love your meatloaf."

"Love yours too," she quipped, shooting him a wicked grin.

"How much time do we have?" He sidled up behind her, placing his hands on her waist, his lips on her neck.

She checked her watch. "Not enough. They're due in fifteen minutes."

"Damn! Still time for a little warm-up, though."

He continued kissing her neck then slid one hand up her chest to capture her breast and the other under her skirt. He squeezed her bottom before running his fingers along the edge of her panties. Carrie dropped the napkins on the table and shut her eyes. A low moan escaped her mouth as she lost herself in his caresses. She gripped a chair to keep from falling as her knees grew weak.

Carrie pushed her hips against him, feeling his erection growing. She chuckled in his ear. "You are so wonderfully wicked," she whispered.

He moved back, a lusty light still gleaming in his eye. "Chemistry. But I have to return to normal. They'll be here soon."

"You could have taken me right here on the floor."

"But now I've got your motor running and as soon as they leave, we'll play."

He shot her his most sexy grin, making her laugh. Before he could reply, the doorbell rang.

"You get it. I'm still...uh, not ready." Grey picked up a large bottle of cabernet sauvignon and held it in front of his crotch.

Carrie moved to the front door but stopped. When Grey gave her thumbs up, she bit her cheek to keep from laughing as she admitted her parents. Hugs and kisses were exchanged. Carrie avoided looking directly at Grey so she could maintain a serious demeanor and not giggle. She had no desire to explain to her parents what was so funny.

Conversation at dinner centered around their wedding. Carrie and her mother disagreed about flowers, desserts, and bridesmaid's dresses.

"I'm only having two bridesmaids, Mom."

"Only two?" Janice's eyebrows shot up.

"This is a small wedding. Delia will be my matron of honor and Leah my bridesmaid. Period. End of discussion."

"Nice to know you're so open-minded," Janice said, digging into her meatloaf.

"Great meatloaf, honey," Grey said.

His cell phone went off. He looked at the display and excused himself. "Sorry, I have to take this." He got up from the table and disappeared into the den, closing the door.

"Does he always get calls during dinner and take them, privately?" Janice cocked an eyebrow at Carrie.

"Mom, don't be silly."

"But, really, Carrie."

"Jan! Let it be. Carrie knows her man. Great meatloaf, Bunny."

"Thanks, Dad."

The silence at the table made the muffled sound of Grey's conversation audible.

"Don't cry, I know how you feel, but."

That was all they could hear. Carrie caught the look her mother shot at her father and decided to ignore it. Grey returned to the table, his face a little flushed. He stopped to kiss Carrie quickly before he sat down. The touch of his lips reassured her.

"Sorry about that. A few details before my trip tomorrow."

"Where are you going?" Janice asked.

"Mother!"

"It's a fair question." Janice shrugged.

"Boston. In fact, I'll probably have a couple of trips up there just for a day or two in the next two months, Carrie." Grey turned to face his fiancée.

"No problem. I can get caught up on my writing. In fact, I have edits to tackle tonight, so we need to make this a quick dinner. I hope you understand." She cleared the dirty dishes from the table.

"Of course, Bunny. An author has to dance to her publisher's tune. I respect that. Read your first book and loved it."

Carrie beamed at her father.

"What's for dessert?" Janice asked.

"Brownies with vanilla ice cream, Grey's favorite," she replied, stopping to kiss him on her way to the sink.

Grey helped clear the table while Carrie prepared four dishes with brownies and added ice cream. She gave her father a larger portion, knowing his sweet tooth.

"Whoa, isn't that a little over the top?" Grey asked.

"Dad has a sweet tooth. Besides, it's his reward for reading my book," she said, adding some whipped cream.

As soon as the last drop of coffee was drunk, Harv took Janice by the arm and headed for the front door.

"We've imposed long enough, Jan."

"But we haven't finished about the bridesmaid's dresses..."

"We have for tonight."

His tone was firm and before Carrie knew what happened, her parents were gone. She looked at the clock, only eight-thirty.

"I'll finish up down here if you want to start your edits," Grey said, rolling up his sleeves.

"How did I find you? Just lucky, I guess." She planted a kiss on his lips.

"Actually, I found you. I'm the lucky one."

Carrie climbed the stairs, undressing along the way. She took a quick shower and threw on a raspberry velour robe before padding down the stairs with her laptop under her arm. She set up on the sofa, resting her computer against her bent knees. Grey brought some papers over and plopped down next to her. He put on his wire-rimmed reading glasses, clicked his pen, and read. The house was quiet as the two lovers turned their attention to their work.

After half an hour, Carrie sighed and stretched her arms over her head. She spied Grey, deep in thought. Carrie took a breath and stopped to admire Grey.

"You're like a handsome, sexy nerd," she said, more to herself than to him.

"What?"

Trying to turn her attention back to her manuscript, she couldn't resist sliding her bare foot up his calf. Her eyes looked up at the same time his gaze sought hers. They smiled at each other and went back to work. Within five minutes, Carrie's foot had moved up slowly. She spied Grey peeking over at her as his hand closed over her foot. Her robe was hiked up to her knees. She wore nothing underneath. Grey's gaze turned toward her legs, then traveled up.

When he connected with her, he took his pen and raised the hem of her robe slightly. She watched him bend a bit trying to see underneath.

"Wearing anything?"

She shook her head. A huge grin spread across his face and a lustful gleam shone from his eyes. Grey's fingers closed around her ankle and then moved up slowly. He squeezed her calf, his fingertips caressing her skin.

"So soft, even your legs. Incredible."

His hand slid up and down her calf, inching higher and higher every time. Pretending to look at her computer, she tried to ignore the tingle he created, though it traveled up to her core. Desire grew as she willed him to bring his touch higher and higher. As if by telepathy, his hand slid up to her thigh. Her breathing became uneven. She saw a few beads of sweat break out on his forehead. Still his hand rose higher, pushing the robe up, out of the way. When it reached mid-thigh, Grey's gaze left her and zeroed in on her bared body. He whistled low and sexy.

"Just the way I like you."

He moved his hand down the inside of her thigh, making her squirm when he pulled it away, teasing her, refusing to touch her where she wanted. Carrie inched her bottom down, closer, enticing him.

"Want something?" He feigned innocence.

"Yeah. You," she breathed.

He couldn't resist. Dumping the papers he was perusing on the coffee table, he lunged upward, one hand closing over her core while his lips locked on hers. At the touch of his teasing fingers coaxing her sensitive flesh, she groaned, opening wider. He kissed his way down her belly, settling between her legs. She gasped when his tongue touched her.

He settled his weight on his knees, nestled comfortably between her legs as his mouth devoured her. She moaned, losing her hands in his hair, moving him to the exact spot to send her desire skyward. He pushed up, his lips kissing a trail to her chest. He nibbled on one breast before settling his mouth over the other. He brought his lips to hers for a soul-melting kiss. Her arms wound around his neck, her body soft, hot, and willing beneath his. When he came up for air, she stared into eyes that burned with fire, radiating heat, warming her blood.

"You make me crazy. I must have you."

"Take me. I'm yours."

"I love you, love you forever." He lowered his mouth, his tongue plunging in to capture hers. Her hands fumbled with the button on his pants but he came to the rescue, unbuttoning and releasing himself quickly. She reached for him.

"God, you're hard as a rock."

"Been thinking about you."

"Do it. Hurry, Grey, please."

A wry smile curved his lips.

"My pleasure, honey."

She raised one leg while he eased up the other one, quickly thrusting into her to the hilt. A gasp escaped her mouth as he filled her.

"You okay?"

Concern furrowed his brow as he hovered only inches above her face.

"Never better, darling." Carrie cupped his cheek.

Grey started slowly, eliciting moans of desire from Carrie. She kissed him and caressed him, her fingers massaging the muscles of his shoulders and back. As her excitement grew, so grew the pressure from her fingers on his flesh. Arching her back, she pleaded with him for more, faster lovemaking but he chuckled and kept up the maddeningly slow pace. A cry from her lips got the response she sought as his hips increased the pace of his movements. He plunged into her harder, causing her hips to move as she panted. His speed stoked her fire to blazing, white hot, spiraling out of control. She cried out his name as her muscles clenched. As her climax took over her mind and body, pleasure rocketed through her body. She lost her fingers in his hair as she came down from her sexual high. Her hips moved rhythmically, her muscles caressing him, coaxing him to completion.

"Let go, Grey. Come for me."

"I'm playing with you," he whispered.

"Oh God!"

Another climax took over her body, causing his control to snap when she came. Carrie hugged his chest to hers feeling him shudder then slow to a stop. Heavy breathing broke the silence in the room. Grey rested lightly on her. The hair on his chest tickled her breasts. Carrie's fingers caressed his back through a light sheen of sweat. Grey moved up on his elbows again to kiss her lightly. A look of love shone through his eyes.

Grey rolled off, almost hitting the floor as the narrow sofa didn't leave much room. He grabbed her, switching their positions, tucking her into his side. She rested against his chest. They lay quietly for a time, basking in the glow of their love.

"Let's turn in," he said.

The lovers climbed the stairs slowly and got into bed. She cuddled into his shoulder, snaking her arm around his waist. Grey pulled up the down quilt to cover their nakedness in the chilly room.

"You're a regular heat machine," she said.

"Saves on heating bills."

"I love you," she whispered.

"I love you too, Bunny."

Carrie sat up in bed, prepared to be indignant until Grey burst out laughing. His laugh was so infectious, she had to join in. Picking up a pillow she struck him playfully. He grabbed her wrists, pulling her down on the bed. After climbing on top of her, he kissed her hard.

"Don't ever call me—"

He planted a sweet kiss on her lips before releasing her hands.

"Don't ever call me Bunny again," she said, striking his back with a pillow before falling back on the bed, laughing. His laughter followed hers. She snuggled up to him again, he replaced the covers and switched out the light.

COLIN HAD BEEN COUNTING the days until Friday when Leah would return for her sixth visit to Pine Grove and his small apartment. It was Thursday night. He'd left wrestling practice early to clean. After being too honest about his reason for leaving early, his team ragged on him about going home to neaten up for a girl.

Several weeks earlier, he bought *girl* soap, as he called it, something that smelled good instead of his standard, whatever was on sale. He'd also purchased extra towels, in pink, so he would know which ones were hers, a pink terrycloth robe—because it's too bulky to pack one for a weekend—and various other female products. He was getting used to having Leah around.

As soon as he was finished with his housework, Colin jumped in his car and headed over to the old Victorian for dinner with his parents. He thought nothing of the invitation as they often invited him for dinner. He enjoyed their company and spent many a Sunday watching football games with his dad and eating his mom's famous chili.

When his father answered the door, he handed Colin an open bottle of his favorite brand of beer. The dining room table was set for four. Who was the fourth? When he walked into the living room, he was surprised to see an attractive brunette he didn't recognize seated on the sofa.

"Colin, this is Mindy Winslow, April Dailey's college roommate. She's visiting for a few days, so we invited her too."

Mindy stood up and shook Colin's hand. He knew immediately that this was a fix-up by his parents. He could feel his blood pressure rise, color come into his cheeks. Anger boiled up in his chest. Feeling like a rat in a trap, he resented their interference in his life. If he'd known, he'd have stayed home. Nothing to do now but make the best of it.

Chapter Thirteen

Colin stared daggers at his mother, who tried, unsuccessfully, to avoid his glare. John carried on a civilized conversation with Mindy, but Colin couldn't focus. Mindy was attractive enough, but he was taken. Why didn't his parents recognize that?

"What do you do, Mindy?" Colin asked, finally able to tamp down his anger.

"I'm an assistant to an editor at a publishing company. I write plays in my spare time. Your mom was telling me you coach wrestling."

"I do. My girlfriend is a clothing designer."

"Oh, really? That must be so exciting! What does she design?"

He realized she didn't know this was a fixup. Now she was caught in this awkward situation.

"She designs lingerie. She's working on a special line now for Madame Jeanne."

"I've heard of her! She's very chic and expensive! What's the line like?"

"She's taken designs from historical romances and reproduced them as nighties, I think."

"Wow, bet they're gorgeous! What a great idea."

Grateful for Mindy's enthusiasm, at that moment, Colin liked her better than his meddling parents.

"She's moving to Paris this summer to work directly with Madame Jeanne."

"You are very lucky to have such an exciting girlfriend."

"I am. Are you attached?"

"Not at the moment. But with work and playwriting, I have little time for dating."

He snickered to himself as he watched his mother's face fall. He wanted to cheer, laugh, and throw it in his mother's face that Colin and Mindy wouldn't be dating. His father shifted in his seat. Colin recognized the move. He'd seen his father do that every time he grew uncomfortable with something his wife had cooked up. Obviously, John had been aware of the plan. Disappointed his father had condoned this fix-up, Colin held Grey in new esteem, knowing his brother would never do this.

"I have one or two more things to do in the kitchen then we'll eat. John, would you give me a hand?"

He got up and followed Fran into the kitchen, leaving Mindy and Colin alone.

"I'm so sorry, Colin. When your mother said you'd be here, I thought you were *in* high school, not teaching high school. I thought this was a friendly dinner invitation, not a fix-up," Mindy said.

"Guess I now know what they think of my girlfriend."

"I'm so sorry." She rested her hand on his arm for a moment. "I'm going to make an excuse."

"Don't do that. Please stay. My mom's a very good cook, and you'll be sorry if you miss one of her meals. Besides, it gives me a chance to torture them a bit."

"Oh, no. I couldn't."

"Please. Please stay. I promise not to make you uncomfortable."

"I could use a good meal. April's still learning to cook. She has a long way to go." Mindy laughed.

Fran returned to announce dinner was ready. Colin and Mindy joined his parents in the dining room. He held out Mindy's chair, noting the look of relief on his mother's face. A steaming bowl of Fran's spaghetti with homemade meatballs was passed around. Garlic bread and a tossed salad also made the rounds. John poured red wine. Then everyone ate.

"Colin, I'd love to meet your girlfriend. Is she coming up to see you soon?"

Colin almost choked but he caught Mindy's eye and played along. Trying hard not to smile, he answered.

"She's coming this weekend. Will you be here? We could grab a drink at Homer's."

"I'm sorry, I have to go back. A friend is performing, and Friday is his opening night. Are you coming to New York?"

"Over spring break."

"Great! I'll give you my number and we can go out, the four of us. I date a couple of actors. You must come and see Harry's new play. He's going to be absolutely terrific."

"That sounds great," Colin said, stealing a side glance at his mother.

Her face always gave her away and it was obvious to him she was not enjoying his new friendship with Mindy. Especially if it included Leah. After a tangy apple dessert, Mindy made her excuses and left. Colin kept his tongue until he and his parents were seated in front of the fireplace in the living room.

"What the hell did you think you were doing? Trying to fix me up with April's friend? I'm in a committed relationship. How dare you?"

"Are you in a relationship, Colin?" Fran asked.

"Damn right I am."

"Watch your language. That's your mother," John warned.

"What right do you have to fix me up without my permission?"

"Leah is much older than you. If you want to have children, which I always thought you did."

"Oh, so that's it! Leah's a couple of years older. She's still in child-bearing age. That's none of your business. I don't care how old she is. I love her, and you can't do a damn thing about it. Stop trying to control me!"

He moved toward the front door. Fran put her hand on his arm. "Colin, I—"

"What? What, Mom? You're sorry? You don't like Leah, don't approve of her. Fine. Then you don't have to see us—ever!"

"Don't say that! It isn't that we don't like her. She's bright, charming, but we thought someone younger might be better for you."

"I don't want someone younger. I'm tired of girls. I want a woman, a real woman. And that's what I have. I've never been happier. Why can't you be happy for me?"

"The boy's right, Fran. We shouldn't have interfered."

"I'm not a boy, Dad. I'm a man."

Silence thickened the air in the living room, like a London fog. John stared at the floor. Fran cast worried glances at Colin who refused to look at her.

"You've insulted me with your disapproval. Rejected the woman I love. I'm going home. We won't be seeing you this weekend." Colin marched to the front door.

"Wait! Colin! Please don't leave angry," Fran called after him.

He hesitated at the front door. "What do you want?"

"I'm sorry. Please don't tell Leah about this. Your father's right. I shouldn't have meddled. It's just that, well, never mind. We've been over that already. If you've chosen her, then we'll accept your choice."

"Great. You'll accept her. Don't overwhelm me with your enthusiasm."

"Take what you can get, son. We're not used to fancy, older women from the city. We'll accept her, like your mom says. She's a nice person and all. No problem there."

"You won't have to worry about her for long. She's going to Paris in a few months."

"Permanently?" Fran asked.

"To live. She's got a job designing there."

"Oh, Colin. I didn't know. I'm sorry, son," Fran said, placing her hand on his shoulder.

"Yeah? I'll bet. We're going to enjoy every minute we have together."

He bent down to pet the pugs, who were crowding him and wagging their tails.

"Of course. Please, bring her around whenever you want. We promise she'll get a warm welcome from us," John put in.

"I wouldn't be comfortable with her here anymore. It's late. I've gotta go."

With that, Colin walked out to his car. He stopped when the door of the Davenport's house opened. Giselle stood in the doorway talking to a man thrown in shadow by the light from inside. She kissed the man on the cheek then he turned to go. Colin slipped into the shadows to avoid being seen. When the door closed, the streetlight shone a dim beam on the man. Colin rubbed his eyes and stared hard. *Damn! That's Grey!*

FRIDAY NIGHT, PINE Grove, NY

Colin put Leah's suitcase in the bedroom and then joined her in the kitchen. She put the kettle on.

"I brought some Chai tea. I thought you might like it. God, it's cold in here!"

She rubbed her hands together and stomped her feet. Colin turned up the thermostat.

"I forget you have Florida blood," he teased.

"Next time I won't need to bring a suitcase, I'll just wear everything," she said.

"I could warm you up in the bedroom."

"But I'd have to take my clothes off. It's too cold!"

"I can start here with your clothes on."

He came up behind her, pushed the collar of her ice blue cashmere sweater out of the way, and nibbled on her neck. Leah eased back slightly, resting against his hard chest. His hands wound around her waist for a moment before moving up over her breasts.

"I've been waiting all week to do this," he breathed.

The scent of her perfume intoxicated him. The ultra-softness of the cashmere over her breasts drove him wild. Never had he touched anything so soft and so sexy at the same time. His teeth captured her earlobe, eliciting a moan from deep in her throat. She placed her hands over his to warm them.

"Getting warmer?"

She nodded.

"You look gorgeous, and you feel incredible."

His hands felt her chest rise and fall faster as his fingers found her peaks, hidden in the rich, dense wool.

"Warm enough to take something off?"

Leah broke from him, took his hand, and led him into the bedroom. The whistling of the tea kettle stopped her.

"Tea can wait." He switched off the stove and followed her into the other room.

Colin ripped his sweater over his head and shut the door.

After making love, Leah pulled the pink robe Colin had bought her tighter and padded into the kitchen. She relit the fire under the kettle. Wearing navy blue sweats, he followed.

"We should invite your parents over for dinner tomorrow." She took down two mugs.

"They're tied up this weekend. Stuff with friends, I think." Lying made him nervous. He cleared his throat.

"Oh, too bad. I like them. Bet I'd like the rest of your family too."

Colin took out the milk as she placed the sugar bowl on the counter. His palms started to sweat. This was not a topic he wanted to explore. If his parents judged Leah to be too old, what would his older sister, Barbara, think? A shudder traveled through his body. He was closer to her than to Jenna, even though he and Jenna were closer in age. At least Grey was on his side. Still, this was no time to get into this with Leah. Staying away from his family would be the best route to avoid trouble.

"Let's be just us this weekend."

"It's going to be cold and windy, let's cook in. I make a great beef stew."

"How about tomorrow? Tonight, maybe we should pick up a pizza."

"Then we have to get dressed. Don't you have any food here?"

Leah started opening cabinets and then peered into the refrigerator. She pulled out some cans and a package of hot dogs from the freezer.

"How about franks 'n beans...and a canned vegetable?"

"Great!"

While they prepared dinner, Colin's cell phone rang. He checked the display.

"Mac Caldwell! Kensington State," he said, aloud but to himself.

He picked up the phone.

"Colin?"

"Hi, Dean Caldwell."

"Hey, we've wrapped up our search for the environmental science professor and I wanted to call you right away."

Colin sank down on the sofa. Perspiration broke out on his forehead, his pulse kicked up until he could feel it in his ears.

"Unfortunately, we found someone who has more college teaching experience than you do. This person was not my first choice, but I was outvoted by other members of the committee. I'm so sorry. Don't lose heart."

"I understand, dean."

"Look, there's going to be a cocktail party in New York City over spring break. I'd like you to come. Some of the other committee members will be there. I want them to meet you."

"Sure. I haven't given up on Kensington yet."

"Glad to hear it. I've got your address. My secretary will send you a formal invite in the mail. You can bring a date, too, if you want. "

"Great. See you then, dean."

"I look forward to it."

Colin closed his phone. Leah sat on the edge of the sofa.

"I didn't get the job," he said.

"Oh, Colin! I'm so sorry, sweetheart."

She moved closer, pulling him into a hug. He closed his eyes.

"Life sucks," he whispered, pushing to his feet and sauntering into the kitchen to attend to dinner. His home, his responsibility to put food on the table, wasn't it?

By six-thirty, Leah and Colin were eating franks and beans at the small dining table. A heaviness in his shoulders weighed down his spirit. His gaze trailed over Leah's beautiful face, down to the place where the robe crossed over, hiding her body from his view. He felt a stirring in his loins as he scooped up another spoonful.

"One of my favorite romantic movies is on tonight," she said.

He lifted his eyebrows in response as he chewed on a piece of frankfurter.

"*Serendipity*. Can we watch?"

"We can watch anything your heart desires, baby."

He loved the way she lit up when he called her that. She was his baby, his one-and-only. And he was hers. She'd said so. Two weeks ago, Leah had told him she wanted to commit to him.

Since meeting Leah, dating anyone else hadn't even occurred to him. So he'd laughed and agreed he would be exclusive too.

After dinner, they cleared up the dishes together. Colin pulled a fleece blanket off the bed and set it on the sofa. Leah scooped out Panda Paws ice cream into two dishes and brought them to the coffee table.

"I wish we had this flavor in the city."

"I don't. Keeps you coming up here to satisfy your craving," he said, filling his spoon.

"I come up here to satisfy my craving for you." She shot him a flirtatious smile.

His mood improved. As he switched on the television, they cuddled together and ate ice cream.

"I have an idea, a crazy idea." Mischief danced in her eyes.

He raised his eyebrows. "Nothing about you could surprise me. Shoot."

"Is it too crazy for you to come to Paris with me?"

Colin dropped his spoon and coughed. "What?"

"Come to Paris with me. Even if just for two months. You have July and August off, right? You can be back in time to start school again and we'll have two more months together."

"Me? Go to Paris? With you?"

"Is that so odd?"

"It's brilliant!"

"You can stay with me, so you won't have to pay for housing."

"I pay my share or I don't go." His brows knitted.

"Okay, okay."

"We're going to Paris!"

Colin jumped up, grabbed Leah, pulled her to him, and twirled her around the room. He stopped so his mouth could descend on hers. He kissed her hungrily, his tongue pressing against her lips until she parted. Her arms wound around his neck pulling them closer together.

Colin stepped back, reining himself in. "Do you really want me to go with you?"

"More than anything. A dream come true, making love in Paris. I won't be alone."

"Are you afraid to go by yourself?"

"A little. I did everything with Hank. I've never moved alone except across town. Going to such a new, exciting place is a little, well, daunting. But if you're with me, I won't be afraid."

"I won't let you down."

"I know."

"Maybe I can find a job there, teaching English or something."

"Wouldn't that be wonderful?"

Leah clasped her hands together, her eyes danced with expectation.

"If I stayed, we could get married, or something," he said.

She stopped. Silence hung in the air.

"Married?" she asked, cocking her head to one side.

"Just—only if I stayed—I mean, otherwise we'd be living together forever. Married is better, isn't it?"

Leah put her fingers on his lips. He stopped talking.

"We've only been seeing each other for three months."

"To some people, three months is a lifetime. I already know how I feel, Leah. You don't have to say anything," he said, pressing his finger against her lips. "In fact, please don't. I'm not saying we should get married or have to get married. But I'd be a liar if I didn't confess that I know my mind."

"Do you? So young?"

"I'm not so young. Plenty of people, men, get married younger than I am. I've been waiting for a woman like you. Now you're here."

"You don't want to wait anymore?"

"Why should I? I'm an adult. I know my own mind."

"Wish I could be as sure as you that you won't someday find a younger woman and—"

"That'll never happen. No one could equal you, Leah." He took her in his arms.

She sighed, resting her head against his shoulder.

"We don't have to talk about that now. Let's watch the movie you wanted to see," he said.

"Let's call your parents and tell them."

"My parents? Why?"

"Why not? Won't they be happy for you to go to Paris?"

"I don't know." Sweat formed in his palm.

Leah picked up his phone and pressed the button that dialed the Andrews family. Colin snatched the phone away but not before his mother picked up.

"Colin? Everything okay?"

"Yeah." His stomach tightened.

Leah made motions with her hands.

"Then why are you calling?"

"I didn't get the job at Kensington State," he blurted out.

"I'm so sorry, dear."

"But instead, I'm, uh, going to Paris."

"Paris?"

"Yup, Paris. With Leah."

His mother's gasp was loud.

"You're following her to Paris? For good?"

"We're going together. Just for the summer. July. August. Then back for school." He spoke quickly.

"Oh. I see." There was a long pause. "Staying with her, I suppose?"

"Of course." He wiped his palm on his pants.

"Well, have a good time."

"I'm not going until after Grey's wedding."

"Then there's time," she stopped.

"Time for what?" Colin cut in.

"To change your mind," Fran said.

"You don't get it, do you? Goodbye, Mom." Colin hung up. Anger filled his heart. Leah sat back against the sofa and stared.

"She wasn't happy?"

He shook his head. "How about that movie?" Colin picked up the remote control.

"Is something wrong?"

"I'd rather not talk about it." Colin switched channels. "What was the name of that movie again?"

"*Serendipity*. Doesn't your mother like me?"

"Sure, she likes you. There it is. Starting in five minutes." He avoided her gaze.

"Then what?" She raised her shoulders.

"Can't we watch the movie and forget about my parents?"

"*Both* your parents? They don't approve of you sleeping with me?" Leah placed her hand on his forearm.

"Not exactly a mother and son topic."

"I don't understand." She raised her eyebrows.

Colin turned off the television.

"Look, it doesn't matter to me what my parents think. I love you, Leah. I want to be with you. Nothing will ever change that. If they're a little old fashioned, well, they'll get over it."

"Old fashioned? About—oh! I see. The age thing? Right, right." She nodded.

He pulled her into his embrace and switched on the television again.

"Watching the movie and forgetting about my parents right?"

"Sure?" she asked, making eye contact.

"Absolutely!"

When she snuggled closer, resting her head on his chest, Colin pulled up the fleece blanket, covering them. She sighed as he stroked her hair.

"Can I tell Carrie?" she asked.

"Why not?" A small smile curled his lips.

He focused on the movie while Leah dialed.

Chapter Fourteen

Grey and Carrie were sitting in front of a roaring fire, looking at hotel brochures for their honeymoon when Carrie's phone rang.

"Hi." Holding the phone, she rejoined Grey on the sofa.

He slipped his arm around her. She rested her shoeless feet on the coffee table and leaned back against him.

"What?" Carrie bolted upright, snagging Grey's attention from the brochure in his hand.

"Really? That's wonderful!" A huge smile spread across her face.

She nodded twice. "Tell Colin I don't care, I'm telling Grey. Right, right. Uh-huh. Perfect!"

A frown furrowed Grey's brow.

"We'll celebrate when he comes down for spring break. Love you too, hon."

Carrie hung up. Her eyes danced mischievously.

"What?" He closed his fingers around a sensitive spot on her waist and squeezed.

Carrie jumped and squealed. "I should never have let you find that spot." She twisted around trying to pry his fingers off, but Grey was too strong for her.

"And I'll never forget it." He grinned. "What are you keeping secret? Tell me and I'll let go."

"It's not a secret. Bad news. Colin didn't get the job at Kensington. Good news, Leah asked him to go to Paris with her for the summer."

Grey slid his hand up from her waist to the back of her head. He drew her toward him for a kiss.

"Colin's going to Paris with Leah?" he asked when their lips parted. She nodded.

"Wow!" He gave an air pump. "Way to go, little brother! She's his, she's his. He's got her. Gotta hand it to him. That old Andrews charm. Women don't stand a chance."

"You're so sure of yourself," she said, laughing.

"Not over-confident. Maybe you could say hopeful? Persistent? I got you, didn't I?"

"Totally."

"Now it's Colin's turn to get the lady of his dreams. We'll be in Paris at the same time."

"We will?"

"Paris is the most romantic place in late June. And this hotel, here, has me salivating. Come and look at what it's got, honey. Just you and me, and all the romance one guy can handle. Whew!"

He pretended to fan himself.

"You are so into this."

"Hey, you've got more than enough help with the wedding. The honeymoon is more my style." He snickered, his gaze traveling the length of her body. "Gonna bring any of Leah's outfits with you?"

"My honeymoon trousseau is a secret." She shot him a wicked grin. He stuck out his lower lip.

"I need to have some surprises left for the wedding night, don't I?"

"Every night with you is like a wedding night, honey." He pulled her close for a kiss which became passionate quickly until Carrie's cell phone rang again.

"Okay, but just for an hour, Mom. I have edits to do." Carrie stared at Grey and licked her lips.

"Your mother's coming over?"

"She has a brochure of flower arrangements and fabric samples for bridesmaid dresses."

"What does Delia think of all this?"

"She threw up her hands. So, I said Mom could have the final say on food because that was her field and Delia on clothes because that's her field."

"So why is your mother coming here with fabric samples? And who handles the flowers?"

"Because Mom can't take direction from Delia or me. And the flowers. Hell, I forgot to assign those. The groom's family is supposed to supply those. Since I haven't heard from your parents, I guess I'll assign them to Mom. I'm getting pretty fed up with her."

"Oh no! If my family is supposed to handle flowers, then I'm calling my mom right now. Do *not* let your mother do that. I don't want her messing with my mom. This could turn into World War Three."

The doorbell rang before Grey could finish. Grey whispered in her ear as she was pushing to her feet.

"Las Vegas."

She chuckled as she folded her cashmere cardigan sweater around her body before she opened the door to the cold air outside. Janice didn't wait for a greeting but barged right in, talking.

"I know you want everyone to look good but the only one who has to look good is the bride, and the mother of the bride, of course. If you put all the others in yellow, no one will outshine you."

"Hi, Mom, I'm fine, how are you?" Carrie rolled her eyes, closed the door behind her mother, and followed her into the kitchen. Janice plunked right down and pulled out a large envelope from the bag she was carrying.

"Got any coffee?"

"Coming right up." Carrie picked up the empty pot under the coffeemaker.

Janice turned to address Grey. "By the way, Harvey wants to get theater tickets for next Thursday night. Our treat. Grey, are you two available?"

Grey pulled out his phone to check his calendar. "I'm going to be in Boston then, but you go ahead, Carrie."

His fiancée shot him a "thanks a lot" look behind her mother's back.

"Boston, again?" Janice raised her eyebrows.

"The deal I'm, uh, closing has hit a snag. Sorry, babe. I won't be more than a day or two."

"Every day without you is like an eternity," Carrie said, planting a kiss on his cheek.

Grey smiled. "You say the sweetest things."

"For a man so in love, you seem to be trekking up to Boston quite a bit."

"Gotta keep the money rolling in for my future bride." A slight blush pinked his cheeks. "Not that I'm not interested, but I hope you'll excuse me. I have some paperwork to take care of before tomorrow. I leave you in good hands."

The smell of freshly brewing coffee almost lured him back. Grey frowned at his future mother-in-law. He found himself wishing Carrie had been adopted. When Grey got up and moved toward the stairs, Carrie stopped him to whisper in his ear.

"Call me upstairs in about twenty minutes."

He nodded and gave her a pat on the rear end. Carrie returned to the kitchen. As he ascended, Janice's voice rang out loud and clear.

"Aren't you worried he flits off to Boston all the time? What's he up to? Is it really business?"

The words *"Shut the hell up, Janice"* echoed in his brain. He shook his head as he closed the bedroom door.

UPTOWN NEW YORK CITY, Saturday, late morning

Carrie chewed a fingernail as she perused her list. "Groceries bought, check. Bathroom cleaned, check. Living room vacuumed, check. Linens ironed, nope!"

Stuffing the list in her apron pocket, she pulled out the iron and plugged it in. Grey appeared wearing a running suit.

"Doing my two miles. Anything you need?" he asked.

"Yeah, to have my head examined. Why did I think bringing Delia and my parents together over dinner tonight would be a good idea?"

"Because you want everyone to be friends. Unfortunately, they don't agree." He brushed his lips over hers.

"I'm such a damned optimist!"

Grey was out the door before the iron got hot. Carrie consulted her list again, put on another pot of coffee, and set up the ironing board.

By six-thirty, everything was set. Her silk-screened tablecloth with matching napkins hung perfectly. Sterling silver flatware gleamed in the soft glow of candles. The crystal twinkled. Carrie flounced down the stairs wearing chocolate brown silk hostess pants and a beige short-sleeved cashmere sweater. The scent of the pot roast simmering in the oven mixed with the spicy aroma of the gingerbread she'd made earlier in the day created a mouth-watering aroma.

Dressed in his navy blue sports jacket and gray slacks, Grey joined Carrie. He stopped dead and sniffed the air.

"Something smells fantastic!"

Carrie joined him, lacing her fingers with his.

"Mom's pot roast. Aunt Delia's gingerbread cake."

"Very politic of you using recipes from both ladies. I'm marrying the smartest woman in New York." He leaned down for a quick kiss. "Hmm, you smell good too."

"Madame Jeanne's new fragrance, *Rendezvous*."

"Honey, I'm ready to *rendezvous* with you, anytime, anyplace."

Carrie fell into his embrace. He held her tight.

"Don't worry. Everything'll be all right," he whispered.

"You don't know these women. They don't back down."

"But you hold the trump hand, it's *your* wedding."

"Las Vegas is beginning to look better every day," she said.

He chuckled. "Just say the word, babe."

"I'm not ready to raise a white flag. Damn it! Can't I have it the way I want it? I'm the bride, after all, I'm not going to give in to their pettiness. I want to have a nice, simple wedding with the people we love."

"Then that's what you're going to have." He stroked her hair, preparing to plant another kiss when the doorbell rang.

"And so it begins," Carrie muttered as she disengaged from his arms.

She greeted Delia Tucker. After a kiss on the cheek, she took her coat and handed it to Grey.

"I swear, Grey Andrews, you're still the handsomest man in the city."

He blushed. "Flattery will get you everywhere, Delia."

Delia laughed. He hung her fur coat up, closed the closet door, and joined the women.

"What are you drinking?" Grey asked.

"Got any of that marvelous cabernet left?"

"Grey buys it by the case now."

"I'd love a glass. Got the fire going. Perfect day for it. April, huh? Feels more like January."

The setting of the sun chilled the air. The wind chill factor made it feel like twenty-five degrees. Delia stood by the fire, warming her hands.

"You really did it, huh?"

She looked directly at Carrie.

"What?"

"Invited your parents here tonight too?"

"Plus Colin and Leah."

"Should be quite a show. I haven't seen Janice and Harv since Jack's funeral."

"Jack?" Grey asked, handing her a glass of red wine.

"Jackson Tucker, my late husband. He was Harv's brother."

Grey handed Carrie the other glass of cab he was holding then retrieved one for himself.

"Let's toast to a peaceful evening," Grey said, raising his glass.

Carrie chewed her lip but clinked her glass with the others.

"Have you always been an optimist?" Delia asked Grey.

The doorbell interrupted. When Carrie opened the door, Colin and Leah entered. Not five minutes later, Janice and Harvey rang. Grey ran back and forth, taking coats. Everyone clustered around the fireplace while Grey took down more wine glasses and opened another bottle of cabernet.

"CAN I HELP?" COLIN asked, standing close to his brother.

"Sure. Hold the glasses."

While Grey poured, Colin spoke in a low voice.

"What are you doing?"

"What? Pouring wine. What does it look like?" Grey replied.

"No, in Pine Grove, visiting Giselle Davenport?"

Grey's hand jerked, spilling wine on the counter. He swore, then wiped it up.

"What were you doing? You have the best lady on Earth," Colin whispered.

"I can't explain now. You have to trust me," Grey whispered.

"Trust you? I know you, Grey. Don't forget that." Colin drew his eyebrows together.

"Then have faith."

"Faith in infidelity?" Colin raised his eyebrows while he kept his voice low.

"Shut up, here comes Janice."

"What are you two buzzing about over here?" Her sharp blue eyes examined the men before she reached for a glass of wine.

"Guy talk. Basketball scores. Baseball picks. You'd be bored, Janice," Grey lied.

"I doubt that," she said, her eyes boring into Grey's.

"Have you met my brother, Colin? This is Janice, Carrie's mother."

Grey left Janice grilling Colin to carry two glasses to guests waiting by the fire. His palms were sweaty, and his stomach churned. Silently, he prayed his brother would keep his mouth shut.

Colin and Janice joined the rest. Grey stuffed a piece of cheese in his mouth. He needed food to keep from getting tipsy and spilling his secret. He picked up a stuffed mushroom and wolfed it down. Leah and Colin were making polite conversation with Janice and Delia. Harv stood by himself, sampling the *hors d'oeuvres*. Carrie sidled up to Grey.

"No blood has been drawn yet," she whispered.

He slipped an arm around her waist. They stood apart listening to the polite cocktail party conversation. Carrie left him to make the last-minute preparations for dinner. Grey took a gulp of his wine and moseyed over to Delia.

"Who you bringing to the wedding, Delia?"

"Don't know. Haven't met him yet."

Grey burst out laughing. He kissed her on the cheek, and she shot him a mischievous grin. "You're one of a kind, lady."

Janice cast a jaundiced eye at the pair. She looked about to speak when Carrie clapped her hands.

"Dinner is served!"

The hungry crowd milled around until Carrie made another announcement.

"There are place cards. Find where you're sitting."

Grey chuckled to himself. How smart of Carrie to arrange the table herself instead of letting people choose their seats! She'd arrange it in the most amiable way possible to avoid a catfight.

Delia had Leah and Harvey between her and Janice. On the other side, Colin sat next to Janice, then Carrie, then Grey, who helped Carrie carry the food to the table. Harvey dug in first.

"Delicious, my recipe, right?" Janice said, taking a bite of the meat. "Right, Mom."

"You're a great cook, Janice. Of course, you don't know crap about fabrics or colors, but you're an expert with food."

"Don't kid yourself, Delia. I know plenty about fabric and colors. Enough to know that the *supporting cast* at the wedding should wear yellow. Make Carrie look good."

"In case you haven't noticed, Carrie doesn't need any help looking good. She's gorgeous. She could wear a burlap sack and still be the prettiest one in the room. And I'm not wearing yellow," Delia chimed in.

"You don't have to be in the wedding, either, Delia. I mean if the bride chooses yellow, I mean, it's *her* choice."

"Right, Mom. And I'm not choosing yellow. Not fond of yellow. It's a hard color to wear. And I wouldn't do anything to keep Delia out of the wedding party."

Janice made a face but kept eating. "The carrots are overcooked." Carrie sighed.

"What color did you have in mind for the bridesmaids?" Leah asked, cutting a piece of potato with her fork.

"Raspberry or turquoise. Those are universal colors. They look good on everybody, right, kid?" Delia piped up.

Carrie nodded, chewing her meat slowly.

"You should let her decide, Delia. After all, it is *her* wedding. You've had one and, from what I've heard, have a number of candidates lined up for number two."

Delia dropped her fork and knife with a clatter. Grey winced.

"I don't know what people have been telling you, but I'm not about to get married. No man can equal Jackson Tucker, present company excluded, of course."

"My brother was an amazing man," Harv put in.

"Not that I couldn't have my choice of a second husband. Believe me, there are plenty of men interested."

"I'm sure they've been busy sampling the goods first," Janice said.

"Can I help it if I'm a desirable woman? You make that sound like a bad thing, Janice. How's your sex life, anyway? Probably a bit dried up, I'd imagine."

Several people at the table gasped. Colin put his head down, focusing on his food. Leah blushed while Carrie paled.

"Mom, Delia, please."

"Tell us all about it, Delia. Any pointers? I'm sure the younger people at the table would benefit from your expertise."

"Are you asking, Janice? Because if you are, I'd be happy to give you some advice, privately. I know how to please a man. Do you?"

"Delia!" Carrie gasped.

"And so do you, Carrie. Obviously or you wouldn't be about to marry this fabulous sexy man sitting here," Delia added.

Grey could feel the color start up his neck.

"How about those Knicks?" Colin asked.

"My husband is perfectly satisfied, aren't you, Harv?" Janice stuck her chin out.

Harvey turned bright red but kept eating.

"I prefer the Nets actually, Colin," Harvey said, training his gaze on his food.

"Maybe Harv would rather not talk. Maybe he's getting his satisfaction elsewhere," Delia commented.

"Delia!" Carrie stood up.

"Down, girl, I'm just teasing my brother-in-law. No harm, no foul, right, Harv?"

Delia waved her hand at Carrie.

Janice turned pale and blinked back tears. Everyone at the table silently finished their food. Carrie put her arm around her mother's shoulders.

"Dessert."

"I think I've had enough. I'm full," Janice said, rising.

"But Janice, gingerbread cake," Harv said.

"I'm sure Carrie will wrap a piece to go, won't you, dear?"

Carrie nodded. Harvey took his plate to the kitchen where Carrie was wrapping two pieces of cake.

"I'm so sorry, Dad."

He patted her shoulder. "Don't worry, Bunny. Your mom started it. She should know by now that Delia always wins. Sorry we ruined your party."

Grey took their coats out of the coat closet and met them at the door. They left quietly. No one at the table spoke. Grey offered more wine and everyone had a refill. After a generous sip, Delia spoke up.

"I'm sorry, Carrie, everyone. I went too far. I didn't mean to disrupt the party, but Janice gets under my skin. I hope I didn't embarrass anyone too badly. Oh, Grey! I'm so very sorry. You turned a brilliant shade of raspberry."

That made everyone laugh.

"Grey's reputation precedes him," Colin said.

Grey shot his brother a look.

"I hope you'll all enjoy the gingerbread cake. It's Delia's recipe," Carrie said.

Delia took a hard look at Colin, then at Leah.

"Haven't seen her so happy in ages. Hmm, I think maybe Colin has some of the same *talents* his brother has."

Colin blushed.

"More wine?" Grey asked, brandishing a large bottle of cabernet.

Chapter Fifteen

Saturday night, last night of spring break, New York City

Colin toweled his hair, standing naked in the bathroom of the luxury apartment owned by Leah's friend. The bathroom was toasty, the mirrors well fogged by the long shower shared by the lovers. Leah sat on the edge of the tub, wringing her hair out.

He rubbed a bit of the mirror and examined his face. "Do I need a shave?"

"This cocktail party is important. Perhaps you should. I like you scruffy but maybe the folks at Kensington State won't."

She ambled over and ran her hand along his cheek. "Hmm."

"You liked it a few minutes ago when it was rubbing up against you."

Leah blushed.

"Yeah. But this is your life, your career, your dream."

"Some dream. Turned down flat."

"What exactly did the dean say?"

"He said they offered the job to someone else."

"Maybe that person won't be any good and they'll hire you next semester when they throw this guy out for, for," she stopped to think, tapping her chin, "for sleeping with students."

He laughed. "I'd never do that!"

"Especially not the wrestling team!" Leah wound a towel around her chest.

"Hey, you're spoiling the view." He tugged on the terrycloth.

"We have to get ready." Leah scooted out of his reach.

"Why are we going to this thing anyway?" he called out.

Leah returned wearing matching white lace panties and bra. "Because it's important for your career. Don't burn any bridges, Colin. You never know."

"Oh yeah? I know one thing. I didn't get the job."

"And that means you can come with me to Paris! Not a bad trade-off."

He grabbed her middle, pulling her in for a hug.

"Not bad at all. You're right. I need to keep up my contacts. Besides, free booze and food. How bad could it be?"

Leah left the bathroom and returned momentarily with a box in her hand.

"What's this?"

"A little present I bought you."

He cocked an eyebrow.

"It's a new tie to wear tonight."

"I have to wear a tie?"

"You don't want to appear to be a hick, do you? You've got a sports coat, right? You need this tie."

He bent down and kissed her. "You think of everything. Thanks."

He opened the box to reveal a stunning narrow-striped tie in teal and dark purple. "Wow! Subtle. I like it."

"Perfect with your coloring."

"You're the fashion expert. Are you going like that? Because if you are, no one will want to talk to me."

She laughed. "Put something on, sexy man, or we'll never get there."

"Okay, okay."

Dressed, he turned to see Leah, elegant in a pink cashmere dress. Colin gave a low whistle.

"You in that dress? No one's going to notice me at all."

She hugged him.

"Flatterer."

"I'm telling the truth. You look amazing."

They hopped in a cab and got out at 68th Street halfway between Park Avenue and Madison Avenue. Colin offered his hand to help her from the taxi. Gold letters spelling out *University Club* on a brick townhouse drew their attention.

They stopped. Colin took a big breath. His palms had grown damp. He plucked his handkerchief from his pocket and wiped his hands. Leah straightened his tie.

"You look very handsome and professorial."

A smile curled his lips. "I hate these things. They always make me nervous."

"You'll be great. And you're not alone. I can handle any party. Let's go."

They joined hands and pressed the buzzer. A butler-type opened the door and Colin showed him his invitation. They stepped inside, into another world.

THE TOWNHOUSE WAS OLD. The ceiling in the foyer was low, Colin ducked his head instinctively. Through an archway to their right was a beautiful room, painted dark red with gold trim. Even the ceiling was red. A fire graced the stone fireplace, and the glow reflected off the walls. Several comfortable chairs and two loveseats were scattered around the room. Silver platters of fancy canapés sat on the dark wood coffee table and sideboard. Men and a few women stood around with mixed drinks or glasses of white wine.

"The bar is right through there," the butler pointed toward another room to the left.

Colin grasped Leah's hand and headed toward the arch.

"Colin Andrews!"

He turned to see tall, slim Mac Caldwell, the dean, heading his way. Grateful for a friendly face, Colin smiled. Mac extended his hand and Colin took it.

"Who is this lovely lady?"

"Leah Golden, Dean Mac Caldwell," Colin said.

Mac shook her hand too.

"Come let's get you drinks."

They followed Mac to the bar. The room wasn't crowded but it wasn't empty, either. People milled around. Some were engrossed in lively conversation while others moved from small group to small group. Leah took a glass of white wine, Colin took red. They followed Mac to a group of four older men.

"I want you to meet our president, John Lawrence."

Mac made introductions. Suddenly shy in front of the silver-haired man who exuded confidence, Colin mumbled, "Nice to meet you, sir."

"Mac tells me that in addition to being an environmental scholar, you're a crackerjack wrestling coach."

"I've been fortunate to lead winning teams for the last three years."

"That's impressive. What's your secret?"

"Hard work."

John Lawrence laughed.

"Yours or theirs?"

"Both."

"I'd love to have wrestling at Kensington State. Seems this fall it's not going to happen but hang in there. Don't lose faith. There's always next year."

Colin worked to keep a look of disappointment off his face while the president turned to resume his conversation with the others in his group. Disappointment sank Colin's spirit. His enthusiasm went out the window.

"What did I expect?" he mumbled to himself under his breath. Impressive Mac wanted the president to meet him, but it ended up meaning nothing anyway. Colin sighed.

"You handled that well," Mac said, patting Colin on the back.

"Thanks."

"There's some great hot food over there if you're hungry. I've got a couple of new arrivals I've got to greet. Be back soon."

Behind them in a room painted robin's egg blue, also with gold trim, sat a table laden with hot and cold appetizers. While Colin's heart sank, his stomach rose to the occasion. Suddenly hungry, he took Leah's hand and approached the table, his eyes taking in the delicious morsels waiting to be sampled.

A huge bowl of the biggest cold shrimp he'd ever seen sat elegantly at the center, with two bowls of hot sauce. On one sat a chafing dish that held tiny meatballs. Next to it was a large platter with small spinach pies, one-bite quiches, and mini eggrolls. His mouth watered and his stomach growled. He took Leah's hand.

"Let's eat."

Leah handed him a plate and took one for herself. He piled up shrimp, meatballs, egg rolls, and tiny quiche.

"Take human portions, Colin. You don't want to look like a pig."

Looking down, he noticed his plate was overflowing. Quickly he popped a quiche in his mouth and chewed. Then he skewered two meatballs on a plastic toothpick and ate them.

"Better?" he mumbled.

"Better."

Colin guided her to a corner where they stood, eating, drinking, and watching the crowd.

"I don't belong here. Finish up and let's go."

"Wait! The dean said he was coming back." Leah put her hand on his arm.

"I'm not hired, not part of the university. I shouldn't be here."

"Don't assume everyone else here is hired either, Colin. You were invited and have every right to be here."

She patted his arm. A man about forty with red hair wandered in their direction.

"Scott Plainfield, new in environmental science," he said, sticking out his hand.

Colin shook it but couldn't find his voice. Could this be the guy who got the job Colin wanted? Leah nudged him in the ribs.

"Oh, uh, Colin Andrews, and this is Leah Golden."

"What's your field or is the beautiful babe the one with the university?"

"She's not a *babe*!" Colin's brow furrowed. Angry color stained his cheeks.

"Sorry, sorry. Right. Who's got the connection?"

"Neither one. We are guests of Dean Caldwell," Leah replied.

"Oh. I see."

"I see you've met Colin Andrews and his lovely lady, Scott," Mac Caldwell said.

Colin looked at his watch.

"Hate to rush off, but we've got a dinner engagement."

"Don't leave on my account," Scott said.

"Colin is an Environmental Science scholar too, Scott. Thought you might have something in common."

"Oh really?"

"Yes, and I coach wrestling."

"Wrestling? With a babe like that, I'd guess you practice every night."

Leah turned pale.

Colin's hand fisted. "How dare you speak like that about her? If we were somewhere else, I'd make you eat those words," Colin said in a low voice loaded with menace.

"Apologize to the lady," Caldwell said.

"I'm so sorry. My libido got the best of me."

Leah gave him a curt nod before moving closer to Colin. He put his empty plate down, slung his arm over her shoulders, then moved toward the door.

"I'm so sorry. That guy's an ass. You can see why I didn't want him for the job. Hang in there, Colin. Maybe he'll self-destruct before the spring semester."

Colin managed a small smile, shook the dean's hand, and then pulled Leah out of the University Club. He took a big breath of crisp air.

"Had to get out of there before I decked that guy. How dare he talk to you like that. Asswipe."

He hugged Leah to his side as they proceeded toward Madison Avenue.

"Let's order in Chinese food and make love. It's our last night. You go back to Pine Grove tomorrow." Her lusty gaze locked with his.

"I'm there, but?"

"Men fighting over me always makes me horny," she whispered in his ear.

"Then what are we waiting for?" Colin raised his hand to hail a cab.

THURSDAY NIGHT MID-May, Pine Grove at the Andrews home

"Set the table, dear," Fran Andrews said, handing her husband flatware.

"Leah's coming tomorrow?" John Andrews asked, putting down his newspaper.

"We have to finalize plans for Paris."

"Paris?" Fran asked.

"I told you, Mom. I'm going to Paris with Leah."

"Just because you didn't get that job at the university?" John asked.

"Not exactly. Since I don't have that job, I have the summer off. Leah invited me to come with her. I might look for a job there, maybe teaching English, coaching wrestling?"

"Go to Paris and maybe never come back!" his mother wailed.

"Now it's only for the summer. Get a grip, Mom."

"Sounds pretty exciting, if you ask me," John said.

"You'll be living with her there?"

"We're practically living together now."

"I don't need to hear that," Fran said, carrying the salad bowl to the table.

"Then don't ask. Geez, I'm almost thirty, not three. Get over it."

"The boy's right, Fran. Gotta let him grow up. He's a man and a man needs a woman."

"John. Enough! Do you both have to rub sex in my face? Dinner's ready. Sit down."

The three took their places at the table. Fran's Dijon chicken was the main course, a favorite of Colin's.

"What can I do to help you prepare for the trip, dear?" his mother asked.

Colin let out a breath. "I think I have everything under control. Leah and I have been brushing up on our French and researching things to see and do in Paris. I'm pretty excited."

"You've got all the luck. Imagine a pretty female taking you to Paris. What I wouldn't have given for an opportunity like that," John said.

"Jealous, Dad?"

The men chuckled. Fran made a face.

"She's a damn fine female too, son. You got good taste, just like me and your brother."

"Speaking of Grey, I saw him coming out of Giselle's house a couple of weeks ago. What's that about?"

"None of your business," Fran snapped.

"If he's cheating..."

"As your mother said, stay out of this," his father said, cutting a piece of chicken.

"I'm going to New York next weekend for a fitting for the wedding tux. I hate those things."

"Me too. Gotta wear 'em 'cause some woman somewhere said so and now look at us. Look like a bunch of penguins," John grumbled into his peas.

"Maybe we'll go with you. Dad has to have his fitted too. And I need to buy a dress. Maybe Leah would take me shopping."

"I'm sure she would. Okay, then we're all going."

After dinner, Colin dried the dishes.

"You know I don't mean to reject Leah. She is lovely, as your father says, and she seems devoted to you. It's taken some time to get used to the idea, that's all."

"Are you used to it?"

"I thought I was. Kind of looking forward to maybe another wedding. Then you tell me she's going to Paris and you're going but only for two months. Is this a fling, Colin? I thought you were serious."

"I am serious, but designing in Paris is her dream. How can I ask her to give that up? I'm waiting to see how Paris goes. Leah's kind of skittish. She's a widow and afraid to make another commitment. I understand that."

"A widow? You never said." Fran handed her son a wet platter.

"I haven't told you much about her because she's a private person."

"But we're family."

"Not yet."

"But you'd like to be?" she asked.

"I can't imagine finding another woman like her. She's everything I want."

Fran smiled. "Sounds like love to me."

"Not a topic to discuss with my mother."

"It's okay. I know all about boys and stuff. I went through this with your brother too. But each child is different. I hope you and Leah can find a middle ground somewhere."

"I hope so too, Mom."

"I only want you to be happy."

At ten o'clock, Colin closed his parents' front door and headed for his car. He noticed lights on next door. He peeked in the window where the curtains didn't quite meet, then crept closer, trying not to make any noise. He clearly saw his brother sitting on the sofa with Giselle. They were drinking wine. Grey made some kind of toast, and Giselle wiped her eyes.

Colin stepped on a twig. At the sound, Grey turned toward the window. Colin bent over and crept away as silently and quickly as he could. He opened his car door noiselessly but pulled it shut the way he normally would. In the quiet of the night, the noise of the slam reverberated, sounding much louder than usual. He spied Giselle's silhouette approaching the window, so he ducked down. After counting to twenty, he turned on the motor and sped away, driving faster than he intended.

MID-JUNE, NEW YORK City, Grey Andrews' townhouse

Carrie paced in the kitchen.

"Stop worrying. This is your party. Go sit down somewhere. You're not supposed to be in here helping. It's *your* wedding shower, Carrie. Come on." Leah took her by the shoulder, then marched her over to the sofa.

"Sit."

"But I—"

"That's an order!"

Carrie plunked down on the couch. Leah returned to the kitchen. She laid out a platter of deviled eggs.

"Your mother and Delia must throw in the towel. The wedding is only two weeks away. They've got to give up fighting."

"Hah!" Carrie snorted, cocking an eyebrow at her friend.

"Where is Grey going to hide out?"

"He's going to be here. Says he doesn't trust those two. I'm glad too."

Carrie sat back on the sofa.

"Marcel did a beautiful job with these tea sandwiches. They look delicious."

"He's French but he makes fabulous food from all countries. Speaking of French, how excited are you about going to France with Colin?"

"I'm beyond thrilled, overwhelmed, excited, scared, delirious." Leah put her hand over her heart while she rolled her gaze to the ceiling.

"He's a great guy, but I thought you weren't going to do the *love* thing again?" Carrie pushed to her feet.

Her friend's cheeks filled with color.

"I was stupid. You can't simply decide never to fall in love again. I had no idea someone like Colin was out there. He's amazing." She wiped off a new platter and laid out more tea sandwiches.

"Worth breaking your rule over?" Carrie cast a questioning glance at Leah.

"Absolutely. I'm happy."

"Hank would be pleased."

"I think he would. He loved me and wouldn't want me to pine away forever."

"You deserve a guy like Colin and happiness, Leah." Carrie squeezed her friend's shoulder.

They were interrupted by Grey bounding down the stairs into the living room. He lunged at Carrie, pushing her back down on the sofa and landing on top. He buried his face in her neck. She giggled wildly until she couldn't catch her breath. His hand slid under her shirt, up her chest, and closed over her breast. Since they weren't alone, Carrie struggled to push him away.

"Ah, the fair maiden struggles, alas, in vain. The rogue has her trapped. He *will* have his way with her!"

"Grey, Grey!" Carrie choked out.

He lifted his head long enough to see Carrie point toward the kitchen.

"Oh my God!" He sat up immediately, pulling her shirt back in place.

"Don't mind me. I'm just the help." Leah kept her gaze on her platter.

"She's practically a sister-in-law, Grey." Carrie chuckled, straightening his hair with her fingers.

A loud clatter of silverware hitting the floor followed Carrie's statement. Grey looked at Carrie, his eyes dancing.

"That's right. Little Colin's gonna be next down the aisle."

"Now wait a minute," Leah began.

"Don't deny it. You're crazy about that little bugger," Grey teased.

"Little?" Leah put her hand on her hip and cocked her head.

"Oh yeah. You're tiny so he must be a giant to you."

"He's a giant in many ways."

"Whoa! Gotta tell him his girl's bragging about his size!" Grey got up from the sofa.

Leah turned bright red. "I didn't mean *that*! I meant, his personality, his intelligence." Leah gestured with her hand in the air but the color in her cheeks only intensified.

"I bet." Grey snickered.

Carrie smacked his shoulder.

"Don't disturb my helper. She's handling the food."

"Seriously, Leah, can I help?" Grey got up and strolled into the kitchen.

"Here, stack these sandwiches on this." She handed him a platter and a box. "Please wash hands first."

"You're in good hands, so I'll go shower and get dressed," Carrie said, moving toward the stairs.

"Maybe you need help with that?" Grey asked, mischief shining in his eyes.

"Oh no, lover boy. I need you. You ain't goin' nowhere." Leah grabbed his arm.

"So tell me, Leah, when is your wedding?" Grey said.

Carrie heard a box hit the floor and the deep laugh of her fiancé as she mounted the stairs.

Chapter Sixteen

As Carrie was coming down, the doorbell chimed. A quick glance in the kitchen told her everything was done. She answered the door, admitting her mother and her editor, Chelsea. Before she could close the door, other guests arrived, including Delia. Leah took Delia by the arm and sat her on the other side of the room from Janice.

Carrie blew out a breath when she saw her mother and Delia mingling, talking with other guests and not bothering with each other. Grey hovered on the sidelines, opening champagne, mixing mimosas, and staying out of the way. Carrie noticed he kept an eagle eye on the party.

The food won high praise, along with Grey's talent for getting just the right combination of champagne to orange juice. The ten women chattered and laughed, making sly references to the wedding night. Carrie spied Grey blushing once or twice when the women's voices rang out. Peals of laughter piqued her interest as well.

"Come on, Carrie, open your presents," Sophie urged.

"Please, please, can't wait until you see what I bought!" Marnie giggled.

"Maybe I'd better leave for this part," Grey said, sneaking into the den and closing the door.

The women sat in a circle munching on mini cannoli and Italian cheesecake from Little Italy. Leah sat near the pile of gifts and handed them, one by one, to Carrie. Champagne raised spirits, shyness melted away, and a few raunchy comments got the women laughing. The alcohol relaxed Carrie. She opened box after box of sexy lingerie and nightwear. The women cheered each one. Comments about each garment and bets on how long it would stay on brought gales of laughter. Carrie spied Grey peeking out of the den wearing a combination of surprise and fear.

"Your friends have some unusual ideas about you," Janice said.

"Not unusual, Janice, spot on!" Sophie said before dissolving into laughter.

Janice fidgeted in her seat.

"Your age is showing, Janice. Can't get a little raunchy with the girls? It's just sex," Delia said.

"Not according to Carrie." Chelsea snickered.

"Carrie? What do you tell these women? What are you doing?" Janice sat upright.

"Nothing, Mom. They're just being silly," Carrie said, unable to stifle a giggle of her own.

"You're so uptight," Delia said.

"Now who's showing her age." Janice sniffed.

"Come, come, ladies," Leah said, taking Delia's hand. "Help me with the coffee, Delia."

Once Carrie had opened all the presents, her friends left. She breathed a sigh of relief that Delia and her mom had not started a big fight. Grey cracked open the den door.

"Safe to come out?"

"All the sex talk is over, Grey." Delia motioned him to join them.

Soon it was only Janice, Delia, Leah, Grey, and Carrie. They sat around drinking champagne.

"Is everything ready for the wedding?" Janice asked.

"Only a few little details to deal with," Carrie said.

"I don't like the raspberry color for the wedding party, Carrie," Janice said.

"Mom, it's too late."

"No, wait!" Delia held up her hand. "I want to hear what she has to say. She's been itching to attack me for weeks. Go ahead, Janice."

"I don't think it's masculine. I mean, the tuxedo cummerbunds are raspberry to match the dresses and I think it looks a little feminine. Raspberry is pink, after all."

"Raspberry is NOT pink! We have a man here, let's ask him. Grey!"

He emerged from behind the bar and held up his hand. "Don't get me involved in this discussion."

"Janice, you have criticized every decision I've made. I've discussed everything with Carrie. She doesn't have a problem with my ideas. Let's get to the root of the problem here. You don't want me to be involved at all, do you?"

Janice shifted in her seat for a moment before answering. "No, I don't. She's my daughter. This is my moment with her. You've butted in, insinuating yourself in a place where you don't belong. You decided not to have children. Your choice, but Carrie is mine."

"No, I didn't, Janice."

"What?" Janice stopped and looked at Delia. "That's what I always thought."

"Well, you thought wrong. Jack and I wanted children. Very much." Delia's voice shook. "After three miscarriages, I had to have a hysterectomy. That's why we had no children."

"Oh. I didn't know," Janice said, her voice quiet. "I'm sorry."

"When Carrie came into our lives, we considered ourselves blessed. She was a joy for us every single day," Delia whispered.

Silence lingered in the air like smoke. A queasy feeling settled in Carrie's stomach. She braced herself.

"I've always been grateful for Carrie's closeness. The fact that you were too wrapped up in your work to give her the proper amount of time and attention was fine with me. I've built a relationship with her while you were busy elsewhere, Janice."

"Why, Delia Tucker, you lying, scheming—" Janice got up to approach Delia.

Grey stepped in. Gently, he eased Janice back to her seat. "Ladies!" The women stopped and looked up.

"I've tried to be patient, kind, forgiving. But enough is enough. I can't believe how selfish *both* of you are. You are upsetting my soon-to-be wife. You have stepped over the line. I've seen Carrie grappling with your prideful, insensitive, controlling behavior for weeks. It's eating her up and I won't have it anymore."

Carrie gazed at him with shining eyes.

When both women tried to speak, he raised his hand, and they fell silent.

"This is her wedding. Frankly, I wouldn't give a damn if she called the whole thing off and flew to Las Vegas with me. Hell, I'd take City Hall. I want to marry this woman, and I don't care if I have to wear a loincloth to do it. I also don't care what the food is like, who's invited and who's not, or anything else. Marrying Carrie is the only thing on my mind. She has my complete blessing to do anything she wants with this wedding, and I will go along happily. The same is not true of you two. One more episode of bickering and I will spirit my fiancée off for a private wedding and leave you to kill each other."

Delia and Janice sat back abruptly as if they had been slapped.

"I mean every word. Ask Carrie. She knows how I am. You've pushed us too far. Now back off or be ready for the biggest disappointment of your life."

In the silence that followed his outburst, Leah and Carrie gathered up the gifts and stowed them in shopping bags.

"You should talk! You're cheating on my daughter!" Janice stood up and hollered.

"What?" Grey turned to face her.

"All those trips to Boston. I don't believe you were in Boston and I don't believe they were business trips, either. And those private phone conversations with someone named Giselle. What were those about?" She sank down on the sofa.

The doorbell rang. Leah answered it, admitting Harvey and Colin.

"I don't have to account for my whereabouts or who I talk to on the phone to you or anyone but Carrie. She hasn't questioned me one bit. Who the hell do you think you are, Janice?"

"I'm her mother, that's who. Carrie, don't do it. I know what it's like to be married to a cheater."

Everyone gasped. Harv turned red.

"Mom, come on. You don't mean—" Carrie began.

"I certainly do. It's about time you took your father off that stupid pedestal you keep him on. He cheated on me. Maybe only once, but once was enough. I know what I'm talking about and I don't want it to happen to you."

"Janice, did you have to do that?" Harvey whined, his hand on his forehead.

"I'm tired of pretending."

"Okay, I admit it. I strayed—once. I was young and stupid. But we've dealt with it and come through it together."

"Maybe you have. But that's a pain that never goes away. I don't want my daughter to go through that."

"Dad, did you really?" Carrie's eyes widened.

"I'm sorry, Bunny. I made a mistake."

"How could you?" Carrie's eyes grew wide.

"I hope you can forgive me." He took a step toward his daughter.

Carrie's eyes filled. She glanced first at her mother, then her father, then Grey before running up the stairs. Grey shot an angry look at Janice and Harv, then followed his wife.

"Maybe we should all go home and let them have some alone time," Delia said.

Janice threw open the door and stalked out, not waiting for Harvey who kissed Delia on the cheek and scurried after his wife. Delia hugged Leah and Colin then followed Harvey out the door.

Leah sank down onto the sofa and let out a sigh. "Wow! Talk about TMI. Things I never ever wanted to know about anyone."

"Janice wasn't wrong about my brother," Colin muttered.

"What do you mean?" Leah asked.

BEFORE HE COULD ANSWER her, his cell phone rang.

"Hi, Dean Caldwell."

Leah sat up.

"What? No. I mean yes, sure. I can."

More silence as Colin stood, nodding his head.

"Wow, really? That's great. Terrific. Uh-huh. Uh-huh. Sure."

More silence.

"When? July?"

Colin swallowed. "Right. Yes, I'll get back to you tomorrow. Is that soon enough? Good. Thanks so much. Yes. I won't let you down."

Colin put down his phone and stood still. Leah held her breath.

"That was Mac Caldwell. That asswipe new professor harassed the lady dean and was fired. I've got the job."

Leah broke into a big grin. "Wonderful! Colin! I'm so proud of you!" She hugged him.

He turned away from her, his face frozen, his gaze avoiding hers.

"But I have to start July first."

"July first? Why? The semester doesn't start until the end of August, right?"

"They want me to start the wrestling program this summer. They're recruiting students for the team now."

Had someone thrust a knife into Leah's gut? There was none there, but the pain slicing through her didn't stop. Tears stung the backs of her eyes as she choked down a sob and took several deep breaths. Leah tried to focus and to force her lips to smile, but they were frozen. She reached out to touch his arm. His gaze followed her hand all the way up to her eyes.

"What should I do?"

"You should take the job! Are you even thinking of turning it down? Why?" Her positive attitude sounded forced. She fisted her hand, pushing it into her stomach trying to stop the agony.

"Because if I take the job, I can't go to Paris."

"This is your dream, Colin. You must go for it. I have my dream and now you have yours too." She touched his cheek.

"But my dream is about us, too, our dream together? Paris—living together."

"We'll see each other at Christmas." She fought to keep the tremor out of her voice.

"That's six months away. A lot can happen in six months." He placed his hands on her upper arms.

Leah turned away, taking another deep breath as she walked across the room. She bit her lip for control.

"We've had a good run. Nothing lasts forever." She bowed her head.

He strode over and whirled her around, holding her still.

"Face me and say that." His voice angry, and his eyes flashed.

Her pulse pounded in her ears.

"Come on, say it again. Speak up, I can't hear you." His hands on her arms held her captive while he shook her. She cringed.

"I thought so. Can't, can you?" He nodded.

"You have to take that job." Her head snapped up, her gaze connected with his.

"I will. But I don't have to be happy about it. What about us?"

"We have two weeks left. Let's make the most of those two weeks." Leah pushed away from him. "I'm not feeling too well. All that drama on a full stomach. I think I need to be alone."

"What?" He grabbed her, squeezing hard.

"You're hurting me."

Colin loosened his grip. "Sorry. I need you tonight."

"Maybe tomorrow?"

"I'm going back tomorrow."

"Logistics. Nina and Clint are in town. I didn't think it would matter because we'd soon be in our own place for the summer, but now."

"You could stay here with me."

She shook her head.

"Why not?"

"Stomach." She wrapped her arms around her middle.

Colin let go of her and stepped back. "You don't seem too upset about this."

"I'm in shock. I'm surprised. I wouldn't do anything to stand in your way, ever." Emotion gripped her sending a tremor through her fingers. Her mouth dried as she swallowed another sob.

"I know you wouldn't. One of the things I love about you. But you don't seem to care."

"If you believe that, you don't know me very well," she said, clasping her hands together to keep them from shaking.

"Then show some emotion." His eyes flamed.

"I can't do this," she said, flinging open the front door and running out.

She ran into the street as tears broke through her defenses. A taxi stopped with a screech, almost hitting her. It was empty, so she jumped in, croaking out the address before her voice gave out. All control gone, Leah sobbed for ten blocks in the backseat of the cab.

"He ain't worth it, lady."

"Yes, he is," she replied.

Light traffic allowed her to make it back to Nina's apartment house quickly. She paid the driver and blew her nose. Lance arrived to open the cab door. He smiled warmly. Leah shuddered, waited a few seconds, then swung her legs out of the cab. He helped her up. Once the door closed and the taxi sped away, tears streaked down her face as her body slumped. Lance cocked his head.

"Missy?"

"Oh, Lance!" Leah threw herself into his arms, sobbing.

Holding her up, he escorted her inside the building and into the back room where the doormen kept their uniforms. He sat her down on a bench. Leah clung to him, crying.

"Did Colin do something to you?"

She shook her head, unable to speak.

"Then, what?"

She took a calming breath and explained what had happened.

He closed his arms around her and held her against his soft belly. Her small arms didn't reach all the way around, but it didn't matter. His presence soothed her.

"What am I going to do? I love him so much. I can't let him go, but I can't stop him either."

"Maybe he'll stick, Missy."

"Six months?"

"He's a good man. Give him some credit."

Leah stepped away from him to search in her purse for a tissue. Lance offered his man-sized handkerchief. She accepted with a feeble smile.

"Can you make it upstairs?"

"I think so." She gulped air as she nodded.

Lance cupped her elbow and accompanied her to the elevator. When she reached her floor, Nina was waiting for her. Leah fell into her embrace.

"What happened?" Nina eased her friend through the door.

"I've lost Colin." Her face contorted in pain, and she laid her head on Nina's shoulder.

Chapter Seventeen

Saturday, June 25, Shelton, Connecticut

Brilliant sunshine burst through the window, waking Carrie on her wedding day. After shoving the sheet down from the bed, she swung her legs over the side, stood up, and stretched. A huge grin spread across her face. Speaking aloud only to herself, she said, "Tomorrow morning, I'll wake up Mrs. Grey Andrews."

A small doubt about Grey's fidelity nagged at her mind. She threw on a cotton robe and padded downstairs. People in every room filled Delia's quiet house completely. Carrie was the first one awake. She checked the clock. Six-thirty! *Coffee.* She filled the coffeemaker and pushed the start button.

Taking a mug, she plopped down on the sofa by the picture window facing the backyard. Colorful tents graced the expansive lawn. Soon people would set up for the four o'clock wedding. She rubbed the goosebumps on her arms, her pulse kicked up. A noise diverted her attention to the stairs where Leah stood, tying the sash on her robe. They exchanged greetings.

"Your wedding day! Can't believe it, Carrie. How do you feel?"

"Nervous, excited, happy. Coffee's ready."

Leah descended the stairs and entered the kitchen. Clad only in sweatpants, Colin came down. The old wooden steps groaned under his weight. He joined Carrie on the sofa.

"So how do you feel?" he asked

"Nervous. Excited." She took a sip.

"Grey is probably shitting himself," he said.

She laughed. Leah returned carrying two mugs of coffee. Colin stood and kissed her.

"Hmm, you guys are next," Carrie murmured.

"I heard that!" Leah said.

"What's the big deal? A little geography getting in your way?" Carrie asked.

"You call the Atlantic Ocean a little geography?"

"Love finds a way, Leah."

"That's what I keep telling her," Colin said.

"Why didn't you wake me? There are a million things to do," Delia said, clapping her hands together as she descended the stairs.

"Carrie, did you lay out your dress? Leah, where's the checklist? Who has the shower schedule? Hop, hop, people we have a wedding today."

Startled, the three by the window jumped before they trained their eyes on her.

"I'm not kidding. I see coffee!"

"Getting you a cup right away, boss," Leah chirped as she scurried toward the kitchen.

"I think the list is on the refrigerator, Leah. Bring it in, will you? Colin, I'm putting you in charge of creating a shower schedule. Carrie gets first pick of a time slot, then the rest of us."

"What's the name of your friend, Delia?" Colin asked, pushing to his feet.

"You mean Stuart? He's British, you know. Lovely man. Oh, and don't forget your parents. Where the hell are they, anyway?"

"Still sleeping, I'd guess. After the one they tied on last night, I'm not surprised." Colin chuckled. "By the way, is Grey showering here too?"

"Horrors!" Delia clutched her heart. "The groom *never* sees the bride on their wedding day until she comes down the aisle. It's bad luck!"

"I don't know these things."

"You have two married sisters."

"I wasn't exactly paying attention back then."

"Well, you should be now since you're next in line," Delia said. Both Leah and Colin blushed.

"Delia! You're embarrassing them," Carrie chimed in.

"Like you didn't a minute ago?" Colin responded.

"Don't they have a shower at that house your parents rented?"

"I'm sure they do. The house is huge. Maybe two or three showers."

"Good, then your brother can shower there. Chop, chop, everyone. Let's go. There's work to be done. Leah, please give me a hand with breakfast. Colin, wake up Janice and Harvey. And Carrie."

"Yes?"

"Do whatever the hell you want. It's your day, sweetheart."

As Delia turned to go, a tall man with light brown hair and gray eyes sauntered down the steps.

"Can I help?" he asked.

"Stuart! My love, come into the kitchen. You can help with breakfast," Delia cooed.

Stuart stopped to kiss Delia before he followed along behind her and Leah.

"I don't know, Colin, Delia may be next," Carrie snorted before scampering up to her room.

It appeared that the smell of bacon woke Janice and Harvey. Wearing robes, they lumbered down the stairs slowly. All seven sat down to breakfast together. While they ate, Delia parceled out jobs and put initials next to each task on her list.

"I have you all on here, so don't think you can weasel out. I'll know who does their job and who doesn't."

"This is beginning to sound like boot camp, Delia," Carrie said.

"You've got to be organized to put this together, honey."

AFTER BREAKFAST, THEY dispersed. Colin and Leah retreated to their room. Together they stripped the bed.

"What time is the limo picking you up?" Colin folded the cotton blanket.

"Nine o'clock. Plane leaves at eleven-thirty. Our last night together." Leah sighed.

"Just for a while."

"Six months." She avoided his gaze.

"But what a night it was," he said, pulling her up against his chest.

"If we don't—"

His mouth came down hard on hers before she could finish her sentence. Leah melted against him as he demanded her surrender. His fingers wound through her hair, holding her head in place while his mouth ravaged hers. A small sound escaped her throat as her fingers gripped his shoulders.

Leah tried to focus her senses on the feel of his chest up against hers, his strong thighs pressing hers and his lips, hard and soft at the same time. She locked the sensations of his closeness into her heart forever.

A loud knock on the door drove the lovers apart.

"No more fooling around in there. We've got work to do," Delia's voice rang out.

Looking sheepish, Colin picked up the sheet he was folding.

"Christmas, huh?" he murmured.

"Yeah. I'll be back at Christmas."

"Will you wait for me?" Colin put down the sheet and picked up a towel.

"I will if you will," Leah said.

"What?"

"I mean, of course I will. Will you?"

"Where could I find another woman like you?" He grinned.

"The same place I'd find another man like you." She got on her tip-toes to plant a kiss.

"Since I'm handling the shower list, I've put myself first."

She threw a pillow at him. He caught it and tossed it back at her. Pillow toss quickly escalated into a pillow fight. He tackled her on the bed, restrained her hands, and kissed her passionately.

"Take that to France with you," he said.

"I love you, Colin. Nothing can change that."

"I love you too. And I won't forget you."

"We can email." Leah took her jeans out of her suitcase.

"Text."

"Call."

"I'll *friend* you," Colin said, stacking the linens on the bed.

"FaceTime."

They hugged and then Colin grabbed his towel and headed for the shower.

Leah tossed on her jeans and a T-shirt and descended the stairs in search of Delia. By now, the caterers had arrived and the backyard was bustling. People set up tables and chairs while others prepared serving areas in the tent.

"How many are coming?" Leah asked.

"Seventy-five, but to see all this, you'd think it was three hundred. What a job," Delia said.

Leah made herself busy helping the caterer's staff, cleaning up messes, and washing and drying dishes. At one o'clock, she scurried upstairs to dress. Colin was buttoning his tuxedo jacket, but his tie hung loose. He faced her and shrugged.

"Can't tie the tie? I'll do it," Leah said.

Memories of tying Hank's tuxedo tie time after time for the myriad of charity functions they attended flooded back. For a second, her breath caught in her throat and her fingers froze. Colin wrapped his warm fingers around her hand and brought it to his lips.

"You okay?"

She nodded, then tied his tie perfectly. He glanced in the mirror.

"Excellent! That ability alone is a reason to marry you," he said.

Leah turned her back to him and handed him her necklace. Colin took his time fastening it, brushing her neck with his fingertips. She broke out in goosebumps. Tears forced their way through her defenses, watering her eyes. She sighed.

"I'll remember the feel of your skin forever," he whispered, his breath warm on her ear.

"So much to do. Delia'll kill me if I'm not downstairs in two seconds."

Colin nodded.

"That's okay. Run away. Someday you'll stop running from me."

Without a little general like Delia at the big house down the street, pandemonium reigned. Jenna, Grey's younger sister, yelled at her husband, Bill, to dry the dishes faster. Barbara, Grey's older sister, cried because she'd lost an earring. Barbara's husband, Earl, on all fours, searched the bedroom for his wife's missing jewelry, and Fran couldn't stop blubbering because her oldest boy was getting married. John sat in the kitchen, his tuxedo tie untied, mumbling about the suit. Grey maintained his cool with no sweat.

He showered and took his time donning his tuxedo. He wanted to remember every little action. *The next time I put in studs, I'll be married. The next time I tie my tie I'll be Carrie's husband. The next time I wear these stupid, shiny shoes, Carrie will be my wife.* He called Colin to check on the ring, then picked up a set of keys and stowed them in his pants pocket.

Jenna cornered him in the bedroom and closed the door.

"You're sure you want to do this, right?"

"Don't you like Carrie?" His brow furrowed.

"I do. I love her like a sister, but I'm not marrying her, you are."

"I've never been more sure of anything in my life."

"That's all I wanted to know. I'm happy for you."

She hugged him.

"I have you to thank, you know."

"Me?"

"You and your marriage list. I never would've found Carrie if it wasn't for you and that damn list." He chuckled.

"Take all the credit, brother. You found her, you won her."

"And it wasn't easy. Isn't she great?" He stopped to stare out the window.

"I can't take all this lovesick mooning. Let's get 'em dressed and out of here," Jenna said.

Grey plopped down on the sofa in the living room of the rented house, chuckling to himself as he watched his family race around.

"Barbara, where is my tie?" her husband called.

"Your tie is on the bed. Don't sit on it! Jenna, do you have an extra pair of earrings to go with this dress?"

"John, don't forget your dress socks."

"Bill! Get dressed, now! You're going to make us late."

Their antics, hollering, frantic behavior trying to pull themselves together to be ready on time, reminded him of newly beheaded chickens, racing around the yard before they collapse. He nursed a second cup of coffee, put his feet up, and smiled.

John joined him. "Nervous, son?"

"Nope."

"Don't know if that's good or bad. Aren't you supposed to be? At least a little?"

"Who knows? This is my first—and only—time getting married."

"I guess when you make a wise choice, you're not nervous."

"Guess so. Were you nervous?" Grey shifted to face his father.

"Nah. Your mother's the best thing that ever happened to me. I knew it then, and I know it now."

"You found her faster than I found Carrie."

"Different circumstances, different times," John said.

"S'pose."

"I like your gal. Smart, independent. Doesn't take any crap from you."

"She's all those things and, well more," Grey said, sensing a blush steal to his cheeks.

"Pretty girl too," his father said as if he could read Grey's mind.

"Very pretty. Beautiful."

"You've got good taste in women, always have."

"You too, Dad."

One by one, the Andrews family members joined Grey and John in the living room. The men first, then the ladies. Grey stood up.

"Everyone ready?"

He opened the door, took a breath of the sweet June air, and smiled. The cloudless sky appeared to be a richer, deeper shade of blue. The group walked along the side of the road to Delia's house. Even from the front, Grey could see bustling activity. John and Fran pressed the doorbell. Delia herself answered, ushering them in with a broad smile and a hug for everyone.

Grey entered last. Janice stood in front of the staircase.

"Groom may not see the bride until the wedding."

Grey chuckled and gave a half bow. Leah came down the stairs, her eyes glowing.

"I've never seen a more beautiful bride, Grey."

"I'm not surprised," he said.

"Smokin', brother," Colin chimed in.

The sun had warmed the air, so Delia threw open the French doors, allowing people to wander outside. She had a terraced stone patio where the ceremony was to take place. Steps led down to a generous lawn, trimmed to perfection. Grey checked his watch. Two o'clock. He motioned to his father, and they strolled over to the bar. They ordered vodka and tonics and then found an out-of-the-way place to watch the doings. Colin joined them.

Grey glanced up at the windows on the second floor. He caught a glimpse of Carrie and waved. He wondered if things were as chaotic in that bedroom as they were on the lawn.

ALREADY WEARING HER strapless wedding dress, Carrie perched on the window seat of her bedroom. She spied Grey with a drink in his hand flanked by his father and brother. As if by telepathy, he looked up at that very moment, smiled, and waved. She raised her hand.

"Who's that? Grey? He's not supposed to see you," Janice snapped.

Carrie moved away from the window. Leah laid out the wedding veil and flowered headpiece. There was a knock on the door.

"Come in," Carrie called.

Janice straightened up and immediately went to the door. She admitted Fran.

"Oops! I didn't mean to pry."

"Come in, come in." Carrie took Fran by the arm and pulled her close to the window.

"It's a lovely day for a wedding," Fran said, gazing out the window.

Carrie hugged her almost mother-in-law, who colored. "Thank you."

"For what?" Fran's eyes got wide.

"For Grey. He's so wonderful. I love him so much. You raised a fabulous son."

Fran blushed. "No false modesty. I agree."

The women laughed.

"Can I help?" Fran asked.

"Just hold my hand."

"Nervous?"

"A little."

Fran sat down at the dressing table while Leah pulled out a brand-new pair of shoes. "Brides always wear new shoes. Don't they kill your feet?" Leah asked.

"When you're in love, you don't feel the pain," Fran replied.

Carrie picked up the headpiece, a band of small white flowers. Janice secured it with two bobby pins. Fran kissed Carrie's cheek then returned to her family on the lawn, taking Leah with her. The bride moved to the full-length mirror on the back of the door, examining her image.

"You can still back out of this, you know. It's not too late."

"What?" Carrie turned to face her mother.

"I know what it's like to live with a cheater," Janice continued.

Chapter Eighteen

"Mom! Grey's not a cheater."

"Are you sure? Are you absolutely certain those trips to Boston were about work? I'm going right now to confront him. Make him tell you the truth" Janice opened the door an inch.

Carrie put her hand on her mother's arm. "You'll do no such thing."

Masculine voices cut the women's conversation short. From out in the hall, Carrie recognized a familiar voice. It was Grey.

"You don't know what you're talking about. Butt out, Colin."

"But I saw you. Saw you with my own eyes, coming out of Giselle Davenport's house. You were supposed to be in Boston. What were you doing there?"

"None of your business. Stop trying to stir up trouble."

"Don't do this, Grey. I saw Giselle kiss you on the cheek. If you want her instead of Carrie, stop this wedding now."

"Are you insane? Shut up!" Grey gripped his brother's upper arm.

Carrie stood there, pain gathered like a lump in her throat. Her mouth fell open a little but for a moment, she couldn't breathe. Struggling for air, she gasped as her eyes filled with tears.

"I told you," Janice whispered. "Thank God it isn't too late."

Grey looked up, his mouth fell open.

"It's not what you think, Carrie. Please, believe me."

Carrie pushed her mother into the hall, shut the door, and locked it. Stunned, she stood still for a moment until she heard the doorknob rattle.

"Go away!"

"Honey, it's me. Come on, open up. You don't believe that, do you?"

"What else can I believe? Colin saw you at the Davenports when you were supposed to be in Boston?" Carrie leaned against the wall.

"I know it looks bad. Please let me explain." Grey's plaintive voice came through the door.

"Drop dead, liar." Anger flared up in her chest.

As quickly as it came, her anger turned to sadness. Carrie slumped down on the bed, crying.

"Oh, honey. Carrie, don't cry, baby, please, don't cry. You're killing me. You know how I hate to see you cry."

"You're responsible." She spat out, reaching for a tissue.

"Please listen to me."

"No!"

There was silence only for a moment before the sounds of whispering and footsteps drifted through the door. Her heart sank.

A moment later, a throat cleared.

"Carrie? It's me, dear." A voice came through the door.

"Fran?" The surprise stopped her tears.

"Please open up, dear. Grey is telling the truth. I know all about what was going on and it was totally innocent. Please let him explain."

Carrie reached for another tissue and blew her nose, loudly. The silence that followed grew heavy as she contemplated Fran's plea.

"I swear. After you hear me out, if you still hate me, I'll let you hit me with a baseball bat." It was Grey again.

She chuckled in spite of herself. "What if I want to stop the wedding?"

There was a pause. She thought she heard a sigh.

"There'd be nothing I could do, honey. I can't force you to marry me. But you'd break my heart. Just hear me out."

Silence again as Carrie pondered opening the door. She waited but not a sound emanated from the other side of the door. She padded over and turned the lock. Still no sound. The metal doorknob was cold in her hand as she turned it.

"Five minutes. You have five minutes." She stepped back, swinging the door open.

Grey strode in, wrapping his arms around her. She resisted the urge to fall into his embrace and be comforted. Instead, she pushed against his chest. Colin, Fran, Leah, and Janice shuffled in quickly right behind Grey. They lined up against the wall, giving the couple some space but no privacy. Delia barged in too.

"Hey! What's he doing here? Carrie's been crying? You'll look all puffy for the pictures. Where are your shoes? What is going on? The judge has arrived and we're supposed to have a wedding in fifteen minutes!"

Grey turned to her. "Stall, Delia. I just need ten minutes with the bride."

"Oh my God! You two are gonna kill me!" She looked at their faces and knew this wasn't a joke. "All right, all right. I'll think of something!"

She turned on her heel and scurried down the stairs.

"Ten minutes? I said five!" Carrie said.

"I know, but you always say I can't tell a story fast, so maybe ten is more realistic," Grey replied.

Carrie sat down on the bed. She looked at her watch.

"Four minutes and twenty seconds left."

Grey reached into his pocket and pulled out a set of keys. His face was pale as his gaze sought hers.

"I know you love Pine Grove and love visiting my parents there. I also know their house is getting a little small. I mean, we're all getting married and soon having kids and stuff. Anyway, privacy is nonexistent there, for the most part."

"It's not *that* bad," Fran huffed.

"Mom, please." Grey turned toward his mother for a moment.

"Sorry."

"So? What's that got to do with Boston?"

"I was saving this for after the wedding because it's your wedding present."

He took Carrie's hand and dropped the set of keys in her palm. She closed her fingers around the cold brass and looked up at him.

"I don't get it."

"I bought the Davenport's house—for you. As a wedding present. All my trips to Boston were really to Pine Grove. I had to deal with Giselle and the estate lawyer. There were some negotiations, requests. Giselle had to keep some stuff. Papers to sign and all that."

"You bought that big old Victorian? For me?"

"You said how much you liked it and with some TLC, it could be great. And it's big, so there's room for us, kids, and maybe even Colin."

"You bought a house for me?" Carrie repeated, still staring at him.

"Yup. And I spoke to Gavin too. He's going to do the renovations. You'll love working with him, he's a master craftsman. You can do all those things you were telling me about when we made our condolence call to Giselle."

"Oh my God!" The tightness in her chest dissipated as tears of happiness gathered in the corners of her eyes.

"I wasn't *seeing* Giselle. There's no one for me but you. I've told you that a thousand times. I'd think you'd finally believe me." He frowned.

"You bought me that wonderful old house."

"You're repeating yourself. It's in your name too. So, you can kick me out any time and keep the house."

"Grey, I'm so sorry. I apologize. I never thought. I mean—wow. I should have trusted you." She wiped the beads of sweat from his forehead with a tissue.

"You did until my brilliant brother opened his big mouth." Grey shot him a dirty look.

Colin squirmed.

"That's the most thoughtful, wonderful gift. I'm speechless." She kissed him.

"I suppose I'd be getting a more tangible show of your gratitude if there wasn't a crowd of people in here." Grey glared at the family members fidgeting on the sidelines.

"And if Delia weren't holding back the crowds who are waiting for us to get married." Carrie opened her hand and stared at the keys. "My own old Victorian. Our old Victorian." She looked up, took his face in her hands, and gave him a passionate kiss.

"I'm sorry I misjudged you. Welcome to the family, Grey." Janice stepped forward.

"Thanks." He gave her a hug.

"I think everyone has heard all they need to hear. Can we give them a moment of privacy before we put the finishing touches on the bride and get on with this wedding?" Fran held the door open and shot stern looks to each spectator until everyone had cleared out.

"I'm so, so sorry. I never should have doubted you." Carrie's gaze settled on the set of keys in her hand. "Can you forgive me?"

Grey took her by the shoulders, stood her up, and pulled her into his embrace. His lips came down on hers gently. When she melted against him, his mouth took hers.

"Does this mean the wedding is back on?"

She nodded, tears of joy caught in her throat.

"No more crying. Delia will have a fit if you look puffy in the pictures," he said.

She laughed.

"I wanted it to be a surprise." He released her.

"It was."

"I was so proud of you not listening to your mother, but then," he began, his thumb caressing her cheek.

"When I heard Colin. I had to believe what I didn't want to believe."

"You never have to worry about me. I'll never stray from you, Carrie."

"I know. I should have let you speak." Embarrassment colored her cheeks.

"Got that right!" He chuckled. "Are we okay now? Do you like the house?"

"Better than okay. I *love* the house! I'm so excited. It'll be so great to visit any time we want, not bother your parents but have our own place."

"*Your* place."

"*Our* place. While you were meeting with Giselle, did you ever find out why she stopped talking to you for a year?"

Grey blushed. "Yeah. I made a pass at her on our first date, and it freaked her out. She thought I was a mover so she stayed out of my way. Said I scared her."

"Guess she had you pegged right."

"Funny thing is I didn't know what to do. I was a virgin when I did that. I did it because I thought I was supposed to do it. Thought girls expected you to make a pass. But look where I am now, about to marry the smartest, most beautiful woman in the world. I couldn't be happier. Giselle did me a favor."

He grinned at Carrie. His love glowed through his hazel eyes. Carrie threw her arms around his neck and kissed him hard.

"I'd better get out of here before Delia kills me. We have a wedding to go to."

Grey kissed her before he stole away down the stairs. Delia, Fran, and Janice came in.

"Let's put this girl back together. My gorgeous daughter, you'll make the most beautiful bride ever."

Delia and Leah hugged Carrie, then left to take their places down the aisle. Carrie took one more look in the mirror. The soft white satin bodice fit her snugly but not too tight. The full tulle skirt was plain, simple, and elegant. A white sash with a white satin bow in the back added interest.

She wore her mother's pearls around her neck and Delia's pearl earrings. A pearl bracelet Grey had given her for her birthday graced her slender wrist. A simple white headpiece with tiny pearls and flowers spanned the width of Carrie's head. Hidden beneath her skirt was a blue garter.

The veil fell gracefully over her face. Her thick hair was pulled back in front and tied with simple white grosgrain ribbon, allowing her locks to flow down her back to her shoulders. Leah had applied light makeup perfectly. Carrie was delighted with the results. She paced, awaiting the arrival of her father. Harvey stuck his head in her room.

"You still speaking to me?"

She stopped walking and turned to face him.

He walked tentatively into the room. "Am I still giving you away?"

"Do I have any other father?"

"I suppose John Andrews would pinch-hit for me if you wanted him to."

"Your turn at bat, Dad."

"You look breathtaking, Bunny. The most beautiful bride ever. Grey is such a lucky man. I hope he knows that."

Carrie chuckled. "I think he does."

"Are you ready?" Harvey offered her his arm.

He helped her down the stairs. Delia and Leah stood on one side of the aisle in lovely raspberry silk dresses. Colin, John, and Grey, looking dashing in their tuxes with raspberry cummerbunds, stood on the other side. Grey took a step toward her until John put out his arm to stop his son.

"Let her come to you, son," he whispered loud enough for all to hear.

A murmur of laughter and giggles filled the air. Everyone stood up when they saw Carrie.

The string quartet struck up Vivaldi's "Four Seasons" as the bride started down the aisle. Harvey pulled a handkerchief out of his pocket to dab his eyes. Carrie smiled and tightened her grip on his arm.

They took their time strolling down the aisle. As soon as she took one step, all her nerves disappeared. She glanced up at Grey, whose encouraging smile gave her strength. Marrying him was the right thing to do. Peace settled into her heart. Calmly, she smiled back. She spied her mother blotting tears and Delia too.

Before she knew it, Grey was offering her his hand. Her father lifted her veil and kissed her.

Carrie whispered, "I love you, Daddy."

He hugged her before giving her to the groom. Losing her hand in Grey's large, warm, dry one was comforting. They laced their fingers before stepping up to the judge. When Grey slipped the ring on her finger, a tingle shot up her spine. Now she was his. She chuckled at the smile of satisfaction on his face.

Putting the ring on Grey's finger made it real. He would be her husband forever, for better or worse. The thought thrilled and reassured at the same time. Within a few minutes, Grey's mouth captured hers while the crowd of family and friends cheered. He tucked her arm into his and led them back down the aisle as a married couple. She had never seen his smile beam as brightly. It warmed her heart.

Time seemed to stand still and to fly at the same time. Her face hurt from smiling so broadly on the receiving line. Colin shoved champagne glasses at them. Leah brought a plate of hors d'oeuvres for them to share. Grey held the plate while Carrie picked up a stuffed mushroom. Desire reflected in his eyes as she fed him. His lips locked on her finger, sucking it part way into his mouth where his tongue caressed it.

Carrie colored. "Grey! People are watching," she whispered.

"I don't care. If I had a magic wand, I'd make them all go away."

She chuckled. "Then I'd have you all to myself."

Before he could continue his verbal seduction of his new wife, the string quartet played more Vivaldi. The aroma of delectable hot food wafted over to the couple. Delia bustled over to them.

"You must be the first in line for food. Then the first dance. Come, come, time for all that stuff later, Grey." Delia gave him a hard look.

"Guess I have a lifetime to seduce my wife." He drew out the last two words.

"You do. Come." Delia grabbed Grey's arm, pulling him along to the long table covered by a pink cloth. There were platters of cold shrimp, cold lobster, and fresh crabmeat salad accompanied by dishes of spicy cocktail sauce and Russian dressing. A huge bowl of choice mixed greens was surrounded by smaller bowls with fixings, like artichoke hearts, bacon bits, cucumbers, raw mushrooms, and a variety of dressings from vinaigrette to blue cheese, fresh coleslaw and finishing the fantastic array of dishes was a platter of fresh sliced tomatoes with gorgonzola dressing. Chafing dishes filled with lobster Newburg, wild rice, sliced filet mignon, fingerling potatoes au gratin, Brussels sprouts, broccoli and cauliflower in cheese sauce, and grilled vegetables took up the last half of the table.

"The only thing I have an appetite for is you," he whispered over his shoulder.

"Are you kidding? Look at all this! Eat, Grey. You'll need your strength. Trust me."

He shot her a questioning glance.

"I have plans for you. Conserve your energy, husband." Carrie sported a wicked grin.

He laughed.

"Can I help you, sir?" One of the servers drew Grey's attention to the chafing dish with rice on one side and lobster Newburg on the other. Carrie's stomach rumbled at the smell of the rich food. Grey handed his plate to the server, who piled it high with one delectable concoction after another.

"Taking me seriously, I see," she said, eyeing his plate.

"I always take my wife seriously, especially when she talks about the bedroom." He chuckled.

They sat down. After only one forkful of the lobster dish, they were forced to dance the first dance. Grey pulled Carrie close. While swaying to the music, she inhaled his familiar masculine scent mixed with piney aftershave and fresh soap. All around people laughed, talked, and ate. Good feeling filled the air.

"I'm glad we didn't run away to Las Vegas. Everyone's having fun," she whispered.

"Delia and your mom can throw a great bash when they bury the hatchet."

A sense of well-being and happiness washed over her as Grey tightened his embrace.

"Are you happy, honey?"

"Deliriously so. Never been so happy in my life. You?"

"Same. Didn't know getting married could be this good."

Suddenly, he stopped. His three best buddies from college stood there, ready to cut in. They called themselves "The Four Horsemen" and were inseparable during their school days.

"You didn't think we were going to let you monopolize this beautiful woman, did you?" Bobby asked, tapping Grey's shoulder.

Grey grinned. "I should have known."

"And when Bobby's finished, it's my turn," Will chimed in.

"And you don't get her back until I'm done," Spence added.

Grey stepped back, allowing Bobby to take Carrie in his arms.

"No funny stuff." Grey wagged his finger at the men.

"Don't you trust us?" Spence asked.

"Not for a second," Grey replied.

The men snickered.

Grey sat back down at his table and tucked into his plate of food. When Delia breezed by, he corralled her. "This is amazing, Delia. Thank you." Grey reached up to plant a kiss on her cheek.

She blushed. "The least I could do."

"You're sending me the bill, as we agreed, right?"

"Actually, Harvey insisted on paying. It's his daughter's wedding after all."

"How about that? They came through in the end. Good enough."

Grey danced with Delia, Janice, and the wives of the other three horsemen. He almost didn't have time to eat. Carrie, shepherded from man to man, ended up with her father.

"Weren't we supposed to be second?" he asked.

"Grey's friends can be a little pushy."

"I have you now."

"Thank you for everything, Dad."

"Nothing's too good for my little girl."

"I forgive you for your infidelity," she whispered in his ear.

"Thank you, Bunny. I broke your mother's heart. I don't think she ever recovered. I regret it every day of my life. Your mother has been a devoted and loving wife. Better than I deserved."

"Don't say that."

"It's true. I know she's difficult with you, but deep down, she loves you. We miss you."

"You know where to find me."

"We'll be back for a visit too if Grey can forgive your mom."

"He's not a grudge holder."

"I think you've found a wonderful man, Carrie. I couldn't turn you over to anyone less."

"Thanks, Dad." Tears pricked her eyes.

Chapter Nineteen

Keeping busy meant Leah didn't have to think about Paris. Being a helper during the wedding had her running up and down stairs, doing Carrie's makeup, making sure there was enough wine, and sending requests to the band. With no time to ponder her own future, she relaxed and enjoyed the food and music. Standing with a plate of lobster, she shoveled forkfuls into her mouth, not even tasting what she was eating but thinking about what she had to do next. A hand closed over her shoulder.

"May I have this dance?" Colin asked.

"I have so much to—"

Before she could finish the sentence, Colin took her plate and placed it on the table then led her onto the dance floor. As his arms closed around her, she shut her eyes, melting into his embrace. His fresh scent seduced her senses. Her arms closed around his neck as he pulled her in closer. Leah sighed. They moved slowly around the dance floor.

"We fit so well together," he said.

She giggled. "Vertically and horizontally."

A laugh rumbled in his chest, the vibration tickling her breasts.

"The wedding is perfect. You did a great job," he said.

"I was only a small part of it."

"Stop being modest and take some credit. God, you smell good."

His lips on her neck made her shiver. "So do you."

The music stopped. Colin took her hand.

"Let's go for a walk. No one'll miss us."

She followed along as he led her down a dirt path and over a little bridge that spanned a stream and led to the woods. A large almost flat rock outcropping provided a perfect place to perch, away from prying eyes.

Colin sank down and pulled Leah onto his lap for a passionate kiss. His hand covered her breast, starting a familiar fire inside her. His tongue slid along the crease of her lips, parting them. Her hands gripped his shoulders as she arched her back, pressing her breasts toward his chest. A groan escaped his throat. His lips moved to her neck on their way south. She pushed away from him and stood up.

"We can't do this." She pushed to her feet and turned away.

"Who will know?" He followed her.

"What if someone comes looking for us?"

"Can't blame a guy for wanting to make love to his girl one last time before she leaves, forever." Colin frowned, turning his gaze to his shoes.

"Didn't we do that last night?" She faced him.

"A couple of times. So who's counting?" He shot her a wicked grin.

"It's not forever. I'm coming back at Christmas."

"Six months from now. You'll probably come back engaged to some hot French dude."

She laughed. "Doubt that."

"Are you kidding?" He stood up and started pacing. "When they see you there in Paris with your stylish clothes and hot...it'll be all over for me."

"I've never met a man better than you." She rested her hand on his forearm.

"Then marry me before you go!" The words rushed out of his mouth.

"What?"

"You heard me. The judge is still here. Then I know you'll still be mine when you come back." He took her hand.

"That's insane. You can't mean it."

"I do. And I've got the ring to prove it." He whipped a small box out of his pocket.

Leah's eyes widened. "Colin...no. We can wait. We have to wait. I'm not going to rush into this. If we can't wait six months, then we shouldn't be together."

"I didn't think you'd go for it, but thought I'd try anyway," he said.

"Don't look so glum. I'm flattered you want to marry me."

"I do. I want to be with you always." He pulled her into his embrace.

Leah rested her cheek against his shoulder.

"Really?" She pushed away and cocked an eyebrow. "You'll be at a university crawling with eligible *young* women. I'll be in the company of women and gay men. We'll see."

"Eligible *girls*, not women."

"I see you're still living by the dating list."

"You know about that?" He jumped up.

"Carrie told me. She dropped something about it, and I wormed it out of her. But don't tell."

"So all this time?"

"Yeah, I knew. Knew you were coming after me."

"How come you didn't hold out?" he asked.

"You're irresistible. Wanted to...couldn't."

"The dating list worked after all? Now we should take it a step further."

She was quiet.

"You think I'm going to find some hot babe at Kensington, so you're afraid to commit! Got it. Not gonna happen."

"How do you know?"

"Because you have my heart. I can't give away what I no longer possess."

His words stunned her. She never expected such a commitment from him. Emotion choked her as his love surrounded her. Suddenly, her feelings broke through her defenses. All these weeks, she had maintained control, especially in front of Colin. But his declaration shredded the wall she had built around her heart into little pieces, like old newspaper. Raw emotion bubbled up in her chest. Hiding her face with her hands, she burst into tears. He was beside her in a second.

"Don't cry, baby. Our love will survive, you'll see."

Big, strong hands rubbing her back soothed her. Colin pulled a handkerchief out of his breast pocket and offered it to her. She fisted the white cotton, holding it to her face.

"And I thought you didn't care," he said.

A big breath brought on a shudder.

"I love you. I don't want to lose you, either," she admitted.

"It would be easier to feel the commitment if we were married."

"If we can withstand the separation then I'll feel confident about our commitment. Hold on to that ring." A small smile lifted the corners of her mouth as she dabbed at her eyes.

"We're sort of engaged?"

She shook her head.

"You're free to find someone else. So am I. If we do, then we're not meant to be. Time to get back to the party."

"Wait, Leah."

She took a shaky step back. He grabbed her elbow, steadying her as her hand wrapped around his biceps.

"And if we don't find anyone else?"

"Then we *are* meant to be. I'll be ready to make a commitment."

An uncertain smile passed over his lips. "Not sure if I like this idea."

"Why? Doubting you'll still want me?"

"Doubting *you'll* still want *me*." He pushed several stands of hair out of her face.

"Then isn't it better to know before getting married?"

"We're talking romance, not logic."

"Our lives, Colin, we're talking about our lives. I don't want either of us to be unhappy. We've sailed into a fabulous affair. Can it last? I don't know."

She took Colin's hand and started back to the party. He followed along.

Grey and Carrie were cutting the wedding cake when the lovers returned. Colin sighed as he slipped an arm around her waist.

"I want what they have."

"Me too," Leah whispered.

The happy newlyweds fed cake to each other. The quartet continued to play while everyone sat down to eat their portion of the beautiful confection. Grey approached Colin.

"We'll be leaving in an hour. Ready, squirt?"

Colin nodded. "When does your limo arrive, Leah?"

"Too soon," she said, looking at her watch.

"Let's dance while we can."

She fell into his arms.

STUART SWEPT DELIA into his arms for a dance.

"Marvelous wedding, my dear," he whispered into her ear.

She smiled. "I'm exhausted. But everyone looks happy."

"Except those two." Stuart nodded toward Colin and Leah.

"In a little while, they'll be parting for six months. Young love, so intense."

He chuckled. "You're pretty intense yourself."

Color stained her cheeks. "I think Carrie had the kind of wedding she wanted."

"Very classy."

"I thought so. Good thing Janice calmed down. I was ready to kill her. Now we're at peace. Isn't Carrie the most beautiful bride ever?"

"She's lovely. You'd make a beautiful bride too, Delia."

She raised her eyebrows.

"Me? My marrying days are over."

"Sure about that?" He eased her into a dip.

"What did you have in mind?"

"Perhaps this isn't the time or place."

"It isn't." She rested her head on his shoulder.

"But later, when the guests are gone?"

Delia giggled. "I love it when you're mysterious."

He leaned over and whispered in her ear, "How about we have the honeymoon first? Before the wedding."

"I like the way you think," she responded.

"Why don't I take you away somewhere romantic, like the Riviera? Or maybe a cruise down the Amazon?"

"Perfect."

"It's not every day a man my age finds a woman like you, Delia. Please forgive me if I want to hang on to you as long as I can."

"Darling, we'll be together after the wedding is over. I'd love to recover with you on the Riviera." She kissed his cheek, then consulted her list. "Hmm, what's next? Oh yes. Almost time to get the bride and groom off on their honeymoon. Then we'll have ours, Stuart."

An hour later, Delia rounded up Colin and Leah. Carrie and Grey came down dressed in street clothes to make the trek to New York City. They were scheduled to stay in a suite at The St. Regis for a night and then catch a plane to Paris. But first, Carrie had to throw her bouquet. Several women were vying for position. Leah hung back. Carrie turned her back, closed her eyes, and gave a healthy toss. The bouquet bounced off the head of one woman and into Leah's arms. Colin burst out laughing at Leah's flustered, red face. Delia smiled as she leaned over to whisper in Leah's ear.

"I'll make the same wedding for you, sweetie."

"Colin! Bring the car around," Grey called, motioning for his brother.

He nodded, turned, and took Leah in his arms for a kiss. Grey stopped, his mouth open slightly as his brother bid farewell to his lady love. Heavy blinking was obvious by both lovers as they parted.

"Good luck in your new job," Leah said, cupping his cheek.

"Thanks. You too."

"Until Christmas," she said, sliding her hand over Colin's.

"Christmas."

He turned abruptly and walked away. Within five minutes, he pulled up in his brother's Jaguar. Grey opened the door for Carrie, bid everyone farewell, and got in the car. Colin took one last look at Leah before he put the Jag in gear and roared away.

Leah's chin quivered and her eyes filled. Delia put her hand on the young woman's shoulder.

"It'll work out. You have an exciting time ahead."

"Just wish I could share it with him."

Delia pulled Leah into a hug. The younger woman hid her face, allowing a few tears to escape.

"I believe what you have is real. Patience. Go out there and show them what you can do, Leah. Shock them with your talent and make Colin proud. This is your time to shine."

Leah smiled at Delia.

"You're right."

Leah's phone rang. "The limo driver," she said.

Harvey came out of the house carrying Leah's two suitcases as the limo pulled up. While the driver loaded her luggage, she got in the back seat.

"*Au revoir*," Delia called.

"*À bientôt*." Leah waved as the limo headed for the airport.

"Ah, young love, so sweet, so pure, so painful." Delia sighed.

Stuart came up behind her and rested his hand on her shoulder.

JULY, PARIS, FRANCE

Email from Leah to Colin.

I finally unpacked. The apartment is small but very chic. The view is of a tiny side street but I love it. How would we fit you into this space? With a shoehorn! Seriously it's quiet and lonely without you. But all of Paris is outside my door. Back later.

Love,

L

Reply from Colin.

Found a great two-bedroom apartment on the second floor of a house in Willow Falls. Unlike your tiny place there's a ton of room here. Enough for me and you. I seem to rattle around here like a marble in an empty shoebox. Trying to focus on preparing my lectures and outlining a program for the wrestling team but my mind keeps drifting to thoughts of you. You'd love it here. Tons of fresh air and room to breathe.

I want to hear all about Paris. Don't meet any hot Frenchmen, okay?

Love,

C

August, Willow Falls, New York

Email from Colin to Leah.

Wow! Paris sounds great! Wish I was there with you. Met any men, yet? Hope not. How's your designing going?

Half of our team is experienced, and half are new. I keep telling myself the new guys aren't dumb, just inexperienced. Still, we have a long way to go. I work out with the team. Keeps me in shape and gives me less time to miss you.

I have my lesson plan completed but I almost blew lunch thinking about my first lecture. TMI? LOL! Guess I'm the newbie there. I hope everyone loves your designs and you haven't met any men yet. Have you? Still missing you like crazy. But I have found a few friends to go to football games with. Harry, John, and Kathy are just as rah-rah as I am about Kensington's team. Wish you were with me too.

Love,

C

Reply from Leah.

You'll be great lecturing the students. It's the anticipation making you nervous. Besides a few nerves will make you better. I have faith in you. And as for the wrestling team, I know you can whip them into shape and win some matches. Keep working out. Makes me look forward even more to touching you again. TMI?

Madame Jeanne has sold my first design! I'm so excited! Everyone is very happy. She's given me a guide, Jean Pierre. He's showing me around the city. We will travel together to other cities to visit great art museums and get ideas for my designs. Wish you were coming with me. I miss you so much.

Love,

L

September, Paris, France

Email from Leah to Colin.

I can't believe Madame Jeanne sold my second design, the one I made up for Carrie. Oops, I think I wasn't supposed to tell about that! LOL. I'm very excited. I've been at the Louvre, sketching, every day this week. There are so many fabulous ideas there waiting to be picked up.

Madame Jeanne has scheduled a month-long trip for Jean Pierre and me to travel to Italy and a few other places. I'll be sketching and trying to take in all the art. I know that seems like a lot of time but it will pass quickly.

Who is this Kathy person? You're going to football games with her? Is it serious? Is this something I should worry about? I love you, Colin, in case you've forgotten.

Love,

L

Reply from Colin.

Don't worry about Kathy. She's only a friend. It's more fun to go to the football games with her than alone. I didn't think about the time change when I set up FaceTime. It seems impossible to talk to you, see you. I wish I could touch you.

You're traveling with Jean Pierre for a month? Do you have separate rooms? When are you leaving? Are you sleeping with him? Please tell me it isn't so.

Lectures and wrestling are okay but I keep thinking of you traveling with this guy. It's hard to concentrate. Of course I still love you. Please tell me you feel the same.

Love,

C

Reply from Leah.

I didn't think about the time change either. I miss talking to you. I'm going to be on the road a lot now, so the timing gets even crazier. I miss you so much.

Love,

L

October, Willow Falls, NY

Email from Colin to Leah.

Hi, Leah,

The wrestling team has won two matches and lost two. We have two guys with star potential and the rest have a lot to learn. I'm hopeful that we can improve and have a winning team next year. The school seems happy so far.

Lectures are going okay. Students seem interested. I'm beginning to remember their names and be more relaxed. Lots of papers to grade at night. Tires me out so I'm sleeping better. I'd rather you tired me out, but I can't have everything.

Our football team is doing better than the wrestling team. Kathy and I bet on every game. So far I've won two lunches at the local pizza place. She's won one.

When are you taking this trip? I'll be worried about you every day you're gone. Only three months till Christmas. I'm crossing the days off my calendar.

Love,

C

Chapter Twenty

R eply from Leah.
 Glad to hear your teams are doing well. A little worried about those bets with Kathy. I hope they don't morph into something more than food. I knew you'd be okay with the lectures. You're a good speaker. Wish I could be there to hear you.

 The trip is planned for October 15 to November 15. I probably won't have internet access then, so don't wig out if you don't hear from me for a while. You'll be traveling with me in my heart—as always. Don't worry about Jean Pierre. He's not half the man you are.

 Madame Jeanne sold my third design. She's not happy with what I'm doing now, though. I'm a little concerned. I'd better find inspiration on this trip or I might be in trouble. Missing you a ton. Will email as soon as the trip is over. I hope you don't find someone else while I'm traveling.

 Love,
 L

PINE GROVE, NY

It had started coming down at noon. By two o'clock, the heavy snowfall tapered off into a smattering of stubborn flakes. The sun was out but an inch had already accumulated. Carrie fisted her hand and wiped it in a circle on the window in the front door of her wedding present from Grey, the old Victorian home in Pine Grove. She pulled her black cashmere cardigan a little tighter to keep out the draft as she looked for her husband.

While shoveling snow off the front walk, Grey looked up and spied her signal and waved. She held up a mug of hot chocolate and motioned for him to come in. He stomped the snow off his boots, put down the shovel, and headed for the front door. When he opened the door, cold snowy air blew in with him. Carrie shivered as she handed him the hot beverage. His cold lips found her warm ones before seeking the drink.

"Lunch," Carrie said.

Grey took off his boots, then his down jacket. He hung it on the peg by the front door before he walked through the living room, freshly painted a dark teal blue with white trim. Winter sunlight streamed in the tall front windows, warming Grey a bit. He followed her into their big kitchen. On the long antique oak table, two places were set. Two small bowls of homemade New England clam chowder and freshly baked bread sent tempting fragrances through the air. Two big slabs of homemade sourdough bread, perfectly buttered, perched proudly on a plate next to the soup. Grey slid into his seat and picked up his spoon.

"Walk is almost finished," he said, blowing cool air on a spoonful of hot soup.

"I still have two pies to make and our cauliflower cheese casserole."

"Mom is in love with that dish. Says Dad only eats cauliflower when it's in your casserole."

Carrie smiled as she joined him at the table.

"Soup is delicious," he said, tearing off a piece of bread.

"Thank you. I was hoping the house would be finished by Thanksgiving, but the holiday crept up on me. We're nowhere near done."

"Is the guest room ready for Colin?"

"It is. I thought he was staying at your parents' place?"

"He might and he might not!" He gave her a mischievous smile.

"What does that mean?"

"Tell ya later." He averted his eye from her gaze.

"Our first Thanksgiving in our own house in Pine Grove as husband and wife." She sighed.

He placed his hand over hers as their eyes connected.

Grey shivered.

"We need to do something about the heat in this place. It's drafty as hell. The kitchen should never be this cold. I'll get on it as soon as I finish the front walk."

"An old house is a lot of work, isn't it?" Carrie said.

"Maybe but it's what you wanted. When we get done here, it's going to be a real showplace, like the townhouse."

"It's going to be a big money drain, isn't it?"

"Nope. John and I have an excellent offer for one of our companies. The income from that deal will more than take care of the expenses for this house for the next ten years. Don't worry."

"I love renovating and decorating."

"I know you do," he said, rising from his chair. "And you have a knack for it."

"I love you, in case I haven't told you in, let's see, the last ten minutes?"

He laughed and kissed her. "My wife. I love saying that," he said, almost to himself.

Grey went out to finish the walk. Carrie followed him and entered the dining room, which was under construction. Sanding equipment, a ladder, paint cans, and various brushes took up residence on a drop cloth. She deftly walked around everything to perch on the window seat where she could see quite a ways down the street. The kitchen faced the backyard with a peek at the lake through the trees.

Carrie pulled a small pad and pen out of the pocket of her apron and started a list. She had responsibilities for tomorrow's Thanksgiving dinner at the Andrews family home. Enjoying the unbroken silence of the country, the sound of tires on slush grabbed her attention. She moved to the living room window and watched Colin pull into the driveway next door, maneuvering his car next to his father's black Jeep. He walked slowly toward the front door, his shoulders seemed to slump a little. She sighed.

She thought back to her last email from Leah:

Email to Carrie.

Jean Pierre and I are going to Florence. I'm going to get ideas from the art there.

He's been so helpful, I don't know what I'd do without him. Don't get to spend

    much time with Madame Jeanne. Planning a big trip to buy fabrics. Will be traveling

    for a month. Not sure about internet. So if you don't hear from me, don't panic.

    Sending hugs.

Carrie hadn't received word from her in weeks. She wondered who Jean Pierre was and why they were traveling together. Is he Leah's new man? Are they lovers or just traveling companions? Carrie shook her head to banish the thought. Grey finished up the walk and opened the front door.

"It's damn cold out there," he said, brushing icicles from his hair.

"Come in, warm up. We've got work to do."

"I have a suggestion how you can warm me up." He snickered.

Carrie glanced at her watch. She wiggled her eyebrows then turned and sprinted up the stairs with Grey close behind.

THE BARKING OF BUSTER and Daisy from the big living room window greeted Colin as he turned up his collar and walked up the path to his parents' house. The door opened and the two pugs charged out, barking and jumping up on his legs. His father motioned him in.

"Shake a leg, boy, we're not heating the whole outdoors!"

Colin smiled to himself. *Some things never change.* He shook his head slightly as he crouched down to pet the dogs. Daisy leapt up to lick his face with Buster following. Colin laughed. When he looked up he noticed his father watching him.

"What?" His eyebrows knitted.

"Nothing, nothing, come in." John closed the door.

Fran appeared from the kitchen, wiping her hands on her apron. She planted a kiss on her son's cheek.

"So happy to see you," she said, studying his face.

"What's everyone looking at?" Colin asked.

"Nothing, nothing," Fran said, trying to hide a smile.

"You're in Grey's old room," John said, preceding Colin up the stairs.

"I forgot. They're next door now. Convenient for the newlyweds, eh?" He smirked.

Colin dumped his bag on his bed then descended the stairs and joined his sister, Jenna, in the living room. She had her feet up on the coffee table with a pug snuggled up.

"Where's Bill?"

"Dad's got him stacking firewood. Now that Grey's got his own house to take care of, and you're living in Willow Falls, it seems Bill's next in line."

"What about Earl?"

"He and Barbara aren't here yet."

Fran carried a tray with cheese and crackers on it into the living room. John followed.

"What ya drinkin'?" he asked.

"Beer?" Colin stood up.

"Sit, son. I'll get it. Then I want to hear how your wrestling season is going," John said.

Jenna sipped a glass of white wine. "I want to hear about your girl-friends at Kensington."

"What girlfriends?" He sat back against the sofa, Buster jumped up and curled up right next to him.

"Come on. There must be a ton of hot coeds there?"

"There's no one," Colin said.

"You? Winner of my *Mover of the Year* award?"

"Last year."

"What happened?" Jenna straightened herself on the sofa.

"Leah happened."

"Oh, the designer lady? The one in Paris."

"Yep."

"What's up with you two? Been separated a long time. It's not like my horny younger brother to be celibate for so long."

"None of your business, Jenna!"

She laughed. "I'm making it my business. Give."

"Nothing to tell. She's coming back at Christmas."

"And?"

"We'll see. Let it go."

"Touchy, aren't we?"

"Leave it!" he hollered, bounding up from the sofa and stalking out of the room.

Colin took the stairs two at a time and burst through the door of his room. He toed off his shoes, stretched out on the bed, and stared at the ceiling, wondering what would happen at Christmas. He hadn't heard from Leah in three weeks. Of course she'd told him there would be no email since she wouldn't have internet. But he hadn't been able to connect via phone, either. Even text messages didn't get delivered. He only had a couple of weeks left to find out if he would win or lose the lady of his dreams. *Jean Pierre, I hate you.*

A knock on the door interrupted his thoughts.

"Come in," Colin said.

"Since Grey's not here—he's busy as hell next door—I wondered if you'd mind chopping a little wood for us?"

"Sure, Dad," Colin said, pushing up off the bed.

They shrugged on their jackets before moving to the yard at the side of the house. John handed his son the axe.

"Go to it."

"How much do you want?"

"Stop whenever you feel like it."

Colin smiled. *He gets it.* John returned to the house. Colin grabbed the axe.

"This is for *Jean Pierre.*"

Whack! Another piece of wood.

"This is for Jean Pierre too," Colin said, wielding the axe.

Whack! Another piece of wood

"This is for all French men."

Whack!

After half an hour, Colin had exhausted himself. He stacked up the wood, filled his arms with split logs, and returned to the house.

Dinner was a quiet affair. During dessert, Barbara and Earl arrived. Barbara glowed. Along with a blast of cold air, they blew in on a tide of good cheer. Barbara was so happy she practically babbled.

"I'm pregnant!" she announced.

Fran's face broke into a huge grin as she hugged her daughter. The men shook Earl's hand.

"Celebration is called for. I'm opening champagne," John said.

"For everyone except Barbara," Fran admonished.

Barbara's face fell for a second, but she quickly regained her good cheer. The next few hours were spent discussing baby names and brands of strollers as well as colors for the nursery. Colin was closest to his sister Barbara, but her life had changed dramatically and he felt distant from his oldest sibling.

He missed being able to talk to her about Leah but understood what this pregnancy meant. Barbara and Earl had been trying to get pregnant for two years. Colin didn't want to rain on her parade or bring her down in any way. Unable to muster a cheerful attitude, he opted for retiring early.

THANKSGIVING MORNING, Colin and his father were the first ones up.

"I'm on for breakfast, what should I make this morning, son?" John poured water into the coffeemaker as Colin carefully measured out the grounds.

"I don't know. Doesn't much matter."

"No appetite? Didn't eat much last night for dinner, either, did you? Must be love, eh?"

"Stop kidding, Dad. This is serious."

"They all say that. It'll work out, you'll see. You have no faith. That Leah's no fly-by-night. I bet she comes through."

"Wish I had your confidence."

"If she doesn't, good-lookin' college professor like you shouldn't have any problem finding another girl. By the way. How's the new job?"

"Fine."

"Happy?"

"I love teaching college kids. That's the best part of my day."

"What about the new wrestling team? How's that going? Win any matches yet?"

"Considering we're a new team, we're not half bad. We've won three and lost four so far this season. I'm pretty happy. The school isn't upset because it's our first season. We will need to step it up next year, though."

"Seems like you've settled in nicely."

"Everything's great except for one thing..."

"Got my fingers crossed for you, son."

"You need any help, Dad?"

"Why don't you start the bacon? Know anything about cooking breakfast?"

"I've learned a lot from you. I've been cooking my own bacon for a long time now."

"Long time?"

"At least a year."

"Oh, I see." John stifled a chuckle as he passed two packages of bacon to his son.

"Grey and Carrie coming for breakfast too?"

"Don't know. Now they're at their own house, can't seem to get them out of the bedroom."

After the Thanksgiving table was set, Fran directed the meal except the carving of the turkey, which was John's job. Family members moved back and forth from the kitchen to the long dining room table, crafted by Gavin Dailey specifically for their large family. Spread out across the table were vegetable casseroles, bowls of salad and cranberries in several forms, a gravy boat, and an empty platter to be filled with fresh, sliced, hot turkey. When the table couldn't hold anymore, everyone sat down. Carrie ended up next to Colin.

A prayer was said with everyone joining in. Colin mouthed a silent prayer of his own. Grey's cell interrupted Colin's thoughts. Grey left the table with nods of permission from his parents.

"Since when has it been okay to leave your cell phone on during Thanksgiving dinner?" Colin asked, passing the mashed potatoes to Jenna.

"Don't be so rigid. Grey told us he was expecting an important call," Fran said.

Frowning, Colin turned his attention back to slicing off a bite-sized piece of turkey. A hunger nagged at his stomach but nothing like his usual appetite at Thanksgiving. For the past few years, he'd won the rivalry with Grey over who could eat the most at the holiday. But maybe not this year. Loneliness washed over Colin when he looked around the table at his siblings with their spouses. Everyone appeared happy. There was room for one more place, next to him, for Leah. Could Leah become part of his family? He sighed.

Grey returned to the table and exchanged a look with his mother. Colin's attention returned to his food. Nothing seemed to taste good. He toyed with the cauliflower on his plate unable to eat more. Instead, he sat silently listening to the chatter of his parents and siblings. Spirits were high, a first grandchild would come along in seven months, and the oldest son had taken a wife. Lines and creases were smoothed as John and Fran radiated happiness.

His chest tightened. He seemed an outsider in his own family, the only one suffering from a broken heart. Emptiness swept through him. Without Leah, the celebration fell flat. Colin sat back waiting until an appropriate time to excuse himself. When they finally finished, Jenna and Bill cleared the table.

"Grey, could you please go to the store for some milk? We don't have enough," Fran asked.

"I bought some this morning, Fran," John put in.

Fran shushed him, putting her hand on his arm. John gave a helpless shrug. Colin watched them without seeing.

"Sure, Mom," Grey said, grabbing his coat and disappearing out the door.

"Colin, come help with the coffee, dear. You're so good with this machine."

He joined his mother in the kitchen and counted the coffee drinkers before measuring the grounds. A heaviness surrounded his heart. He wished Leah could have been there for Thanksgiving, an important Andrews family holiday, the one holiday reserved for family only.

When Grey returned, pies were loaded on the table. Jenna brought out dessert plates. Barbara passed out coffee cups.

"Oh my, what's wrong with me? I forgot my special pumpkin pie. Colin, would you mind getting it? It's on the front hall table in our house. The door's unlocked," Carrie said.

She turned pleading eyes to him.

He had nothing better to do, so why not? "Sure."

He shrugged into his jacket and went out the front door. The cold air revived him as the bright light from the streetlamps, appearing brighter against the blackness of the night, stabbed his eyes. A burst of energy propelled him quickly through the frigid air. Hurrying to get into the warmth of Grey and Carrie's house, Colin wrapped his fingers around the brass door jamb, opened it, slipped inside, and spun around quickly to close the door. Behind him, he heard a throat being cleared. The sound stopped him while he faced the door. Slowly, he turned, and there she was.

Leah.

LEAH'S PULSE KICKED up, her heart beat out of her chest as the door opened to admit Colin. He turned so quickly to close the door, he didn't see her standing there in her fur coat, white wool beret, and high-heeled black suede boots. She cleared her throat. He stopped dead, turning slowly.

"Leah?" His voice was almost a croak.

She smiled, emotion swelling in her throat, preventing speech. Tears burned her eyelids. Rapid blinking kept them at bay. Two deep breaths restored her voice.

"Colin?"

"It's really you?"

He closed the distance between them in two long strides, arms open, but then he stopped abruptly.

"What are you doing here? Someone die?"

She shook her head, restraining her urge to jump into his arms.

"Explain?"

"I'm here to see you," she choked out.

"To tell me you're going to marry Jean Pierre?"

"What? No!" She chuckled.

"Why is that so funny?" He bristled.

"Jean Pierre is gay. I thought you knew."

Colin released a huge breath of air, and a smile slowly spread across his face.

"What about you? That girl, Kathy? You went to football games with her?"

"She's just a friend."

"Really?" Leah cocked an eyebrow.

He chuckled. "You're jealous of Kathy? She's engaged. Her fiancé is getting his Ph.D. at Indiana University. We were catching a game or two together, two lonely souls. That's all."

"Good."

"What happened to your job?"

"I was too miserable missing you."

Before she could finish, he lunged across the space separating them, pulling her into his embrace. He closed his arms around her, burying his face in her hair.

"You've come back to me?"

"Yes."

His lips sought hers for the most tender of kisses. Leah slipped her coat off her shoulders, letting it fall to the floor. Colin pulled one arm and then the other out of his, also leaving it on the floor. He grabbed her waist, forcing her right up against his chest. She sighed.

"So what happened?" Colin asked, plaiting his fingers through her hair, gazing into her eyes.

"Well, I was working hard, coming up with new designs. Madame Jeanne sold my first three designs right away. She had people waiting for more. I traveled, but my heart wasn't in it. She saw that my newer designs were not as good. They were missing the heart—the *romance* she called it. She could tell I was unhappy, missing you. We made a deal. I get to work from here for ten months and travel for her in Europe the other two. I jumped at the chance."

"You can be here and work for her?"

"As soon as she made me that offer, she said she saw a huge improvement in my designs. I must confess when I knew I was coming back to you, I captured the *romance* again, and it showed in my work. But I didn't know if you were still single. Through my travels the last few weeks, I haven't been able to be in touch with you and Kathy. She had me worried."

"You're actually coming back but still designing for Madame Jeanne?"

"Weren't you listening?"

"Guess I didn't hear anything beyond you were coming back to me."

She smiled. "If you still want me."

Colin dropped to one knee and pulled out a small, burgundy-colored velvet box. He snapped it open to reveal a beautiful, shiny, round-cut diamond ring.

"Will you marry me, Leah?"

The tears she had held at bay burst forth, streaming down her face. Her pulse beat wildly.

"Well? Will you? Why are you crying?" He pushed to his feet.

"I will. I will marry you. I'm crying because I'm happy."

She flew into his arms, hugging his chest with all her might.

"I love you so much. I missed you, Colin," she breathed.

"I missed you too, baby. Every day. I thought about you every day."

Again his mouth came down on hers hard. He demanded her surrender and she happily complied, melting against him, opening her lips to him. He took her mouth.

When he lifted his head, he stared into her eyes.

"I can't believe it's real. You'll be living here, with me, as my wife, designing for Madame Jeanne."

"I guess I am lucky, I'm getting both my dreams at once."

"So am I."

He took her hand, leading her to the stairs.

"There's a guest room upstairs."

"Won't your family miss you?"

"I have a feeling they already know all about this. Did Grey pick you up at the bus station?"

"Didn't he tell you?"

"Said he was going out for milk. It doesn't matter. You're here."

They climbed the stairs to the second floor.

"I saw a *for sale* sign on a beautiful farmhouse with twelve acres of land. Looked like it needed a little work but—"

"A farmhouse?" Her eyebrows shot up.

"Four bedrooms. Plenty of room for our family."

"Family?"

"Kids. I thought you wanted to have kids?"

He stopped on the second floor. She hugged him.

"You know I do."

"Let's practice, eh?"

He shot her a wicked grin before he pulled her into the room and closed the door.

Epilogue

Across the path, the Andrews family sat down to dessert.

"Where's Colin?" Bill asked.

Jenna shushed him.

"He won't be joining us for dessert," Grey said, a little color staining his cheeks.

Fran smiled as she looked down at the end of the table.

"Good thing I have service for twelve. Enough for all the in-laws and a couple of grandchildren too. Hmm, that spot on the corner will be perfect for Leah."

"You always plan ahead," John said, patting her hand.

"We're complete now. Ready for the next generation, John?" She cocked an eyebrow.

"With you by my side, Fran, I'm ready for anything."

THE END

About the Author

Jean has over 70 books published in ebook and print and 22 in audio. She writes fulltime, never far from her secret stash of black licorice. An avid bird and dog lover, she has a special fondness for crows and pugs. Jean has two adult sons, one granddaughter, and lives in New York City.